"How did I get so lucky?" Jack asked. "I'm the lucky one," Melinda said quietly.

She touched his face as if to assure herself that he was real, then brushed a stray lock off his forehead. He caught her hand and brought it to his lips.

"Where is everybody?" he asked, and she knew the question was not an idle one.

"Gone," she said quietly, jingling the keys. "I have to lock up."

"So we're all alone?"

"Completely."

Jack grinned, and he didn't have to tell Melinda what he was thinking. "Well, Ms. Myles," he said, assuming the tone of a patron of the arts, "I believe this calls for a command performance."

"And just what did you have in mind?" Melinda teased, as beguiled as he was by the endless prospects.

"I don't know exactly. I'm casting for a very important part."

"Really? What is it?"

"Sexiest woman in the world. Care to audition?"

"I'm a star, Mr. Bader," she drawled. "I don't usually have to audition. I'm play or pay."

"Well, how do I know if you're right for the part?"

"Check my résumé."

"Just what I had in mind," he whispered, taking her in his arms.

Books by Leah Laiman

Bride and Groom
The Bridesmaid
Maid of Honor
For Richer, for Poorer
For Better, for Worse
To Love and to Cherish

Published by POCKET BOOKS

BRIDE AND GROOM

Another Summer of Love

LEAH LAIMAN

POCKET BOOKS

New York London Toronto Sydney Tokyo Singapore

This book is a work of fiction. Names, characters, places and
incidents are products of the author's imagination or are used
fictitiously. Any resemblance to actual events or locales or persons,
living or dead, is entirely coincidental.

An *Original* Publication of POCKET BOOKS

 POCKET BOOKS, a division of Simon & Schuster Inc.
1230 Avenue of the Americas, New York, NY 10020

ISBN: 0-671-53406-8

First Pocket Books printing September 1995

10 9 8 7 6 5 4 3 2 1

POCKET and colophon are registered trademarks of
Simon & Schuster Inc.

Cover art by Punz Wolff

Printed in the U.S.A.

BRIDE AND GROOM

❧ 1 ❧

The smoke was visible from twenty miles away. Riding in the back of the limousine that had met them at the airport, wedged to one side by the skis sharing their space, they could see the shroud of black vapor curling over the horizon.

Glued to the window with the natural curiosity of a six-year-old, Moira Symington spotted it first.

"Look," she announced, taking no heed of the fact that her parents were snoozing, nestled in each other's arms, "a fire!"

Andrew Symington reluctantly opened his eyes and stretched. He looked at his young daughter and couldn't help smiling. She had inherited her mother's lustrous red hair, but on Moira it was spun with gold instead of copper. Her blue eyes, wide with the possibility of adventure, came from him. She was kneeling on the seat facing them, her face pressed excitedly to the window. Leaning forward, he peered in the direction she was pointing.

"Somebody must be burning leaves," he said and leaned back again, sinking once more into the comfort of his wife's shoulder.

Not opening her eyes, Samantha Myles Symington snuggled against her husband, intent on holding onto the dream fuzzily winding through her mind. They had spent a glorious week in Aspen. It had been Moira's first time on skis, and she had taken to the sport immediately, happily joining the children's group on the bunny slopes and more than content to remain with them through a day of activities in and out of doors.

Recognizing an opportunity when they saw one, Sam and Drew had spent as much time in their room as on the slopes. Since the first time they had seen each other, when Drew was heir apparent to the D'Uberville Motor Company fortune and Sam was an unknown assembly line worker who had to be content to indulge her genius for designing cars in a spare garage, their ardor for each other had remained undiminished. Steadying a rocky marriage that had survived a disinheritance, a kidnapping, and an ill-advised liaison, they had passed the seven-year mark itching for no one but each other. And with their lives finally on a forward track, they had decided to work on increasing their family.

The powder was good, and mornings were spent skiing. But after a lunch in front of the fire in the lodge, and with a good three hours before Moira was scheduled to be picked up from ski camp, they had been willing to forego outdoor sports for indoor activity. And now Samantha, glowing as much from the light within as from the winter sun, was dreaming that she was holding an infant in her arms, the happy product of afternoons spent on snowy sheets instead of trails.

"They must be burning a lot of leaves, Daddy." Moira's voice interrupted Sam's reverie.

"Uh-huh," responded Drew without looking, reluctant to leave the warmth of Sam's languid embrace.

But the words had broken through to Sam, and rousing herself, she pulled forward to see what was so fascinating to her child.

"In the middle of winter?" Sam questioned her husband. "Why would anybody be burning leaves in winter, with snow on the ground?"

"It's a fire," said Moira solemnly, unwilling to relinquish the dire threat of her first pronouncement.

"Could be," acknowledged Drew, giving up all hope of further sleep and joining his wife and child in scrutinizing the skyline.

The black clouds had gathered density in the few moments since he'd first observed them. And now, even with the windows closed, the acrid odor of burning matter began to seep into the pine-freshened recirculated air of the limousine.

"Looks like a big one," offered the driver, adding, "I hope it's not going to louse up traffic before we get to your place."

"Can we go see it?" asked Moira, entranced by the prospect of viewing a disaster up close.

"No, sweetie," said Sam. "We might get in the way of the firefighters and make it hard for them to do their work."

"I want to see," Moira complained. "I've never seen a real live fire."

"Out of the question," Drew said, adding his admonition to Sam's. "Number one, it could be dangerous, and number two, it's not nice to watch when other people are having trouble."

"We might not have a choice," sighed the driver as they pulled past the Woodland Cliffs town limit, and a fire engine, siren blaring, went streaking by them, turning, a hundred feet ahead, directly into the street where they were going.

Sam felt a knot in her throat and gripped her husband's hand. Even Moira suddenly fell silent and, leaving her own backward seat, where she had insisted on sitting alone, wedged herself on the opposite side, between her parents.

"Shit," said the driver as they turned the corner and their passage was blocked by a squadron of fire engines disgorging black-coated men who quickly snaked their hoses off the backs of their trucks. "I can't get past this. How far down the street is your house?"

"That *is* our house," said Drew quietly, sounding more calm than he felt.

"Oh, my God," gasped Sam, opening the door even before the car had come to a full stop.

"What?" asked Moira, shock replacing her animated curiosity. "Is our house on fire? Are all our things going to burn up?"

"Stay in the car with Moira," Drew ordered Sam,

4

pulling her back inside and stepping over her onto the street. "Let me just see what's happening."

She nodded, cradling her daughter who had begun to quietly whimper, soothing her with simple words. "It's going to be all right. The firefighters are here. They can take care of it."

"Where's Daddy? I don't want him to get burned."

"No one's going to get burned," Sam said emphatically as she nervously watched her husband move quickly past the fire trucks and out of sight.

A crowd had gathered. Even in fashionable neighborhoods like Woodland Cliffs, where the average mansion was worth well into the millions, everyone found the lure of a fire engine irresistible. Driven by equal parts fear and fury, Drew shouldered his way through the throng of curious strangers, ignoring their outraged remarks at the rudeness of his press to the front.

It was worse than he had imagined. Even the smoke filling the sky did not prepare him for the panorama of classic horror, of tongues of fire lashing from the windows of a house, his house, while firefighters, in full battle regalia, sent rivers of water, arcing like rainbows, into his home in a futile attempt to beat back the flames.

He stepped around the sawhorse that had been placed at the gates of the estate to hold back the sightseers. Instantly, a policeman was upon him.

"Hey, get back. Why do you think that thing's there?"

"This is my house," Drew explained, trying to get around the cop's outstretched arm.

"What?"

Drew couldn't be sure if he hadn't been heard or wasn't believed. "It's my house. Belvedere. I live here."

The policeman eyed him suspiciously, taking in his ski jacket and worn jeans. He'd had to turn back quite a number of tourists, some of them claiming to be journalists, others begging for just one picture. No one had been bold enough to profess to living here.

"What's your name?" he asked. There was always the risk of looters. With the chaos of a fire, it would be pretty tempting to sneak into a place like this and grab what you could.

"Andrew Symington," responded Drew, trying not to lose his patience. The man was only doing his job. But he'd be damned if he'd watch his house turn into an inferno while submitting to the third degree from some functionary who didn't know who he was. "Who's in charge here? Mulcahey?"

Suddenly, it didn't make a difference. He didn't care who was in charge or whether people were just doing their job. He was hardly aware that he had shoved the policeman aside and was running down the circular gravel driveway to the blazing mansion. He didn't hear the cop's shouted threat or see his shoulder shrug as the man concluded Drew must indeed be who he said he was or he wouldn't be acting so irrationally. All Drew knew was that he had seen Ian Taylor, his brother-in-law, stumble out of the burning house, coughing and blackened with soot. And Ian was alone.

By the time Drew reached Ian, they had hustled him away from the building, past the singed lawn to a safe zone. He was gulping oxygen from a portable tank as Drew raced over to him. Not caring who saw or what it looked like, the two men embraced silently, both near tears.

"I have to go back in there." Ian sounded desperate. "Sarah . . ." His voice cracked with a sob.

"She's in there?" Drew asked, but he knew the answer. It was what he had feared when he had seen Ian emerge alone. "You can't go back. You're too weak. I'll go."

He started running back toward the house again. He knew it made no sense. But he felt like he'd been given a second chance, a chance to redeem himself. He hadn't been able to save his sister before. He hadn't been able to stop the unspeakable horrors of their father's abuse. Two years younger than she, he had been jealous and hated her all the more for complaining of her "special" time with Daddy from which he'd been excluded. There had been no one to protect her then, and she had learned to defend herself, splitting into alternate personalities that shielded her and fought for her and almost destroyed her. But Sarah had battled her way back to sanity, conflating her characters into a single entity, fragile but whole, who only recently had started to appreciate the gift of life. And this time, Drew thought, he could not let it be torn away from her. He had a second chance. This time, he would save her.

"Get out of the way, mister," someone shouted, bumping him back into reality.

For the first time, he noticed the increasing intensity of the heat as he approached the house. Even the ground was hot, searing his feet through the thick soles of his boots. Firefighters were everywhere, inside and out. He was choked with a futility more impenetrable than the smoke that emanated from the fiery building. There were twenty-seven rooms in the house. It was clear that the fire was confined to the east wing, where Ian and Sarah made their residence, and if Sarah were in danger, that was where she'd be stuck. But that still left ten rooms with access only through a wall of black smoke and orange flame. What chance was there of finding her? What hope of rescue? Still, desperation propelled him forward. He would not ignore his sister's unheard cry for help again.

"I'm sorry, Mr. Symington. You're going to have to move back from here."

Hearing his name stopped him in his tracks.

"Chief Mulcahey!" He clutched at the man with relief. "I've got to go in there," he said, too distraught to recognize the irrationality of his demand. "My sister's in there."

The fire chief nodded in agreement, even as he positioned his broad torso in front of Drew and delicately edged him backward. "We know that, sir. We've got men inside going after her. They've got emergency equipment to get her out safely. She's got a better chance with them than with you," he added bluntly. He'd had more than enough experience with frantic relatives and had become adept at combining persuasive confidence in the professionalism of his men with gentle discouragement of civilian heroics. It worked with Drew as it had with others, and he allowed himself to be led back to reason and to safety.

The two men had met before in unhappy circumstances: once, when arson had razed the factory where Drew, estranged from his father and banished from his place at the family-owned D'Uberville Motor Company, had planned to build his own company with his wife. Their second unfortunate encounter had come when Drew was back at the helm of DMC and an explosion at the plant had destroyed the manufacturing unit of a new car that Sam had designed. Both had been acts of sabotage that had had serious impact on the future and stability of the company. But Mulcahey didn't have to be told that nothing would equal the loss if one of his men didn't walk out of that house with a breathing Sarah Symington Taylor beside him.

"I know it's a hard thing to ask," Mulcahey said as he brought Drew back to the first aid station, where Ian waited, still sooty but breathing on his own. "But I need both of you to just stay here. We're working on getting Mrs. Taylor out safely, and anywhere else, you two would just get in the way."

"But Sarah . . . I have to . . . ," Ian stammered, fear making him incoherent and irrational.

Mulcahey interrupted. "This is no time for heroics. All you can do is put yourself in danger, put my men in danger, and make it harder for us to help your wife. And if you can't promise me that you'll stay put, then I'll have to have an officer remove you." He knew he sounded harsh, but there was no time for argument.

Distressed as he was, Drew understood. "It's okay, Mulcahey. We won't move."

Someone put a blanket around Ian and gave them coffee, which they held but did not drink. They could not look at each other, could not speak. They tried not to think, not to feel, and, each alone, each shared the other's fears.

Drew had no idea how long they'd been there when Sam joined them. Mulcahey led her to them and only shook his head at their unasked question before returning to his duties. Activity around the mansion was slowing down, the smoke had paled from dense black to steaming gray. It was clear the conflagration was coming under control. And still, no sign of Sarah.

"I took Moira over to my mother's and had the driver bring me back," Sam said quietly at Drew's questioning look.

"Good. She didn't need to see this."

Sam moved to Ian and put her arms around him. Until he had come to Oakdale a few years ago looking for his biological mother, Sam hadn't even known she had a brother. Now she couldn't imagine her family without him.

"Can you talk?" she asked him gently. "Can you tell me what happened?"

"I don't really know," Ian answered forlornly. "It was just a regular Sunday. We had breakfast, read the paper, took a nap. I woke up coughing. There was smoke everywhere. And Sarah was gone. I tried calling her, looking for her, but the smoke got too bad."

"Well, maybe she's not even in there," Sam said hopefully. "She could have gone out somewhere. Shopping or . . ." She didn't want to go on. There was a time when Sarah would slip out on a regular basis without informing anyone. But those were the days when she'd transform herself into one of her multiple personalities and go out to bars to drink and pick up strange men. Since the discovery of her disorder and the integration of that angry, self-destructive persona, the disappearances had stopped. Sam wasn't sure what would be worse for Ian to contemplate: Sarah's being trapped in the burning mansion or the horror of a recurrence of the disease that had, at times, endangered them all. Ian gave her the answer.

"Sarah wouldn't have gone out without telling me," he said adamantly. "I mean, we were really happy. We had a great weekend. We sent everyone home, did our own cooking, and just had the whole place to ourselves. It was like a honeymoon."

Sam smiled, understanding completely. She could count on her two hands the number of times that she and Drew had been really, truly alone, and she cherished every one of them. It was one of the few downsides of living on a fully staffed estate with extended family. Even though you could always find a room to be alone in or take a solo walk on the grounds, you could never really wallow in the self-preoccupation that only true solitude allows.

"She could have just gone to buy something special for lunch. To surprise you. Or maybe she left a note, and you didn't see it." Sam knew she was grasping at straws, but there was no point in watching Ian give himself up to despair before they really knew what had happened.

He brightened for a moment, but then his face fell again. "Even so, she'd be back by now."

Sam fell silent, knowing he was right.

Mulcahey approached. He had obviously been in the building. His features were melded into a mask of grime punctuated by streaks of sweat. Only his eyes were clear, and they were grim. Sam felt a collective shiver as she huddled between her husband and her brother.

"The fire's out," Mulcahey began, but there was no jubilation in the announcement. "We've found a body."

Sam gasped aloud and felt the two men tense beside her.

Mulcahey went on. "In a small room, looks like it might have been a library, off the hall down from the master bedroom in the east wing."

"That was Sarah's office," Ian said. His voice sounded like it was coming from very far away.

Mulcahey nodded. "I'm sorry, Mr. Taylor. I know how hard this is for you, for all of you. They're bringing the victim out now, and I know it's a horrible thing to ask, but we'd like one of you to identify the body. It's . . . she's been badly burned."

It took Sam a moment to realize she was crying. All three of them were. No one had even asked if it was Sarah. They hadn't needed to.

"I'll do it," Drew said, breaking from their tearful three-way embrace.

"No." Ian was vehement. "I have to see her."

"Why?" asked Drew hoarsely. "It's awful enough as it is. Remember her the way she was before . . ." His voice broke. "Do that for yourself."

"Mr. Symington's right," Mulcahey volunteered. The husband would suffer enough without a vision of the charred remains of his wife's body etched into his memory. He was only sorry he had to inflict such a task on any of them. But with the condition of the body, it would make things a lot easier if they could get a positive identification from a next of kin.

Ian forced himself to sound calm. He didn't want them to think he was hysterical. "I don't care what she looks like," he said quietly. "She's my wife. And unless I see her, I'm not ever going to believe that this could have happened."

"I'll come with you," Drew offered.

"Please," Ian implored, "I know it sounds crazy, but I don't want anyone else to see her this way." It's, like, the only way I can protect her now."

Drew fell silent, and Sam felt her heart breaking. But they let Mulcahey lead Ian away. When he returned, his haggard face told them all they needed to know.

"They think she was probably reading and fell asleep," he told them, filling in the facts. "The fire started in an electrical outlet. She was probably unconscious from the fumes without ever waking up. That means she wouldn't have felt anything, wouldn't have been afraid."

"It's better that way," responded Sam, knowing it was a stupid platitude, but at this point they needed something positive to hold on to no matter how minimal or how clichéd.

But it was harder for Drew, carrying the guilt of the years she had suffered and he hadn't known. "Damn," he said, not bothering to hide his anger or his tears. "Things were just getting good for her. It isn't fair." And holding each other tightly, they all silently agreed.

* * *

The play was supposed to be a comedy, but so far, the only laughs seemed to come when the actors flubbed their lines. Melinda Myles reminded herself that they were only in the second week of rehearsal; it was too soon to expect things to come together. But she had to admit that she was nervous. More than anything, she didn't want her first foray onto the legitimate stage to be a complete and utter flop.

The production, by a young playwright named Gilbert Gruen, who was also directing, was called *The Truth about Hortense.* Melinda, aware that she had been cast because of her movie star ability to draw box office rather than her sheer talent, had the title role. And, in fact, though the play had been originally scheduled for the one-hundred-eighty-seat Old Vat Room of the Arena Stage, once her participation had been announced, demand for tickets had been so high that they decided to move the production to the larger five-hundred-seat Kreeger Theater.

At least working with the experienced ensemble players of the Arena Stage proved to be a treat. She had expected a certain amount of hostility at the beginning because she might be considered a Hollywood interloper, but instead, she found them all familiar with her film work and quite respectful of her acting skills, even though her experience was exclusively in film and she'd never worked on the stage before. Still, she had a strong sense of her own limitations, and a great fear of overstepping her range.

"Listen, Gil," she said as she approached the writer-director when rehearsal had ended and the cast members had gone their separate ways, laughing and promising to do better the next day, "I know I've got a contract, but if you don't think I'm getting this, I won't sue or anything if you want to let me go."

"Thank God," Gilbert joked before turning serious. "Aren't you enjoying this?"

"Are you kidding? I don't know when I've had so much fun. The other guys are so great, and they're being really kind to me. But so much of the humor falls to Hortense, and I'm just not sure I can carry it. It's such a fabulous play. I'd hate to ruin it."

Gilbert smiled. It had been a long time since he'd heard an actor, let alone an Academy Award–winning leading lady, assume any responsibility for something that wasn't working. The usual tendency was to blame the writing, the directing, the audience, the political atmosphere, anything except one's performance. It was refreshing to meet someone so talented and unassuming who was more concerned with the work than with her own ego. Especially since, as far as he could ascertain, she was doing a great job.

"Let me put it this way," he said. "If you even think about leaving my show, *I* will sue *you*."

She laughed. "You like courting disaster, don't you?"

"What are you talking about? You're great for this part. Hortense is beautiful, a little insecure, smart, not always sure she's doing the right thing. It's typecasting."

"But I'm not funny."

"Wait," he said with confidence. "It always starts like this. There's too much to think about at the beginning to concentrate on the laughs. Once everyone knows their lines and the action is blocked, you'll see. Everyone will relax, and it will all just fall into place."

"Promise?"

"I promise." He hugged her for reassurance, then let her go. "Are you lost?" he joked, realizing the rest of the ensemble had long since decamped. "Do you need a lift somewhere?"

Like everyone else who ever read a gossip column, he knew that Washington was still relatively new to Melinda. For two years she had been married to Diego Roca, the president of San Domenico, a small island-nation in the Caribbean, whom she had met when they had fought side by side to overthrow the dictatorship that had preceded him. They had a child together. But when Melinda realized her husband was turning into the same kind of tyrant he had deposed, she had stolen their son away in a daring maneuver and returned to the States. The rescue had been arranged by Jack Bader, an old flame who was now her current husband. And, Gilbert was aware, it was because of Jack's burgeoning career in the State Department that Melinda had chosen to forego the money and acclaim of Hollywood in favor of doing Gilbert's important—he liked to think—but still rather small play in Washington.

"I'm waiting for Jack to pick me up. He's late as usual," Melinda explained. She noticed Gilbert glance at his watch, a worried frown furrowing his brow. "Is there a problem?"

"Since rehearsal was late today, I sent the janitor home, said I'd lock up."

"Oh, I'm sorry. I'm holding you back. I can just wait outside."

"No, no," he said hastily. "With the windchill factor, it's something like ten degrees out. I can't have my star freeze her butt off. I wouldn't even mind waiting with you except I'm supposed to meet someone."

"Well, can I lock up for you?" she volunteered. "I'm pretty trustworthy."

"That would be okay." He looked hopeful. "Except that means you'd have to be the first one here tomorrow."

"Just tell me when," she said, holding out her hand for the keys.

He hesitated for a moment, then looked at his watch again. He had recently begun an affair with the young, beautiful wife of an older cabinet minister, a major contributor to the Arena's yearly deficit. She was meeting Gil at his apartment. If Gil kept her waiting, he could lose both her affections and her patronage.

"Well, if you're sure. You don't have to do anything except lock the door behind you when you go. I'll turn off all the lights except for the stage light that stays on all the time. Rehearsal's at ten, so if you could be here at, let's say, a quarter to?"

"No problem," she said, accepting the keys in her hand and a kiss on her cheek.

Melinda sat on the edge of the stage, her feet dangling over the footlights, watching him hurry up the aisle and disappear into the shadows of the auditorium. She heard a series of clicks, and suddenly, the darkness had spread except for a small circle of light that reached out to her from the single bare bulb on its stand. His footsteps receded, and then the door slammed shut, introducing a surreal quiet.

She stayed where she was for a moment, losing herself in the serenity of the empty theater. Then she remembered the monologue with which she was supposed to bring down the act one curtain and shuddered. She turned to the page in her script. She read it silently, smiling to herself. On paper, it was funny and charming, but in her mouth, the words seemed somehow lifeless. She got up and started to say the lines, quietly at first but then, remembering she was alone and no one would hear her anyway, louder and more confidently. Realizing she had long since memorized her part and only fear kept the script in her hand, she threw it into the wings. It was, in fact, a delicious speech, and she had always felt it cried out for a healthy dose of overacting. In rehearsals, embarrassed by her own inclination toward melodrama, she had underplayed it. But now, with no one watching, she let loose with every histrionic bone in her body, banishing all subtlety and declaiming her comic emotions to the rafters. It was working; she could feel it. She knew exactly where the laughs would come, and once or twice, she even imagined she heard them. Ending with a flourish and a pratfall, she envisioned herself bringing the house down in a barrage of laughter and applause. And then she realized, with sudden sickening clarity, that the laughter and applause were no fantasy. There really was someone out there in the dark, laughing and clapping at the sight of the movie star making a fool of herself.

"Jack?" she called, peering out over the stage, praying it was him and no one else. She was relieved to see her husband come forward into the light, grinning from ear to ear.

"I've never seen you like that," he said as he ignored the steps and hoisted himself onto the stage beside her.

"And if I had known you were there, you wouldn't have seen it this time either. Why didn't you tell me you'd arrived?"

"You were busy."

"I was just trying something out. I'm having trouble with the part. Obviously."

"Why do you say that? You were great. Really, really fantastic."

"Do you mean it?" She was taken aback but pleased. "You're not just saying that because I'm your wife and you don't want to ruin the evening?"

"Didn't you hear me laughing? You were hilarious. And totally believable."

"You know what? I don't care if you *are* just saying it. It's exactly what I want to hear."

"So the evening's a go?" he asked slyly.

She punched him. "You meany. You *were* just saying it."

He laughed and caught her in his arms. "No, I wasn't. I'm just teasing. It's still hard for me to believe that anybody can be as gorgeous and as talented as you are and not know it. How did I get so lucky?"

"I'm the lucky one," she said quietly.

They looked at each other, both aware of how long it had taken them to reach this moment. When they had first met, Melinda had been a naïve secretary in

Oakdale, having an affair with her boss, Forrest Symington. Jack had been a ponytailed assembly line worker, concealing his education and his law degree while he helped Melinda's sister organize workers' demonstrations against the very man that Melinda professed to love. She had gone to Hollywood and become a movie star, then had an ill-fated marriage to Diego Roca. Jack had cut his hair, become a high-powered lawyer in Washington, and was prepared to marry a smart and beautiful socialite named Daisy Howard when Melinda had come back into his life. At the time, they had both thought it was too late for them, but Daisy, with her intuitive wisdom, had known better and courageously stepped aside to let Melinda take her place at the altar.

Now, at last, Jack and Melinda were together, and neither one of them could believe their good fortune. She was still beautiful, with lush chestnut hair and a flawless ivory complexion. But life's lessons had matured her, and now, instead of the hungry ambition that had once brightened her hazel eyes, she was lit from within by a vital awareness of what really mattered: her hometown husband and the little boy, nearing his second birthday, whom he had accepted as his own son.

She touched Jack's face as if to assure herself that he was real, then brushed a stray lock off his forehead. She let her fingers linger in the sun-streaked silkiness of his golden hair, a legacy of his California youth, that she knew frequently made female undersecretaries at the State Department try to assume more than diplomatic relations. Regular workouts in *tai kwan do* had kept him from losing any of his vigor, and in spite of the time he now spent behind a desk, his body was still toned and muscular. He caught her hand and brought it to his lips.

"Where is everybody?" he asked, and she knew the question was not an idle one.

"Gone," she said quietly, jingling the keys. "I have to lock up."

"So we're all alone?"

"Completely."

Jack grinned, and he didn't have to tell Melinda what he was thinking. He had never been interested in a life in the theater, but the stage seemed, suddenly, a very enticing place to be.

"Well, Ms. Myles," he said, assuming the tone of a patron of the arts, "I believe this calls for a command performance."

"And just what did you have in mind?" Melinda teased, as beguiled as he was by the endless prospects.

"I don't know exactly. I'm casting for a very important part."

"Really? What is it?"

"Sexiest woman in the world. Care to audition?"

"I'm a star, Mr. Bader," she drawled. "I don't usually have to audition. I'm play or pay."

"Well, how do I know if you're right for the part?"

"Check my résumé."

"Just what I had in mind," he said, slipping his hand under her sweater. Her breasts, full but able to support themselves, were soft and warm. He could feel her heartbeat quicken, and as his fingers grazed her nipples, he heard a sharp intake of breath. "You definitely have the right credentials," he whispered in her ear, breathing in her scent. "But how well do you take direction?"

"Try me," she said, her voice husky.

Deftly, he moved his hand under her short skirt, circumventing the tights she had worn to protect against the cold. Barely moving, she accommodated him, letting him feel the moist heat and the pliant flesh that told him she was ready to play the part.

"I see you're very responsive," he said between tiny kisses that brushed her lips. "I like that in my leading lady." With a sweep, he lifted her in his arms and placed her on the edge of the table where only hours earlier she had sat with the entire cast reciting their lines. She flicked her shoes to the floor, and with a single movement, he slid her tights down her shapely legs and tossed them out of the way. Pushing up her skirt, he buried his head in the nirvana between her thighs.

Edging toward completion, she stopped him, forcing herself to pull away. "You know," she said, not having forgotten the game they were playing, "an actor of my caliber gets to pick who she works with. How do I know you're the right director for me?"

"I'll tell you the truth," he said. "My past experience wouldn't qualify me. You're the only one I could do my best work with. I'll show you what I mean." With the speed that comes with desire, he slid out of his pants.

"I see," she said, taking him in her hands and bringing him to her. "This is going to be one powerful performance."

Standing between her knees, not rushing, he guided

himself into her. Slowly, almost languidly, he teased her with his body, bringing her closer, then letting her go. Finally, she could stand it no longer, and, wrapping her legs around him, she locked him to her, clinging to him as their play reached its climax. And though the only applause was in her heart, looking over the footlights into the silent theater, she knew that here in her husband's arms, she had at last found a role she would be content to play for the rest of her life.

"I'm going away," Ian announced to his sister and brother-in-law two days after his wife's funeral.

"I hope you know you can stay in the west wing with us until the house is fixed. It's still your home," Drew told him.

There hadn't really been time yet to assess the damage or get estimates on how long it would take to renovate the decimated east wing. But the west wing, where Sam and Drew resided with Moira, was largely intact except for some smoke damage. Informed of her daughter's horrible death, Mathilde D'Uberville Symington had returned from the south of France in time for the funeral and was occupying her usual suite, trying to recover from the shock. But there were still plenty of empty habitable rooms in the mansion where Ian could be comfortable.

"Thank you, I know that," Ian said graciously, but in fact, he didn't feel that Belvedere was his home at all. It was the estate that Forrest Symington had built for his own ego gratification. To him, it had been proof that he was richer, smarter, more important, than any of his neighbors. But to Sarah, his unhappy daughter, it had been the pampered prison where her misery had begun. It was here that her damaged soul had sought to shelter itself in an elaborate fortress of multiple personalities, and it was here that she had lost control and nearly been done in by the very forces created to protect her. Ian had thought, after the therapy had worked its painful miracle and forged her shattered spirit into a tender but whole unit again, that they might still make a life here. That Sarah might be able to look out over the lush grounds and regard it as her rightful legacy—the abundance she deserved for the agony she had endured. But fate had robbed her of that right.

He knew it was irrational, but he blamed them all. The dead father, the absent mother, the concerned brother who did not know and could not help. The facade of extravagance that encouraged the impression of coveted perfection, while underneath, ugly secrets festered, just as rotting wires hidden behind elegant silk-covered walls had sparked the flames that took his beloved's life. He felt that if he stayed there, he would die himself or, worse, explode and try to exact revenge, burning down the rest of the edifice, because if Sarah couldn't be there to relish it, why should they? And because he knew it was irrational, he knew he had to leave.

"I just think it would be better for me to get away" was all he said to Drew.

Drew nodded, understanding. Even accepting the responsibility of rebuilding his ancestral home for his family's future, it was painful to regard the wreckage that had claimed his sister's life. He could only imagine what it did to her husband. "Where will you go?"

"I have a friend that I used to teach with in Seattle who's been running a boarding school in the suburbs of Paris. He's leaving his position as headmaster and recently wrote to me, asking if I was interested in taking it over. Sarah and I were talking about it when . . ." His voice cracked, and he pretended to cough while he recovered. "Now, I'll have to go alone."

Drew wasn't going to try to dissuade him, but he wanted his brother-in-law to be aware of all he controlled. "If you want to do this, I understand. But I just want you to be aware that Sarah's death hasn't altered your position at DMC. If anything, it's strengthened it. You stand to inherit all her holdings—"

"No." Ian cut him off. "Even though you were kind enough to make a place for me in the company, I never belonged in the auto industry. I'm a teacher. In the realm of big business, it may not seem very important, but it's what I do."

"On the contrary," Drew assured him, showing his respect for the man who had given his sister the only true love she had known, "it's the most important thing there is, and if that's where your heart takes you, then bless you."

Ian smiled gratefully. "That's really all I need to take away from here. Your prayers."

"You're a good man, Ian. But with your permission, I'm going to have the lawyers go over things and put whatever assets are coming to you in a trust. You go do what you have to do, but know it'll be there for you when you want it."

"I don't—" Ian began to protest.

"I'm not listening to any arguments," Drew interrupted. "It's yours. You're the only person who ever made Sarah truly happy. She'd want you to have it. And if you don't use it yourself, then I'm sure, along the way, you'll find a good use for it."

The two men hugged and for the third or fourth time in as many days let the tears roll unashamedly down their cheeks.

Since Ian had booked himself on a night flight to Paris, they decided to have a farewell dinner for him before he left, but it felt more like a wake. For the first time in her adult life, Mathilde did not bother to dress for dinner. Even though they had all agreed that attire at a time like this was totally inconsequential, it was a shock to see their elegant matriarch sitting at the table in black slacks and a sweater and no makeup. Suddenly, she looked old, and it made them all the sadder to see how time, in a devastating few days, could march relentlessly forward, trampling them all.

Melinda and Jack, who had come for the funeral with baby Nico in tow, stayed for the dinner, feeling a need in this time of disbelief and despair to be a part of the family. Harvey and Diane Myles were there, too, wanting to confirm their position as Ian's parents even though long-ago mistakes had sent him into the loving care of an adoptive home. For Moira, who had been staying with her grandparents in Oakdale and was just now returning home, it was a confusing time. Her joy at being back with her parents and finding her baby cousin there was tempered by the knowledge that something bad had happened and the grown-ups were all sad.

"Is Uncle Ian going to be with Aunt Sarah?" Moira asked her mother after her aunt Melinda had taken the overtired and cranky Nico off to bed.

"I told you, sweetheart," Sam explained. "Sarah is in heaven now. You only go to heaven when you die." They had been gentle in breaking the news to Moira of her aunt's death, and they hadn't let her come to the funeral, wanting to protect her as much as possible from the trauma of what had happened in her home. But except for her grandfather Symington, whom Moira had seen in his wheelchair only a few times, no one she knew had ever died before, and she was having a little difficulty grasping the concept.

"Doesn't he want to be with her?"

"Yes, sweetheart. But he can't quite yet."

"Are you going to die?"

"Not for a long, long time."

"Good. Because I want to be with you right now."

"Me, too, pumpkin." Sam hugged her daughter close to her, a silent, unarticulated prayer filling her soul.

Ian left with two suitcases and a box full of books, not much more than he had had when he arrived what seemed like eons ago, seeking his biological mother. He had been a timid young man then, uncertain of his reasons for wanting to find the woman who had given him away, even though he viewed Frank and Elise Taylor, the couple who had lovingly raised him, as his real parents. But before he could complete his mission, he had met and fallen in love with Sarah. And when the search eventually brought him to Diane Myles and her sordid secret, Ian and Sarah had been terrified that the love that they could not deny was to be forbidden to them. The discovery that Ian was, in fact, Harvey Myles's son and not Forrest Symington's, as Diane had believed when she gave him up for adoption, had freed them to be together. From that moment on, Ian had begun to change and grow.

It was as if he had been creeping through a dark, cramped tunnel, unaware of his appearance, confused in his direction. Suddenly, Sarah had brought him into the open, where he could stand tall and flourish in the light. In almost imperceptible ways, without thought or design, even his appearance had been transformed. With Sarah's encouragement, his tousled hair, darker than Melinda's but with the coppery glint of Samantha's, had been styled to look trim but still allow some tantalizing curls to stray over his forehead. She had bought his clothes and, without altering his essential style, had brought him to a state of casual elegance. He had replaced his wire-rimmed glasses with classic Armani tortoise frames, which enhanced the green eyes he shared with his mother and sister. But most of all, Sarah's presence in his life had given him confidence, the knowledge that he could be and was loved; and it had turned him into a remarkably handsome man.

Saying good-bye to the family he had so recently

acquired wasn't easy, and Ian hugged them each in turn, the turmoil of emotions from the last few days evident in each embrace.

"Keep in touch," said Diane. "We don't want to lose you now that we've found you." She knew it would be impossible for her to have the kind of real mother–child relationship that she had with the daughters she had raised, but she still loved him profoundly from the minute he announced himself to her.

"Let us know where you're staying as soon as you get there," added Harvey, still a little awkward with this son he had never known.

"I will," Ian promised them all. "I'll call once I'm settled."

"Come back when you want," Drew reminded him. "Your assets will be in order, waiting for you."

"Thank you," Ian said, certain that he would never be able to touch the wealth that had cost Sarah so dearly.

Melinda came back downstairs still holding Nico. "You take him," she said, handing him to Jack. "Maybe you can get him to go to sleep. I can't. He cries whenever I put him down." Jack reached out for the baby, who interrupted his bottle sucking to smile at the man he called Daddy.

Melinda turned to Ian and kissed him on the cheek. "You can be an honorary member of the Myles Militia."

Sam seconded the motion with a kiss on his other cheek. "Be aware we've never offered that to anyone before."

He laughed and thanked them and kissed them

back. Then he got into the waiting car, not the limousine that had been offered, just a cab he had called to take him to the airport. Driving down the gravel drive to the gates, he looked out through the back window and watched as the family—his family—stood and waved. He waved back, and in his heart, he said good-bye: to them, to Belvedere, and to a way of life that now repulsed him as much as the ugly burnt-out rubble that scarred the still elegant mansion where his wife had died.

"Does this look pink to you?" Sam asked Drew, holding the test tube up to the light.

She had bought the pregnancy test a week ago. There had just been too many people around and too much going on for her to feel comfortable using it. But the morning after Ian had gone, Jack and Melinda decided to head back to Washington. Cranky and not eating or sleeping well, Nico seemed to be coming down with something, and Melinda wanted to be near her own pediatrician in case he did. Mathilde, still in deep mourning for her lost daughter, had stayed in her room. And Diane had picked up Moira to take the child away from the unhappy household, promising that Harvey would help her build not just a snowman, but an entire snow family in their backyard. Finally Sam had the privacy she needed to retire to her own bathroom and take the test. She jiggled the vial again trying to ascertain if there were any further changes in hue.

"I guess it's pink. I don't know," said Drew. "Is it supposed to be?"

"Do you think it's really pink? Or do you think that's just the reflection of the light?"

"It could be the reflection of the light," Drew was forced to acknowledge.

"That's what I was afraid of." She looked at it, shaking her head. There was no sense in pretending. It wasn't pink, and she wasn't pregnant. Again. "Shit," she said.

Drew put down the socks he'd been about to pull on his feet and padded over to his wife barefoot. He put his arms around her, and she sank into his shoulder. He kissed the top of her head. "Don't let it make you crazy, honey. We've got Moira."

"I know, and of course, I adore her. Which is all the more reason why I want another baby. Don't you?"

"Yes, if it happens. But if it doesn't, I've still got the two of you. I really can't ask for anything more."

"I can," pouted Sam, disgruntled. She knew it was her fault. Both she and Drew had had all the tests, Drew subjecting himself to the humiliation of closeting himself in a little cubicle with nothing but a pile of old *Playboy* magazines to ejaculate into a bottle so they could test his sperm, while Sam had been probed and prodded, her tubes painfully injected with dye so they could be X-rayed. The results had shown Drew's sperm to be more than adequate, high in volume and vigorously motile. And even though no obstruction appeared in Sam, the doctor had been left to surmise that there might be some sort of hidden problem inside her that they were not catching. All her life, Sam had battled the odds, figured out what needed to be done to get where she wanted to go, and forged ahead. For the first time, she felt herself out of control, unable to reason her way to success.

"Well, if there's something you want me to do, I'll do it," said Drew, hating to see his wife unhappy. He knew she had hoped that all the skiing they had traded for sex in Aspen would pay off.

"There's nothing else you can do. The next step is for me to get a laparoscopy. Dr. Norris has already told me that."

"What is that?"

"They cut a hole near your belly button, go inside with a little microscope, and look around."

"That sounds awfully unpleasant. Are you sure you want to do this?"

"No, I'm not," she said truthfully. "I don't know what I want to do."

He looked at his wife still in the oversized T-shirt she'd worn to bed, holding a test tube of not-quite-pink urine, the corners of her mouth pulled down in a major mope. She was still the most enticing creature he had ever seen. Holding an imaginary cigar, he wiggled his eyebrows at her. "Would you like me to make a few suggestions?"

"No, I would not," she responded, trying not to smile. "I'm supposed to be upset, so don't try to cheer me up."

"Madam, please," he said, shaking the ash of his nonexistent cigar in a fairly good imitation of Groucho Marx, "what I'm proposing is no laughing matter. In fact, if we do it right, I could keep you down for days."

"Ha ha," she said, pretending she was not amused. "Anyway, you're already dressed."

"Not completely," he answered eagerly, quickly pulling off the socks he'd just put on a minute ago. "See?" He waved his bare foot at her.

Now she did start laughing, and it was all the encouragement he needed. In the blink of an eye, he had removed the rest of his clothes and was pulling her T-shirt over her head. Still giggling, Sam let him back her onto the bed, falling into the pillows. But then he was on top of her, and suddenly, they were no longer playing. This time, there was no need for foreplay, no need to tease each other with caresses that would inflame, but not consume their passion. This time, they both felt the urgency, the desire to couple in every sense of the word. She was already wet when he entered her, and it was she who guided their rhythm, pushing him up and down with her hands while she moved her body beneath him. And when she could not maneuver exactly as she wanted, she pushed him off her and onto his back, then mounted him so that, on top, she could control the pace and the position to her satisfaction. He let her lead the way and do what she wanted, his excitement growing as he watched her achieve her own. It took only minutes. Then, crying out, she collapsed on his body, quivering with pleasure. Only then did he grab her hips and lift her once, twice, thrusting quickly and finishing just seconds behind.

"Mmmmm," she murmured. "It wasn't days, but it was good."

"There's something to be said for just getting right down to it," he agreed. "Do you feel better?"

"No."

"You're lying."

"Okay, a little."

"For heaven's sake, what else do you need?" He pummeled her with a pillow in mock astonishment.

"Maybe just a haircut," she answered, throwing the pillow back at him.

He held up his hands in surrender. "Okay, go get your hair cut." He sat up on the edge of the bed, looking disgruntled.

"What?" she asked. "You don't want me to get a haircut?"

"No, go. It's fine. If you do, I'll spend the day with my mother."

"Oh, that's what that look is for. Do you want me to stay with you?"

"No. I owe her some time. I've never seen her like this. She wasn't like this when my father died."

Sam was tempted to tell him that nobody cared when his father died, but she knew that was beside the point. Instead, she sat beside him on the bed while they both silently acknowledged a moment of guilt for still enjoying life and each other while a veil of tragedy hung like a shroud around their house.

Sitting and waiting for Edward to finish with the client before her, Sam tried to leaf through a copy of British *Vogue,* but all the clothes seemed silly and pointless, and she began to lose patience. She dropped the magazine and looked up to find a woman watching her. She was blond and stylish, with the same softly feathered cut that Edward liked to give to all his long-haired women. A little disconcerted, Sam smiled at her politely.

"Don't let them cut you," the woman said, not even bothering to introduce herself.

"What?" asked Sam, totally baffled.

"Don't let them cut you."

"I'm just getting a trim," replied Sam, and the woman laughed.

"I don't mean your hair," she said, "which actually looks great anyway. I mean the doctors."

Sam did a double-take. She was at a complete loss for words.

"Are you planning an operation?" the woman asked.

"Well, no, yes, sort of. My doctor wants to do a laparoscopy. But how did you know?"

"I'm psychic," the woman said as if declaring that she was a college graduate or a natural blonde or any number of other innocuous things. "Don't let them do it. There's nothing wrong with you."

"I don't know what to say," said Sam.

"Do you want me to read your cards?"

"Sure." If the woman could tell that much about her just by looking at her face, who knew what else she might be able to fathom?

"What time is your appointment?"

"Oh, the hell with my appointment. My hair is fine."

"My name is Christine Zeller," the woman said as they headed out of the salon together.

"I'm Samantha Symington. Or did you already know that?"

Christine laughed. "No. I'm not a mind reader. I can just sometimes read things in people's auras."

"Really," said Sam politely, having no idea what

she was talking about. "Do we need a special place for this?"

"Just somewhere we can sit and not be bothered."

They chose a quiet tearoom within walking distance of Edward's and settled into a booth in the back. The waitress brought them their tea and then lingered at a nonintrusive distance, fascinated as Christine pulled out a deck of tarot cards from her purse.

"Here," she said, handing them to Sam. "Hold them and really concentrate on what you want to know. Then cut the deck and give it back to me."

Sam followed her instructions, closing her eyes to focus more completely on her question. Then she split the cards and handed them to Christine.

One by one, Christine started to lay them on the table, forming an upside-down pyramid pattern. Sam watched, saying nothing, waiting for Christine to speak.

"You're in good shape here. This card represents your husband." She pointed to a medieval-looking figure on a horse. "This star shows great prosperity."

Sam nodded. It occurred to her that it was possible that Christine had indeed known who she was before she spoke to her and was going to spout back to Sam all the things she'd picked up about her in the tabloids.

"This is your child," Christine went on, pointing to another card. "You have a little girl. She's blessed. No problems there."

Good, thought Sam, *but not news.*

Christine went back to her deck and pulled out three more cards, laying two on the bottom and one on top. "You should have another child," she said, and Sam caught her breath. "There's a spirit around you that's waiting for you to let him into your life. But something is stopping you."

"What?"

"I don't know. It's not physical. This card says you're all right. An operation will tell you the same thing. The baby isn't coming because you're not letting him be born."

Samantha squirmed. It wasn't comfortable to be told that she was responsible for her own destiny, although a part of her believed it. "What am I supposed to do about it?" she asked, hoping that Christine wasn't going to tell her that she needed to sacrifice live goats and pay her thousands of dollars.

"Change the way you think, what you feel, how you perceive. Be conscious of what you want and what's stopping you from getting it."

"Easier said than done," scoffed Sam.

"I know someone who can help you. He runs a place called the Institute of Creative Epistemology. It's what they do."

"Oh, please," said Sam, trying not to sound too dismissive. "I'm just not into that sort of self-help thing."

"Luke is different. Why don't you just talk to him? If you don't like it, you don't have to stay. Just see. It's easier than having someone cut open your belly, and you seemed willing to do that."

Sam thought she had a point. "Fine. Give me the number of this place, and I'll look into it."

"Listen, I was going over there after this anyway. If you've got nothing pressing, why don't you come with me? The guy really is amazing. Check him out. You've got nothing to lose but a few stitches."

Sam wished Christine wouldn't keep harping on the surgery thing. Considering that Sam was contemplating a rather invasive procedure, going to see someone seemed a little enough commitment. "Okay."

"Great. I'll just call and tell him I'm bringing you along."

Christine insisted on picking up the check for the tea and then offered to take Sam in her car, promising to drive her back to Edward's parking lot anytime she asked. But Sam didn't want the pressure of having to politely wait on someone else's good will if she felt the need for immediate escape. Instead, she followed Christine in her own car, questioning her own gullibility and finally telling herself it didn't matter. Whatever happened, she could chalk it up to another adventure and turn it into a funny story for Drew at dinner tonight. And maybe, just maybe, it would change her luck—or whatever it was that was keeping her from holding a newborn in her arms.

"I'm warning you," Sam said after they had parked their cars adjacent to each other, and Christine was leading her through a well-kept garden to a small white apartment building with the classic lines of an early Frank Lloyd Wright, "I'm not taking this entirely seriously."

"That's all right," Christine said. "Luke has dealt with skeptics before. It doesn't matter whether you believe in him or not. I just want you to listen to him."

They entered the lobby of the building. It was spare but attractive. The primary adornment seemed to be fresh flowers that were gathered in huge vases on narrow tables lining the walls. A young woman sat behind a light wood desk that had a smaller arrangement of flowers. She looked at them and smiled, then rose to greet them. She was dressed simply but fashionably in black slacks and a cropped poppy red mohair sweater, and her dark hair was cut in an attractive bob. Sam found herself pleasantly surprised. She wasn't sure, but she thought she might have been expecting someone in a saffron robe with a shaved head.

"Hi, I'm Mandy," the young woman smiled, putting her hand out to Sam. "You must be Samantha."

Sam shook her hand and returned her smile, then gave a sidelong glance at Christine. Obviously, she'd prepared them. Sam just wondered what exactly for.

"Luke's with a group," Mandy said. "Would you like to watch?"

"I'd love to," said Sam, relieved. Maybe this way she could get a preview of what the man was up to. Then, if he seemed dangerous or distasteful, she could plead a sudden headache and flee before she even had to meet him.

"You know your way, Christine," Mandy said, pointing to an elevator at the back of the lobby.

"Sure do," said Christine, sounding just a little too enthusiastic. Sam wondered how much of this performance had been engineered in advance. Still, she was curious as to what she would find.

"Am I getting special treatment?" Sam asked Christine casually as the elevator made its way to the top floor.

"Everybody gets special treatment here," Christine said with a shrug.

The doors opened onto a quiet corridor with white walls and deep blue carpeting. Everything in the place seemed designed for ultimate tranquility. Sam didn't trust it, but she couldn't help liking it. At the end of the hall, Christine silently opened a door and led her into a large room. Sam gasped. She hadn't been expecting this. The room had the same white walls and blue carpet as the rest of the building, but one wall was made entirely of glass and looked out over a snowy meadow, replete with a forest of glistening trees and a family of deer poised at its edge. A group of about ten people sat silently facing the window, watching. For a minute, Sam thought it might be some kind of trick, a *tableau vivant* of a nature scene projected on the back wall somehow. But then, the deer moved, loping gracefully back into the woods, and the group sighed and laughed and turned their attention back to each other.

"Exceptional beauty," said the man who faced them, "is everywhere. If you allow yourself to see." His voice was melodic and pleasant, as though inviting you to listen rather than insisting on it.

"That's Luke," whispered Christine unnecessarily.

From the instant he had turned his face toward her, Sam had been certain of his identity. He was younger than she had expected, not conventionally handsome but with strong features that somehow conspired to give him a pleasingly dynamic face. He had light brown hair of no exceptional length or style, but it shone with cleanliness and health. He was wearing a pair of jeans and a nondescript sweater that made him look like an appealing graduate student. Again, she was surprised. With no clear image of what she was going to find, she had envisioned perhaps a guru in white robes or, at the other extreme, an evangelist in an ill-fitting suit and slicked-back hair. But Luke would have seemed like just a regular guy except for the inordinate charisma that emanated from him like a magnetic field. It was indefinable, but it was absolutely compelling.

He was leading them in a meditation exercise, but instead of telling them to close their eyes, he was instructing them to focus: to choose a point and look at it, absorbing every detail of it without trying to name or define it. Then he asked them to be conscious of their bodies, to feel the air around them. He made them open themselves up to every sound, from their own breathing to the most distant hint of noise. Without meaning to, Sam found herself following the exercise, and, to her amazement, she suddenly became conscious of her senses opening up as her body let go. Embarrassed, she shifted and broke the spell, then lifted her eyes to find that Luke was looking at her and smiling. For some strange reason, she found herself smiling back.

After a few moments of silence, there seemed to be a collective, spontaneous sigh, and then, smiling and talking softly to each other, the group began to disperse. A few went over to Luke, and he hugged them each warmly, sometimes sharing a thought or a laugh. Sam waited with Christine until everyone had left, then they moved to the front of the room to greet Luke. He met them halfway.

"This is Sam," Christine announced after he'd taken a few moments to ask about her family.

"I'm pleased to meet you," Luke said, sounding as if he really meant it. "Let's go talk," he said without further preamble.

It was a signal to Christine, and she took her leave, winking conspiratorially at Sam and quietly adding, "Don't be afraid. He doesn't bite."

"I'm not," Sam laughed uncomfortably, reluctant to admit that, in fact, she was.

Christine left through the door they'd entered, but Luke led Sam to another door that opened into the most tranquil office she had ever seen. It had all the accoutrements of the modern office, a desk with a computer, a small sofa and matching chair, a bookcase, which she noticed after a quick glance contained a diverse selection of interesting titles from *The Tibetan Book of the Dead* to the complete works of Henrik Ibsen. Here, there were fresh flowers, too, small bright bunches in pretty vases distributed around the room like exclamation points of nature. There were paintings on the walls by unknown artists but clearly selected by a knowing eye. A statue of a laughing Buddha reigned in the corner, lending an air of benign humor to the atmosphere. It was hard to think that anything bad could happen in a place like this.

Luke motioned her to take a seat on the sofa and sat in the chair facing her. "Do you want to talk about the problem?"

"How do you know I have a problem?" she asked.

"Because that's why most people come to me. One

isn't usually looking for answers if one doesn't have questions."

She laughed. "That's true. I've got plenty of those."

"You don't have to talk about them if you don't want to. But I sensed with you that you're a woman who likes to get to the point. You've probably got a busy life, and you didn't come here to exchange small talk with a stranger."

She looked at him. In fact, she had wondered how she could avoid wasting time with pleasantries and get right to the point without being rude. He had made it easy.

"You're right. I'm here because I've been having difficulty getting pregnant, and Christine thought maybe you could help."

He nodded thoughtfully. "What made you turn to Christine for advice?"

"It seems silly, really," she said, embarrassed to admit that she was a sucker for all that fortune-telling hocus-pocus. "I'm not usually into this sort of thing, but I was at the hairdresser's, and Christine came up to me and said, 'Don't let them cut you,' just out of the blue. At first I thought she meant my hair, but then she said she was talking about doctors. As it happened, I was about to have a laparoscopy, so I let her read my cards. I don't really believe in that psychic stuff, but . . ." She trailed off, wondering if she was offending him.

He surprised her by saying, "Neither do I. But it's just too tempting not to want to hear it."

"That's exactly how I feel," she said with a laugh, "although my husband would think I'm out of my mind."

Luke smiled and shrugged. "Men aren't usually in touch with that side of themselves. You can't be pragmatic all the time. Sometimes you want your dreams and your hopes confirmed."

"Yes," she said emphatically. "Even if you don't believe someone can tell your future from the cards, it's interesting to see what they surmise about you from your face."

"So what did Christine tell you?"

"She told me that there was nothing wrong with me. I don't need a laparoscopy or any more tests or operations. She said the reason I wasn't getting pregnant was that I was stopping myself."

He nodded sagely. "That is usually why people don't get what they want. They put a big red light at the starting line and then wonder why they're not in the race. The trick is to make the light turn green and keep it that way."

"Is that what you do?"

"No," he said modestly. "That's what *you* do. I just show you ways it might be accomplished."

"I'm sorry . . . uh . . ." She hesitated.

He understood. "Luke. Just call me Luke. Everybody does."

"I'm sorry, Luke. Christine never really told me what you did. She just said she thought you could help. Are you a therapist?"

"In a manner of speaking."

"Are you licensed? Do you have a degree?"

"No. Does that trouble you?"

"If you claim to be a therapist, it does."

"Samantha, I don't claim to be anything but a guide. The Institute of Creative Epistemology only offers a ground plan to navigate the complicated interconnected routes of mind, body, and soul. Since I've been through the maze, I can sometimes offer a map of the hazards and wrong turns that threaten to keep you from finding what you're looking for."

"Whatever that may be," said Sam, not exactly sure what he was talking about.

"Exactly!" he said exultantly as if her natural understanding had suddenly made her his prize pupil.

She felt inordinately proud, but a second later, she almost laughed out loud. She could see what he was doing. Charm, confuse, flatter, make it look like you've got the answers without bragging about it. Then, when they're completely disarmed, hit them up for the big bucks.

"And just how much does it cost to attend the Institute of Creative Epistemology?" she asked, cutting to the chase.

"Nothing."

She was taken aback. "Well, then how . . . ?" She swept her hand around the room, including the system, the building, his involvement, everything, in the gesture.

"The building was given to us by a member. Volunteers keep it going. Donations are made."

"Oh, donations," she said, sounding more accusatory than she had intended.

He laughed. "Don't worry. I'm not going to ask for one from you. We don't solicit."

She sat quietly for a few seconds, at war with herself. But the real question wouldn't let her go. "Do you think that if I came to the institute I'd be able to get pregnant?"

"I think—no, I believe with all my heart that if you came to the institute, you could do anything you damn well wanted to do."

I've got nothing to lose, Sam thought, not quite sure if she believed it herself.

"Poor little Nico," Melinda crooned softly as she rocked her fussy baby. She had hoped that being home might improve his disposition. But he had cried almost nonstop on the plane to the dismay of the other passengers, and even in his own familiar surroundings, he couldn't seem to calm down.

"Do you think he's hungry?" Jack asked, standing in the doorway of the nursery. They had taken over the house on Thirty-first and Q Street from Sam and Drew, and with a change of accessories from pink to blue, the little room next to the master bedroom that had been renovated for Moira was perfect for little Nico. Jack went to them, and the child, seeing him, grabbed his hand and held it to his cheek, wanting both his parents to stay with him. Even though he had been born Sebastian Nicholas Vincenzo Roca, son of the president of San Domenico, at two years old, he knew himself only as Nico Bader, a normal little boy growing up with loving parents in Washington, D.C.

Melinda looked at Jack, shaking her head in desperation. "He won't eat anything. He hasn't eaten properly in days."

Jack looked lovingly at the baby, who had stopped crying but still looked miserable. "He doesn't seem to be losing weight."

Startled, Melinda studied the baby. She had noticed herself that he seemed to look puffier than usual but had dismissed it. "Something's wrong" was all she said.

Their appointment with the doctor was in the afternoon, and they went together. Following the doctor's instructions, they had given Nico plenty to drink and were able to manage to get a urine sample for the doctor. The baby began to wail the minute Dr. Lebow walked into the room, but the doctor wasn't concerned. It was age-appropriate behavior, and she simply ignored it and got on with her examination as rapidly as possible while his parents held the squirming child and tried to soothe him to no avail.

Afterward, in the waiting room, waiting to hear the doctor's pronouncements, they tried to interest Nico in the toys that usually delighted and distracted him. But he lay listlessly in Melinda's arms, spent and exhausted, pale beneath the feverish pink of his cheeks, until, eventually, he fell asleep. It seemed to take an exceptionally long time for the doctor to call them back to her office. When she did, the look on her face told them it was not good news.

"I'm going to send you to a specialist," she informed them immediately, "but I want to tell you what I think is the problem."

They listened attentively, leaning forward in their seats. "Nico," she went on, "appears to be having a problem with his kidneys. That's why he looks so bloated and puffy even though he's not eating. He's retaining fluid. He's excreting an abnormal amount of protein in his urine, which is another sign."

They were stunned into silence. Melinda instinctively held the baby a little closer to her bosom. Finally, Jack, collecting himself, asked, "What exactly is wrong, and what can we do about it?"

"We're going to need more tests, and that's why I'm sending you to another doctor who specializes in pediatric kidney diseases. At this point, because it came on so subtly and seems to be progressing rapidly, my educated guess is nephrotic syndrome, which is a catch-all phrase for a collection of symptoms that appear without a specific cause. There are various courses of treatment depending on the severity of the disease, ranging from steroid drugs to dialysis. In extreme cases, a transplant might be necessary."

Melinda began to cry, and Jack put one hand on her shoulder while the other reached out to stroke the sleeping baby's brow. He could not have loved Nico more if Nico had been his biological son, and his heart was breaking as much as hers. The doctor gave them time to compose themselves, then she handed them a slip of paper with the name and number of a Dr. Alexander Stein. "He's a good man," she said, "one of the best. I've already called his office and told them about Nico. He'd like to see him right away if that's all right with you."

They nodded and thanked her. If something was wrong with Nico, they absolutely wanted to take care of it as soon as possible.

"Remember," she told them encouragingly as she walked them to the door of her office, "a lot of progress has been done in this area in the last few years. With a little luck, Nico will still be able to have a normal, happy life."

From the moment they met Dr. Stein, Jack and Melinda had a profound belief in his abilities. He was a handsome British expatriate in his early forties, and both his knowledge and his commitment to his young charges seemed all-consuming and absolute. But even he was unable to stop the terrifying nightmare of the next few weeks.

Dr. Lebow's educated guess had turned out to be accurate. Further tests showed that Nico did indeed have nephrotic syndrome. Dr. Stein prescribed a number of medications, which one after another proved to have little effect on the child's deteriorating condition. Finally, with no other recourse left, they had taken the baby to the hospital for a kidney biopsy.

The news was not good. "His disease is progressing," Dr. Stein told them gently. "At this point, there are two ways to go. We can insert a catheter into his abdomen and start him on peritoneal dialysis, which might slow the disease, but I don't think it will stop it." Both parents winced. The image of their poor little baby enduring this ordeal without hope of relief was terrifying. "Or," the doctor went on, "we can go directly for a transplant."

Transplant? Melinda was reeling. How could her baby be so sick?

"If he has a transplant and it works, will he be fine?" Jack asked, knowing he had to be the spokesman because he could see that Melinda was on the verge of choking with tears and could barely speak.

"If it works, there's a good chance his life will be almost as normal as any child's."

"Almost?"

"With any traumatic procedure, careful monitoring is necessary. We don't understand the body as well as we'd like to, and sometimes it does things we don't expect. He'll also need to take immunosuppressive drugs, but there's been great advancement in that area, and we've managed to get the doses down low enough so there are few side effects."

Jack forced himself to say the words, "Could getting the operation kill him?"

"Let me put it this way. He's more likely to die without it."

"Let's do it," said Melinda, her mind and her throat suddenly clearing. For the first time in weeks, she felt lucid. Here was a solution she could work with. "He can have one of my kidneys."

Dr. Stein nodded. "If you're both willing, we'll test you both. For an infant whose immune system is more active than an adult's, we try to go for the best blood and tissue match possible to minimize the chance of immunological rejection. Often, one parent is a better match than the other."

"Actually," Jack said with a look at Melinda, "Nico is not my biological son."

The doctor raised an eyebrow. "You're so good with him, and he seems so close to you, I just assumed . . ."

"As far as I'm concerned, you assumed correctly. I'm crazy about that kid. And believe me, if it's possible, I'd be happy to donate my kidney."

To be on the safe side, both Melinda and Jack went through the battery of tests to determine compatibility. But they were not prepared for the results.

"Did you know, Melinda," Dr. Stein asked her when they met to discuss the next step, "that you have one undersized kidney?"

"What?" asked Melinda, displaying her ignorance of the situation. "How did that happen?"

"It appears to be congenital. You were just born with it. But since you only need one kidney to function, it never really mattered. The only thing it means is that we can't take out the good one you've got, and the other one won't do us any good."

"What about mine?" asked Jack hopefully, wanting to step into the breach.

"Unfortunately, your blood type is wrong. You're type A. Nico needs O."

"Then what about getting him on the regular kidney transplant waiting list?" asked Melinda.

"Unfortunately, for type O, it could be a year before his name got to the top."

"I thought O was a universal donor," said Jack. "Doesn't that make it easier?"

"I'm afraid not. All it means is that all other blood types accept their own plus O. But O has antigens against A, B, or AB, which means Nico would automatically reject an organ from anyone but an O. At the same time, the highest percentage of the population has blood type O, which means donor organs from type O are the most sought after. Nico will have to get in line."

"What if he can't wait?" asked Melinda ominously.

"We'll start him on dialysis. That should help. But if there was any way we could get him a kidney and avoid that, it would be good. Dialysis is hard on a toddler, who has limited vocabulary and can't really understand what's happening to him."

"Can we get someone else to donate?" asked Jack, trying to think whom to approach. He had a feeling that both Sam and Drew would be receptive to help-their little nephew, but it was a difficult thing to ask.

"If they have the right blood type, that would be fine. Probably the best bet now is really his biological father. Is there any possibility of getting him to consider it?"

"No, there isn't." Jack's answer was quick and vehement. "His father is out of our lives."

"Yes, there is," said Melinda more quietly but just as fast. "If it means saving Nico, I'll do it. We'll let you know very soon," she promised as she stood up to go, and Jack, more upset than he cared to admit, followed.

"The man was ready to kill you," he hissed at Melinda as they were driving home.

"Me," she acknowledged, "but not Nico."

"You don't see the State Department reports on San Domenico the way I do. He's become a monster. He might not even consent."

"I won't know unless I ask," she said evenly.

"Melinda, I love Nico, you know that. But I don't see what good it will do to make Diego Roca a part of our lives. It's too dangerous."

"I don't want to make him a part of our lives. I just want him to give Nico back his life. Nico's the one in real danger."

"We could look for another donor first. Someone with the right blood type."

"Number one, we don't have the time. And number two, no one in the world could be a better match than Nico's own father. Don't you want to give him the best chance he could possibly have?"

"Yes," said Jack quietly, suppressing his own fears. "You're right."

"I'll write a letter," she said, already composing it in her head as Jack pulled up in front of the house. "Can you fax it from the State Department?"

"Of course," he said.

"I'll do a first draft, and then you look it over. Okay?"

He nodded and watched as she hurried to the computer. He paid the baby-sitter and went to the nursery, where Nico lay listlessly in his crib. His heart melted at the sight of his son, and when the little boy reached out his arms, Jack picked him up and held him close.

"We're going to get you better, big boy. And no matter what happens, Daddy's going to stay with you."

"Daddy," said Nico as he put his arms around his father's neck, "Daddy stay."

"Forever and ever," said Jack as he tenderly kissed the top of the sweet little head that rested on his shoulder.

3

There were sixty-two students boarding at the American School in St. Denis, ranging in age from thirteen to nineteen, in a demanding high school program that prepared them for the best colleges throughout the world. Many of the students were the children of American diplomats posted throughout Europe. Since the school combined the cachet of an elitist European boarding school with a progressive American education, it provided the perfect balance for nervous parents seeking a competitive edge for their children. Some of the students were of European gentry, whose parents had decided a knowledge not only of the English, but of Americans, was necessary for the kind of monumental international success they expected of their offspring. A very few were local children, most on scholarship, whose superior abilities had brought them to the attention of the foreign school on their native soil. The latter group, a handful in each of the four grades, did not sleep in and tended to stick together, doing the same work as the others but somehow giving the impression that they were not really participating, lest they call attention to themselves and their differences.

The building itself was impressive, a classic nineteenth-century chateau that had been converted into classrooms on the bottom floors and dormitory rooms on the top. The children were clustered by sex and grade in eight large, spare, but comfortable rooms, with either a live-in teacher or a privileged senior student occupying a separate but adjacent room, acting as monitor for the evening hours. A small but comfortable caretaker's house had been renovated into the headmaster's home, allowing some distance and privacy while, at the same time, keeping authority on the premises within easy reach. The grounds included a basketball court, four tennis courts, an Olympic-size swimming pool housed in its own glass building, several small gardens, and a forest that was off-limits to all students except those with assignments to search for particular botanical specimens during specified daylight hours.

Ian loved it all from the minute he saw it.

"It's a great place," Paul Kogan, Ian's friend and departing headmaster, confirmed. "Of course some of the kids are brats and pains in the ass, but once you figure out how to deal with them, its all very manageable."

A local school custodian from the village of St.

Denis had picked Ian up at Orly, carrying a handwritten sign with his name. Avoiding Paris and driving straight to the countryside, they had carried on a halting conversation in French, and Ian had been grateful for even the limited amount of exposure he had had to the language with his mother-in-law. His driver had assured him over and over, since they didn't have enough common language to talk about much else, that *"c'est beau."* But nothing had quite prepared him for the sheer beauty and the complete serenity of the school itself and its environs.

"It's just what I need," sighed Ian, overwhelmed with gratitude toward his friend and whatever fates conspired to bring him to this tranquil place at the time of his worst distress.

"It probably is," said Paul, genuinely moved. "I'm sorry about your wife. It must have been an awful blow. But you can forget a lot of things here. Which can be both good and bad," he added with a laugh.

"It'll be good for me," said Ian. "Thank you."

"I should be thanking you. We're only an hour and a half away from Paris here, but it can seem like another world. It was time for me to get back into the real one."

At a faculty tea, Ian was introduced to the rest of the small staff. The math teacher was a hale American named Bill Kaminsky, who lived in, supervising the senior boys. The sciences were covered by a young American couple, Tim and Vera Bolen, who were recent Ph.D. graduates from Stanford, looking to experience the world before settling down in some small American university town. They rented an apartment in St. Denis, to which they repaired after each day's lessons. History was taught by an American in his fifties named Arthur Corbett, who hadn't been back to the States in twenty years. The English literature teacher and the classics teacher, who also taught Greek and Latin language, were both Britons. The romance languages were taught by a beautiful woman named Naomi Varenne, whose mother was American and father was French. Mademoiselle Varenne, as the students called her, was one of the live-in teachers, her room adjacent to the freshman girls. Ian could only imagine what the thought of her one floor away must do to the senior boys at night. But as far as he could ascertain, her English was impeccable and she spoke French, Italian, Spanish, and German all fluently, and in spite of, or perhaps because of, her provocative good looks, she was considered one of the best and most popular teachers in the school. Responding to the informal introductions made by Paul, all the teachers seemed politely friendly and accepting of Ian's presence. But exhausted as he was by the trip and the emotional chaos of the week before it, Ian could register very little of whom exactly these people were or what they offered or expected from him.

Paul noticed. "You must be ready to collapse."

"That's putting it mildly," Ian conceded. "Do you think anybody would be insulted if I . . . ?"

"Not at all," Paul broke in, understanding. "Go ahead. Get yourself settled, take a hot bath, go to sleep. You'll have plenty of time to get to know everyone."

"Um . . . where . . . ?"

"In the cottage, of course. That's where the head-master lives."

"But you . . . ?" Ian was aware he was talking in sentence fragments, but he couldn't seem to muster the energy required to create both a subject and predicate.

"Hey, I'm out of here. I've got a flight to L.A. tonight. I'm leaving in half an hour."

Ian's head reeled with confusion. "Tonight? But I just . . . Who . . . ?"

"Oh, don't worry, pal. You'll do fine. You've met the staff already. You'll see the kids tomorrow. And Colette will be here to show you where to go and tell you what to do."

"Colette?"

"Colette Simard. She's been my personal assistant for the past three years, and she's consented to stay on for you. That is, if you want her. But you'd be a fool not to. I'll admit to you and no one else that my success at this school has been directly related to Colette. I'm telling you, she knows better than anyone what has to be done. So you'll keep her on, won't you?"

"Well, sure, I—"

"Great. Then you've got nothing to worry about. She'll be here in the morning, and you'll be home free."

Ian knew there was something missing in this hasty transfer of power, but he was too tired to argue. Besides, watching Paul check his ticket for the third time in as many hours, he realized it would do no good. For the first time, it occurred to him to ask, "Why . . . in the middle of the semester . . . ? I'm glad, I mean, for myself, but . . ." He was becoming increasingly incoherent, but it didn't seem to bother Paul.

"Actually, I was supposed to go at the beginning of the year. But the guy that was hired to take my place didn't work out the way we'd hoped. So that's why I was so happy when you said you wanted the job and would take it right away. Of course, I'm sorry about your circumstances, losing your wife and all."

Ian nodded. He had no words left with which to accept the expression of sympathy. So, as exemplary as Paul had told him he was, he was not first choice. And considering his predecessor's precipitous departure, he was not surprised that Paul had no intention of sticking around to see if he acclimated or not. But it didn't matter. Ian made his way to the headmaster's cottage and found the bedroom where someone, presumably his custodian-driver, had left his bag. He threw all his clothes onto the floor and climbed into bed. He had already convinced himself that for the time being, the American School at St. Denis was the perfect place for him to be.

He fell asleep immediately and dreamed, as he always did, of Sarah. This time, he dreamed they were having a picnic on the grounds of Belvedere. At first, they were alone and having a wonderful time, but then, somehow, other family members had started to appear, and the day had gone from sunny to overcast. Ian wanted to get Sarah inside before the deluge, but Forrest wouldn't let her go, tugging her from one side, while Ian held fast to the other. Harvey and Diane were there, and Ian tried to enlist their aid, but Diane kept pushing him away, explaining she couldn't be disloyal to her boss, while Harvey just seemed lost and confused. It began to rain, and Ian was surprised at the warmth and gentleness of the drops, thinking perhaps he had been wrong to be afraid, that this would be a warm and healing rain. He loosened his grip, and then suddenly, a flash of lightning struck and swallowed his wife, leaving him screaming for her not to go.

"Why should I go, *monsieur?* I have just arrived."

Ian opened his eyes, keeping the rest of his body completely still. A woman of indeterminate age, neither old nor young, dressed in a simple navy blue skirt and sweater stood at the foot of his bed. Her dark hair, which showed no sign of gray, was pulled back from her face with a wide velvet headband and hung loosely to her shoulders. At first glance, he thought she was rather plain. But further reflection brought him to the realization that his assessment was due more to the severity of her demeanor than the configuration of her features, which, in fact, were rather pretty.

"Who are you?" Ian asked. "And why are you here?"

"I am Colette Simard. And I am here because you are due to address an assembly of the students in one hour. I thought you might want time to prepare." Though it was clear it was not her first language, her English was perfect, with a slightly British accent.

He sat bolt upright. "Oh, jeez. Nobody told me."

"I'm telling you. That's my job. Didn't Kogan tell you that?"

"He mentioned you arranged things and that I'd find you indispensable. Which, obviously, I already have. I should have set an alarm or something."

"I woke up Kogan most mornings, too."

"Well, you won't have to do that for me from now on." He noticed the clothes that he had left on the floor had been folded and placed over the back of a chair. He was profoundly embarrassed. "You won't have to pick up my clothes either. That's not in your job description, is it?"

She shrugged. "My job is to take care of the headmaster. Whatever that requires."

He looked at her sharply. There was more than one way to interpret that statement, not all of them innocuous. But she met him with a level gaze that gave no hint of hidden meanings.

"Okay, Miss Simard . . ."

"Call me Colette."

"Fine, Colette. Then you must call me Ian. Give me fifteen minutes to shower and get dressed and I'll meet you . . ." He trailed off. He had no idea where to meet her.

"I've prepared breakfast in your kitchen. When you're ready." She walked out before he could thank her, and he was left to ponder what exactly her duties as personal assistant entailed.

He showered quickly and put on the least rumpled suit in his still packed bag. Nervously, he ventured out of the bedroom to be greeted by a heavenly scent of fresh croissants and rich French coffee.

"Oh, Colette," he sighed, dropping into a chair by the small table off the kitchen that constituted the dining room, "this is exactly what I needed."

She smiled a little smugly and poured. "I knew it would be."

While he ate, she took out some papers from a briefcase and, consulting them, gave him his schedule. "Don't you want anything?" he interrupted, indicating the overflowing basket of breads.

"I've eaten," she said tersely and continued with her litany of his daily activities. "After you speak to the students, you will meet some members of the school's board of directors who will attend the assembly."

He groaned. The last thing he wanted on his first full day in France was to try to impress a bunch of doddering do-gooders who would no doubt insist on giving him their own views on education. "Do I have to do that today? Couldn't it wait until I'm a little more settled in the school and I've had a chance to assess the situation and what I want to do with it?"

"They sign the checks," she said, and he knew the case was closed. "I've made some notes for you for your speech," she added, handing him a sheaf of three-by-five index cards.

Ian was taken aback. Perhaps Paul hadn't been joking when he said that his success was due to Colette. But Ian had no intention of being a puppet headmaster. "That's very kind of you," he said, trying not to sound officious, "but I think I might prefer to prepare my remarks myself."

"Whatever you wish," she said, and he could not tell if she was insulted by his refusal or merely acquiescent. "There are just some areas you might want to cover."

More as a courtesy than with the intention of using

them, he glanced at the notes. They were typewritten with headings and spaces that made them incredibly easy to read. Flicking through a few, he saw that they did indeed cover areas he needed to touch on—and in such a cogent and concise way that, beyond foolish pride, there was no excuse not to follow them.

When the time came, she led him to the small but elegant auditorium that had been fashioned from the chateau's former ballroom and waited in the wings while he took to the podium on the stage in front. With Colette's index cards as a guide, he was able to make an informal, but at the same time relevant, speech, injecting some of his own humor along the way. Although there was no way of really knowing, the students seemed responsive enough, and he promised that he would be spending time in each of their classrooms, getting to know them on an individual basis. When their teachers led them back to their classrooms, a few shyly waved at him and called out their welcomes. For the first time in a long time, he felt imbued with hope and good spirits. In his time as a member of the extended Symington family, doing his well-financed tour of duty at the D'Uberville Motor Company, he had forgotten how much he loved to teach and never realized how much he missed it.

Ian's feeling of well-being ended abruptly as Colette came toward him leading a triumvirate of dour officials whom he rightly assumed to be the board members. The first two, he noted, as Colette introduced them, were as he had imagined. Mrs. Austin Beckworth was the fiftyish wife of an entrepreneur who had made fortunes with a chain of video stores, designed after the American prototype, all of them featuring endless copies of the Jerry Lewis oeuvre available for sale or rental. While they had no children, Mr. Beckworth had contributed half the yearly budget of the American School to keep his wife busy with charity fund-raisers both at home and abroad. Maurice Menton was a direct descendent of the Frenchman who had purchased the chateau and begun the school in deference to his American wife who was always threatening to go back to Chicago so their children could have an American education. He seemed pained and bored, and Ian noticed that every once in a while, he'd take a nip from an engraved silver flask when he thought no one was looking. But the third board member was entirely unexpected. She was young and beautiful, with the platinum hair of a movie star and the figure of a model. She was on the board, Colette explained, by virtue of the fact that she was connected to someone in the American embassy, which was an ex-officio sponsor of the school. But she seemed genuinely interested in its curriculum and its students. And though Ian hadn't quite caught her name, since Colette had said it so dismissively, he enjoyed talking to her about his philosophy of education and what he envisioned for the school. It was not until she was turning to leave with her colleagues that he realized why she seemed so familiar to him.

"Daisy Howard!" he proclaimed as though he'd just made quite a startling discover, which he had.

"Yes?" she turned back to him, not comprehending the victory in his voice.

"You're Daisy Howard," he elaborated, realizing a little belatedly that this would not be news to her.

"Yes. We were introduced, weren't we?" she asked politely, knowing full well that they had been.

"Yes, of course," apologized Ian. "But I didn't realize until just now that we know each other."

"We do?"

"I'm Melinda Myles's brother."

"Oh, my God," she said, now as aghast as he was. "Ian Taylor. Of course. I never put it together. I can't believe we didn't recognize each other."

"There's no real reason why we should have," he said, excusing them both. "We only met once at your wedding . . . uh . . . that is . . ." There seemed to be an awful lot that was awkward to say between the two of them.

She had the grace to laugh. "My wedding that never was, you mean. I'm afraid I never got a chance to know Jack's friends. Although you must be seeing quite a bit of him now that you're all family."

"Well, he and Melinda are still living in Washington, but they came to the funeral."

She put a sympathetic hand on his arm. "I heard about what happened at Belvedere. I'm so sorry. I know how hard it must have been for you to lose your wife."

"Thank you," he said, grateful that he didn't have to explain.

Mrs. Beckworth and Maurice Menton had already gotten into the waiting car. She tapped impatiently on the window.

"I'd better go," Daisy said. "Can't keep the old fogies waiting. They didn't even want to come in the first place, but the embassy shamed them into it."

"Are you working at the embassy now?"

"Reluctantly. My mother's been ill, and my father's been pressing me to come to Paris to take over her duties. After aborting my own wedding, I didn't have a lot of excuses left, as you can imagine. But I have to admit the work is a lot more interesting than I had imagined. I thought it would be mostly eating and greeting, but I've been able to get involved in some truly worthwhile causes, like your school, and I actually like it. So nepotism does pay off," she added in her self-deprecating style.

"Don't be embarrassed on my account. I went from being a teacher to an auto executive because of my family connections. But I have to admit, I'm happy going back to being a teacher."

"From what I heard today, I'd guess you are a good one."

"Well, if you really want to judge, let me invite you to come back. Without the old fogies. Spend some time and see how I'm doing. Then you can give the embassy a real report."

There was another tap on the window.

"I'll take you up on that," said Daisy, hurrying to get into the car. "Don't worry, I'll call in advance. I don't believe in surprise inspections."

He laughed. "It doesn't matter. Nothing's going to beat the surprise I had seeing you here today."

"A bientôt," she called out, rolling down her window as the car pulled away.

He waved. "Daisy Howard," he said to himself. "What an incredibly small world." He turned, surprised to see Colette, whom he had forgotten was right behind him, waiting.

"Would you like to get on with your day now?" she

asked. "There's quite a lot still that I have to show you."

"Yes, of course," he said, following her as she took off at a steady clip, making a mental note to try to be more considerate of her in the future. In spite of her severity, she was so mutely accommodating that he could see how easy it would be to start taking Colette for granted.

"Burn the fields," Diego Roca screamed at Guillermo Valdes, his minister of agriculture. "Burn every single one of those fields!"

Valdes blanched. "You cannot do that. It is their only cash crop. It would be a disaster for those farmers."

"Listen to me. I don't care if it's the whole goddamn island and we all go bankrupt. I did not fight a revolution to turn my country into a drug farm for American dope dealers."

"Be realistic, *Presidente*. It's not as if we have a lot to export. This could serve us well. We can tax the farmers on their profits. We can charge a heavy export duty to the traffickers. The farmers make money. The country makes money. Everyone is happy."

"And what about the users?"

"What concern are they of ours? As long as they're not in San Domenico."

"It is against our law. It is against international law. We are not going to become exporters of death. Cocaine is not an option," he said with finality.

Valdes turned away, trying not to let his commander know how irritated he was. He cursed the aide who had suggested *el presidente* try to get back in touch with his discontented citizens by driving through the countryside as he used to and reconnecting with the common people. It was on one of these drives that the coca fields now in dispute had been spotted. Valdes had hoped that making a case for the poor growers might convince *el presidente* that this was an altruistic venture. But the truth was that he had already made a deal that would deposit over three million dollars in his personal account, and he was not about to see it go up in smoke.

He tried another tactic. "If you are concerned about the international ramifications, there are ways to make certain that the drugs are not connected to us. The raw materials can be routed to some other country for processing. Also, let me just add, *Presidente,* that for your consideration, I am sure a sizable contribution to your personal campaign fund could be arranged."

"Are you insane? Do you think I would take a bribe from drug smugglers? And did you think I would let you profit from it?"

"Me? I have no interest here except in seeing that the needs of the farmers are met." Valdes's outraged tone was clearly meant to convey the height of right-eousness.

Diego Roca looked at him, almost snorting with derision.

Valdes flushed with anger. "Fine. You want to burn their fields, go ahead. Then what are you going to give them to grow? More coffee? Nobody even wants what we have already. You think these people care about the revolution anymore? You think they are worried about international law? They want to grow something they can sell so they can buy food to eat. Is that such a sin?"

"Burn the fields," said Roca quietly this time but with the same conviction. "Take a regiment of soldiers to the area and burn the fields. On second thought, I will take the soldiers myself. I don't trust you."

He stormed out of his own office, leaving the minister behind. He had no illusions about Valdes's self-interest in the matter. In fact, Diego Roca had very few illusions about himself or anyone else in his cabinet. The fabric of his dream for San Domenico lay in tatters, and he knew that he had to accept responsibility for being the first to slash at it. Given the authority to govern by a democratic vote, he had immediately moved to restrict democracy. Not out of megalomania, as some had accused, but because he believed that when a society was weak, when years of poverty and malnutrition, both physical and spiritual, had eaten away at the core, then any disruption, no matter how just, could end up being fatal. He had lost much because of this conviction: his wife and child, the trust of some friends, the faith of his fighters. Still, he believed. And somewhere behind the dogma and the discord, he still had hope that, however long it took, when San Domenico was stable and its population no longer hungry, he would be proven right and win back all that he had lost.

If he had stopped to analyze his aspirations, he might have seen that they were naïve. But he could not afford to. Even though he knew she had remarried, every day, without fail, in the continual times of stress and the all-too-infrequent moments of triumph, he thought about Melinda and Nico and missed them both with every fiber of his being. His fury at her for abandoning him, for not understanding his mission, for depriving him of their son, was unabated. But so, too, was his love. Unable to alter his conduct, he lived for confirmation of the course he had chosen, so that he could convince his wife and child that he was worthy of their return.

But he knew without a doubt that none of it could happen if he allowed his country to become a haven for the scum who fed off the weaknesses of others. If it had merely been a question of taking food out of the mouths of the peasants, Valdes would never have put up resistance. But taking money out of his pocket, no matter how dirty, was another question. And in doing so, Diego Roca was aware that he had made an enemy of Guillermo Valdes for life.

Pacing the office of *el presidente,* Valdes was already mourning the loss of the new Mercedes he had recently ordered from Germany in anticipation of the profits that Diego Roca now saw fit to incinerate. Until today, he had felt only contempt for the leader of his country. Now he hated him. Valdes had fought with the rebels during the revolution, but only because he knew that eventually they would win. He had served loyally in the postrevolutionary cabinet, not because he shared Roca's particular vision, but because he thought he could benefit from Roca's potency. While others had complained about the president's tyranny, Valdes had faulted him for not going far enough. Maintaining autocratic control for the greater good was a pointless endeavor. It made you enemies and gained you nothing. The only point of having position was to benefit from it. Now, *el presidente's* spineless intervention had caused Valdes to lose his benefits. He would have to find some way to return the favor.

The drone of the fax machine brought him out of his reverie and delivered his solution. Ambling over to the machine, he saw that the missive was from the U.S. Department of State but was marked *personal* and *confidential.* Waiting impatiently for the machine to haltingly spew its message, he was intrigued to realize that this was not an official communiqué, but was, in fact, a letter from Roca's estranged wife in America. Cocking his head to one side, he read each line as it appeared.

"Dear Diego, Although we did not part on the best of terms, I must write to you now with a grave request that concerns us both. Our son Nico has fallen critically ill with a kidney ailment. The doctors inform me that without a kidney transplant, he has little chance of a normal life. Although I would gladly give him one of mine, unfortunately, I have learned that one of my kidneys does not function properly, so I cannot be a donor. Since he has no brothers or sisters, as his closest relative, you would probably be his best match. I know that it is a lot to ask of a father who has not seen his son in two years. But I trust that the love I know you felt for him has not disappeared with his absence. In spite of all that has happened between us, I beg you to please give him the gift of life for the second time. Obviously, there is much to discuss and to think about, but time is of the essence. If you are even considering my request, please contact me immediately so that I can give you all the information. Remember, Diego, he is still your son. Please don't let him die."

Smiling at his good fortune, Valdes ripped the slippery sheet off the roll. Since his English was good but not perfect, he read it once more to make sure that his initial understanding had been accurate. Valdes pondered the Bible's sanction of an eye for an eye. What about a son for a Mercedes? It seemed like a fair exchange to him. Laughing, he crumpled the paper until it was a small ball in the palm of his hand and slipped it in his pocket as he left the room, not bothering to close the door behind him.

When two days had passed with no response from Diego Roca, Jack had a secretary at the State Department call San Domenico and confirm that the fax had been received. The secretary reported that she had checked with Guillermo Valdes, Roca's closest advisor, and that he reported he had personally put the fax into *el presidente*'s hand. When Jack told Melinda, she knew that her plea had failed.

"Maybe we just need to give him some time," Jack said, trying to give her hope, though he had little himself.

"We don't have time," Melinda reminded him testily.

"Nico's already been put on the donor waiting list. Maybe something will come up. There's nothing else we can do."

"There's something I can do," Melinda said adamantly.

"What do you mean?" Jack asked, not liking her tone of voice.

"I'm going to San Domenico."

"No! Absolutely not."

"I have to," Melinda pleaded, fully aware of how much this was upsetting Jack. "You know what the doctor said. With Nico being a type O, he's not going to get to the top of the waiting list for a long time. We've already checked with everybody else in the family. There are no other O's. Diego's the only one."

"Diego is a murderer."

"I don't care. He's Nico's father. That's got to count for something."

"Well, obviously he doesn't think so. He's not exactly beating a path to our door offering to save his son."

"That's why I have to go to him. I can convince him to do it."

"How? What are you going to offer him to make him change his mind?" Jack knew he must sound jealous and petty, and he hated himself for it.

"Is that what you're afraid of? You think I might put out for him and you can't bear that thought? Well, I'll tell you something. If it would save Nico's life, I would. I'd sleep with the devil himself if it would help. And if you were his real father, if you loved him as much as I do, it wouldn't make a damn bit of difference."

The instant the words were out of her mouth, she regretted them. She hoped that in the heat of their

argument, Jack would just dismiss them as a mean-
ingless expression of her exasperation, but she saw
from his face that he could not. He was pale and
almost doubled over, as if someone had just delivered
a sucker punch to his solar plexus.

"I'm sorry," she said, close to tears herself. "I
didn't mean that. I know you love him. You're the
only father he's ever known, the only one he calls
Daddy. I'm just so scared." Warily, she reached out to
him, half expecting him to smack her hand away.
Instead, he let her come to him and folded her in a
gentle embrace.

"I'm scared, too," he said. "For Nico. For you. And
yes, for me, too." But as he pulled her closer, holding
her so tightly she could barely breathe, he knew he
would have to let her go.

"Blood is thicker than water."

It was a simple statement, and Sam would have
thought no response was required. Yet Luke seemed
to be looking at her expectantly. Uncomfortable, she
looked around at the others in the room. They had
been doing their meditation exercise, bringing all
their senses fully into focus, and Luke's words seemed
to rouse them. They were all nodding and smiling,
whether because of what Luke had said or because the
exercise made them feel so good, she could not be
sure. She had joined the group too recently to be able
to read her colleagues. Playing it safe, she nodded and
smiled.

"Family will never let you down."

Again, Luke had spoken as if stating a simple fact.

Sam looked around at the others, still nodding and smiling. She had no idea what the point of this exercise was, but at the moment, it seemed to make no sense. "I disagree," she said. "Not all families are good families."

"Thank you," Luke said, beaming at her as though she'd taken first prize. "I was waiting for someone to point that out."

Feeling a little sheepish, Sam glanced around at the others, wondering if she was going to get a hostile reaction for being the "show-off" new girl. If anything, they were nodding and smiling even more, showing no evidence of animosity. Christine winked at her. It had been Christine who had convinced her there was no harm in joining one of Luke's classes. And, indeed, in the few she'd attended so far, Sam had found them, if not overly instructive, at least ecumenical. The other half-dozen participants ranged from a young medical student who was trying to learn as much about spirituality as he knew about anatomy, to an elderly woman whose life was a perpetual search for truth that had taken her from a convent in Spain to an ashram in India and who considered Luke just another lesson along the way.

"Why don't we all have good families?" Luke was asking her easily, aware it required little deductive reasoning.

"We don't get to pick them," Sam answered obligingly.

"Exactly," said Luke, again rewarding her with one of his beatific smiles. "When we find ourselves in a situation we don't like, what do we do?"

"Leave," said the medical student.

"But if we don't like our families, can we leave?" he challenged them.

"We can walk away," said Christine. "But we take the baggage with us."

"Yes," Luke agreed fervently. "And that's what we have to learn. To focus on the present, on our own senses, our own reality. The family baggage weighs us down. If we can leave it behind, we can move ahead more quickly."

"What if we do like our families?" asked Sam. "What if we don't want to leave them behind?"

"Good point," said Luke. "I'm glad you brought it up," he added enthusiastically. "Let's say you're on your way to paradise. The gate is a mile from the ticket counter, and you've got to run to make the plane. You've packed all the beautiful clothes you think you're going to need in a gorgeous matched set of Louis Vuitton luggage your mother gave you. Someone comes breezing by. He's wearing a nylon backpack, and that's it. He tells you he's been to paradise, and all you really need there is a pair of shorts and a bathing suit. No one wears anything else. He also tells you that this is the last plane to paradise, and it's leaving in three minutes. You look at your luggage. You love it, but it's heavy. And it's making it hard to move. And this guy has just told you you won't need any of your stuff. What do you do? Hang on to it because it's beautiful and miss the plane? Or do you let it go? Drop it. Go to paradise!"

He paused. There was a reverential hush in the room.

"What if he's lying?" Sam asked, breaking the silence.

"What?" Luke seemed not to expect her remark. She noticed him frown for the first time. Obviously, he wasn't often questioned on this point, and he didn't like being caught off guard.

"What if the guy who says he's been to paradise is lying? What if he's never been there and only says he has? What if it's not the last plane and there's another one tomorrow?"

"You can always buy new clothes," Luke said quietly. "And imagine taking a chance at missing out on paradise because of a suitcase?"

Put that way, her objections did sound kind of foolish.

"Think about it," said Luke gently. His eyes shone, lit with kindness again. "Good families make it even harder. If you don't like your parents, as difficult as it is, you can dismiss their values and create your own. But if you love them, as most of us do, if your brothers and sisters and husbands and wives mean the world to you, how many of our choices are based on *their* expectations, how much of what we do is to compensate or assuage or emulate?"

They all nodded. It certainly made sense. But something didn't sit right with Sam.

"I still don't get it. What about all the perfectly good families out there?"

"Another good point worth examining." This time there was no trace of displeasure in his tone. Either she was back in synch with his script or he had become inured to her taking the opposite point of view. "Why are you here?"

"What?" Now she was caught off guard.

"Why did you come? Aside from curiosity. Everyone has an underlying reason, something they need to solve. What's yours?"

She stammered a little. They could see she was embarrassed. Christine put an arm on hers. "It's okay. Everything stays within these walls. Think of it like group therapy."

Sam shrugged. She didn't exactly have a terrible secret. "I've been trying to get pregnant," she said, "and I haven't been able to."

"Have you ever been pregnant before?" Luke asked, completely straightforward.

"Yes, I have a six-year-old."

"Have you been to the doctor? Is there anything physically wrong with you?"

"Well, not that the doctors can see at this point."

"Has anyone in your family ever had a similar problem?"

She suddenly felt uncomfortable; a knot of anxiety twisted in her stomach. "My sister-in-law," she said. "She's my husband's sister and is . . . was . . . married to my brother. They lived with us."

Luke smiled, "Kind of a double family. What happened to her?"

"When she couldn't get pregnant, she went to a hypnotherapist, who uncovered memories of her father abusing her. Then it turned out that she had multiple personality disorder. And after finally getting her life back on track, she died in a fire just last month."

There was a collective gasp. "This is your happy family?" Luke asked quietly. He was not mocking her, but it hardly needed saying. Sam was silent.

"Given that history in someone who was close to

you in so many ways," he went on, "would it be surprising for your unconscious to put on a few brakes?"

"We were very different," Sam said, her voice a whisper.

"Of course you were." Luke's voice was filled with tenderness. He came and stood in front of her and placed his hand gently on her shoulder. "And what happened to her isn't going to happen to you. But you can't just forget about it, can you?"

"No," Sam whispered.

"You loved her. And you love your brother. And you love your husband."

"Yes."

"And they're all connected, aren't they?"

"Yes."

"They're all family."

"Yes."

"And does it seem possible that all this pain in your family could be part of what's keeping you from getting pregnant?"

"Yes."

"If, for you, pregnancy would be paradise, then what does that make of your family history?"

"Baggage," she said quietly, star pupil that she was. She focused on her hands clenching and unclenching in her lap. She felt his hand on her chin, feather light, barely touching. She raised her eyes and saw that he had knelt in front of her so that his face was next to hers, close enough to feel intimate, but not so near as to be uncomfortable. Tears sprang to her eyes although she wasn't sure why. He put his arms around her, and she let her head fall to his shoulder.

"Let it go," he said quietly. "Let the baggage go, and get on that plane to paradise."

Her body trembled, and then, for all the time she'd been trying so hard to conceive, for the fire, for Sarah's awful death and little Nico's terrifying illness, she broke down and cried.

4

"I can't let you go to San Domenico alone—"

Melinda cut Jack off before he could finish. She knew she was screaming, but she didn't care. "We've been through this. I have to go. Nico's too sick to move, and you have to stay with him. Stop being so goddamn selfish and worrying about your petty jealousy and start thinking about Nico."

He was losing patience. "Has it ever occurred to you that maybe that's exactly who I am thinking about? Do you think the only reason I'm raising objections is because I'm paranoid about your sleeping with your ex-husband? Jesus, Melinda, give me some credit."

"Well, how is it going to help Nico if I don't go to San Domenico?"

"How is it going to help him if you do go and you

get thrown in jail for being a traitor and they won't let you out?"

"Diego wouldn't do that."

"You don't think so? He's the one who called you a traitor."

"But he loves Nico," she said quietly, not really knowing if it was still true.

"Maybe," Jack softened. He didn't want to crush all her hopes. "But what about the people around him? From what we're hearing in the State Department, Diego Roca is losing control. What if they want to make an example of you? There's no American embassy there. No one there can protect your rights."

"All the more reason why you have to stay with Nico. If anything happened to me—"

"Stop. I have no intention of leaving Nico. And I'm not going to let anything happen to you."

"But how . . . ?"

"If you'll just shut up for a minute and listen. We just got word at the State Department that Roca is making an unofficial visit to Israel. Apparently, he's trying to get an arms deal going. I have a friend in the Mossad, the Israeli secret service. He'll get you to see Roca in Jerusalem."

Melinda's mouth dropped open. She was sorry she had flown off the handle. She should have known Jack would find the best thing to do. He hadn't failed her yet. "Why didn't you tell me?"

"I was trying to."

"I'm sorry," she said. "It's just that . . ." She didn't go on. She didn't have to. She knew he was feeling the same way. From the minute they'd received Nico's prognosis, they'd been on an emotional roller coaster.

One minute, they were crying in each other's arms, the next, they were yelling at each other for no discernible reason.

"I've got you on a flight tonight. Roca's only going to be there for two days. My friend's name is David Armon. He'll meet you at the airport. Don't ask him any questions; just do what he tells you. I trust him. He'll take care of you."

"Jack," she whispered, "thank you." Tears started falling from her eyes. Lately, it seemed that they were never far from the surface, and almost anything could let loose the flood.

He kissed them away, tasting the salt on his lips. She put her arms around him, and he felt something stirring inside him. It had been weeks, maybe months, since they'd last made love. When they were together, it was hard to concentrate on anything besides Nico. But suddenly, it seemed important to both of them to connect on another level.

"The baby?" Jack asked.

"He's sleeping. He had a pretty good day. I don't think he'll wake up, but we'll hear him if he does."

It was all the encouragement Jack needed. With a romantic flourish, he swept her into his arms and carried her up the stairs to their bedroom, making her laugh with delight and desire. Not bothering to pull down the quilt, he gently laid her on the bed, then wrapped his body over and under hers. They undressed each other slowly, even solemnly, sensing that this was somehow more than just the usual coming together of a husband and wife. It was a covenant they were making, a bond meant to connect them through their bodies and into their very souls. They let their passion build slowly, allowing the promise of their commitment to infuse their every movement. And finally, when the intensity of their connection was unbearable, instead of losing themselves in individual satisfaction, they clung together, feeling each other's desire and perceiving each other's need.

Less than two hours later, hair still wet from the shower, Melinda was on a plane. She had barely had time to pack a small overnight case and kiss her sleeping child before a car had come to take her to the airport. She and Jack had said little to each other before she left, but they had understood a great deal.

"Don't worry," she had told him, covering a myriad of grounds for concern.

"Do what you have to do. Just come home safely," he answered, allowing for a host of possibilities.

"Take care of Nico."

"I will."

"I love you," they both said in unison, and then she was gone.

Reclining in her chair after takeoff, Melinda was grateful that the seat beside her was unoccupied. All her arrangements had been made in the name of Mrs. Jack Bader to protect her from an ambush of paparazzi. With her face bare of makeup and a hat pulled low over her wet hair, she had managed to sneak through the airport without attracting attention. People often didn't see a movie star unless they were expecting one, and the last thing she wanted to do right now was explain why Melinda Myles was taking a sudden flight to Israel.

Although she rarely took pills of any sort, she had decided to make this trip an exception. Anxious over confronting Diego, aware of the consequences if her supplication failed, the prospect of eleven hours alone with her thoughts was too terrifying. Asking the flight attendant for a blanket, a pillow, and a glass of water, she swallowed two capsules and was asleep before takeoff was completed.

She slept a heavy, dreamless sleep, the buzz of the plane providing a white noise buffer that kept the sounds of the inflight service away from her consciousness. She missed two meals and two movies and woke ten hours later when the rising sun bounced its orange gleam on the silver wing outside her window and delivered a fiery wake-up call into her eyes. She drank several glasses of water to relieve her throat, parched by the dry recirculated air, and went to the bathroom to splash some cold water on her face and brush her hair. When she returned to her seat, the pilot was waiting for her. Apparently, while she slept, the flight attendants had had time to study her face and had come to the realization that Mrs. Jack Bader was the movie star Melinda Myles. They exchanged a few pleasantries, and Melinda was vague about her reasons for coming to Israel, politely regretting that her trip would be too short to take in all the wonderful sights he recommended. She gave him an autograph and then cheerfully passed some out to the flight attendants, who had been kind enough to protect her in her sleep. Then, mercifully, they were preparing for landing.

Coming out of customs and into the arrivals terminal of Ben Gurion airport, she spotted him almost immediately. He was tall and muscular, with the even features, sandy hair, and tanned skin that spoke of the

European heritage and Mediterranean influence of many native-born Israelis. He was dressed casually but smartly in slacks and an open-necked shirt, with an oversized Italian leather jacket. A pair of dark aviator sunglasses hid his eyes. He held a sign that read Mrs. Jack Bader, but the minute he saw that she had seen him, he put the sign down and came to greet her.

"I'm David Armon," he said, flashing perfect white teeth in a broad, friendly grin. "And you are Jack's wife." He reached out one hand to shake hers while with the other placed in the small of her back he expertly steered her through the crowd.

"How did you know?" she smiled back, forgetting, as she often did, that there weren't too many people in the civilized world who hadn't seen her face magnified many times over on a movie screen.

"I recognized you, of course," he reminded her.

"I'm glad no one else seems to. Thank goodness I'm not that popular here," she mused self-deprecatingly.

"They're just not looking," he said. "Israelis are far too impressed with themselves to be bothered with anyone else."

She laughed but looked around and saw that he was right. All around her, people were hugging and shouting and calling out to each other in several different languages. The young soldiers, boys and girls still in their teens, wearing their open-necked khaki uniforms, with their ever-present Uzis slung over their shoulders, stared intently around their periphery, looking for danger, but their concentration obviously did not include her in their focus.

He ushered her into a black Mercedes parked

illegally in front of the terminal. She held her breath while he turned on the ignition and waited for the air-conditioning to kick in. Leaving the airport behind, they began the forty-five-minute drive through the Judean hills, past the rusted relics of burned-out jeeps from the war of '48, into Jerusalem.

Traffic was slowing as they approached the city. She had, of course, seen pictures of Jerusalem, but she was not prepared for its charm. All the buildings, old and new, were constructed of the same golden Jerusalem stone that gave the city its character. On the horizon, she could see the golden Dome of the Rock and, below it, the walls of the ancient city within the modern one. Even the smoke emanating from the buses stalled in the snarled traffic and the honking horns of impatient drivers vying for position could not lessen the effect.

"I am taking you to your hotel now," David said as they pulled in front of the bastion of the King David Hotel, built by the British in 1930. "You can shower and rest. Or if you would like to see some of the city—"

"Excuse me, David," she interrupted. "I don't mean to be rude. Jerusalem is beautiful and very impressive. But I didn't come for a tour. I have a very specific reason for being here."

"I understand. You have a meeting tonight. I just thought until then—"

"A meeting with . . . ?"

"Yes. It's all arranged. I will take you to him. He doesn't know that you are coming with me. He thinks I'm bringing an independent arms dealer. I was afraid that otherwise he might not agree."

"Oh, David, thank you." She took his hand in an

88

act of contrition. "Please forgive me for being so short. I seem to be on edge all the time lately."

"Don't apologize. I have a little boy. I can only imagine what you and Jack must be going through."

"You're very kind."

"Jack's a friend. And I hope now you are, too."

She smiled her assent. "How do you two know each . . . ?" she began but then, remembering Jack's dictum against questions, stopped herself. "Just tell me what time you want me to be ready," she said instead as he helped her out of the car.

David checked her in under the name of Mrs. Jack Bader, but she saw from the desk clerk's eyes that she recognized her. She peered at the name tag on her starched white blouse and hoped she was pronouncing it correctly.

"Dorit," she said, "I'm going to need your help."

"Yes?" Dorit's eyes shone eagerly.

"You see, I'm only going to be here for two days to talk about doing a project in Israel. It's still a secret."

"Really?" asked Dorit, thrilled to be privy to the private life of a star. "What is it?"

For a minute, Melinda was stumped, but she covered quickly and said, "It's about Moses' wife. You know, the Exodus and all that from her point of view. The female version."

"That's fascinating," said Dorit, uncertain, but going along.

"But the problem is that if anybody finds out I'm here, the whole thing might fall apart. I could lose the role."

"Oh, but that would be terrible," said Dorit, getting it. "You *are* Moses' wife."

"That's so nice of you. I think so, too. So you'll help me? You won't let anyone know I'm here? And if anyone asks, just deny it. Could you do that for me?"

"Absolutely. You can trust me."

"I won't need a porter." Melinda beamed at her. "I can handle this myself. I'm trusting you."

"Don't worry." Dorit made a motion of zipping her lips.

They moved to the elevators. "Moses' wife?" David asked, laughing.

"She caught me off guard. Moses' wife seemed a better choice than Mary Magdalene. Did he even have a wife?"

"Yes, but she had a pretty minor role."

"Not if I'm playing the part," laughed Melinda.

Her room was spacious and tastefully appointed in brown and cream furnishings, with an elegant old-fashioned writing desk adding to the gracious decor. But its most impressive feature was a huge picture window that afforded a stupendous view of the Old City. As she was irresistibly drawn to the panorama, David came and stood beside her, as awed as she was.

"It does look just like the postcards," she said, "except, of course, it's more stunning in real life."

"I've lived here all my life," he said with reverence, "and I can still weep at the beauty and, yes, the holiness of this place."

She looked at him, surprised at the poetry of spirit in a man whose life in the Mossad, as she understood it, brought him in daily contact with death-dealing intrigue. It was the contradiction of this place and its people, and it moved her.

"I'll be back at nine," he told her, purposely breaking the spell. "The food at the hotel is pretty good if you want room service. Try to eat something."

She called home and talked to Jack, telling him how much she liked his friend and that he had arranged a surprised rendezvous for her with Diego Roca that evening. Jack told her that Nico had had a good night and was doing fine although they both missed his mother. He had taken a few days off from work and was staying home until she got back. They left a lot between them unsaid, but the distance was too great and the subjects were too painful to make casual conversation. After she hung up the phone, she took off her clothes that smelled of airplane air and drew a bath, dumping a bottle of thoughtfully provided bubble bath into the hot water. Then she sat in the tub for an hour and cried.

When the water had turned cold and she felt both dust and emotion had washed away, she got out and dressed in a simple pair of slacks and a sweater. To cover the red of her eyes and to pass the time, she put on a little light makeup. She brushed out her hair and bunched it into a knot of soft curls at the nape of her neck. Turning away from the mirror, she had no idea that unstudied and unassuming, she still had the ability to dazzle. But David, coming to pick her up shortly before nine, could only think how lucky his friend Jack Bader was to have her and how foolish Diego Roca had been to let her go.

"Where are we meeting him?" she asked as they walked out of the hotel.

"A private place. On *Har Tzion,* Mount Zion. We can walk if you'd like."

In the absence of the blistering Middle Eastern sun,

the air had cooled considerably and the night had turned pleasant. She realized that except for the few gulps of sweltering dust she'd inhaled taking the few steps between car and building, she'd breathed nothing but recirculated air-conditioning and moved no more than a few paces for twenty-four hours. A walk sounded like a good idea.

He led her down side streets to the Old City, its ancient stone walls illuminated against the night sky. At the Jaffa Gate they turned right and wandered down a narrow stone path lit by winsome glass lamps edged in gilt. Occasionally, David broke the silence to point out a place of historical significance. Like most Jerusalemites, he knew his city well and took pride in its archaeology. Crossing a narrow alley, they came upon a doorway, and passing through, she saw a stone staircase with rusted metal railings ahead of them.

"This building is a perfect example of our complicated history," David said. "On the ground floor, beneath the courtyard, which used to be part of a medieval monastery, is the Tomb of David. On the second floor is the Room of the Last Supper, which is where Jesus was supposed to have had his last Passover seder."

"Is that where we're going?" she asked as she followed him up the stairs.

"No, we are going to the third floor, which is the ruins of a mosque." He led her out again into the glow of Jerusalem at night. She caught her breath, for, indeed, laid below her with its luminous stone, both ancient and modern, it looked like a city of gold. To one side were the hills of Judea, to the other, the hills of Hebron. She appreciated the view for a few moments, then looked around. As far as she could tell, they were alone on the roof.

She looked at David. "Where . . . ?"

He pointed past a mound formed by the former mosque's dome to the remains of the minaret. "Behind the minaret is a small room. It is called the President's Room because years ago, before the Six-Day War, when Jews were not allowed to go to the *Kotel,* the Wailing Wall, this was the closest they could get, and the president built this little room for people who wanted to come and look at the wall and pray. Now they can go to the wall, so the room is locked. But not tonight. He should be there."

She felt her heartbeat quicken. "I think I should see him alone."

David nodded. "But I'll be out here. There's another Mossad agent here, too. The one who brought him. You'll be safe."

"I don't think he'd hurt me," she said quickly.

"You don't know what he'd do," David said, and she knew that he was right.

She stepped to the door of the little room while David moved discreetly into the shadows. She thought she saw the flicker of a lit cigarette and heard the murmur of voices and realized he must be greeting his Mossad colleague. Then she turned the handle and opened the door.

Diego was standing, facing the door, framed by the view of the night-lit city behind him. His hand was hidden in his jacket, she presumed resting on his gun. A chair had been knocked to the floor, and she surmised that he had been sitting, watching the view, when he heard the doorknob and leaped to his feet, ready to defend himself. Everything registered on his face when he saw her: confusion, shock, and then unmistakable longing, all within a matter of seconds. She had forgotten how charismatic he was.

"Melinda," he whispered. It was both prayer and reproach.

"Hello, Diego." Her voice was shaking, and for the moment, she didn't trust herself to say more. She had loved him as much as she had loved any man—and she had hated him more.

He resisted the temptation to take her in his arms, knowing it was inappropriate and she would not welcome it. He could not fathom how she had come to be in this place, but looking at his watch, he saw he did not have time to ask. "You shouldn't be here," he said. "I am waiting for someone."

"You are waiting for me," she answered simply.

"I have a meeting arranged," he insisted, still not comprehending. "These are not people to whom you would want to be introduced."

"I'm sorry to fool you, Diego," she said. "A friend in the Mossad set this up. There are no arms dealers coming tonight. Only me."

"What are you talking about?"

"When you didn't answer my fax, I was afraid you'd refuse to see me. I had to talk to you."

"What fax? I received no fax from you."

"I know you did," she insisted. "We were told that Valdes gave it to you."

"Valdes gave me nothing," he said angrily.

She didn't know whether to believe him or not, but she knew better than to argue. "Nico is dying," she said without preamble, knowing that if he were telling the truth and he did not know, this was a cruel way to find out. His face told her nothing, so she went on. "He needs a kidney transplant. I can't give him mine because I only have one that works. But you could give him yours. As I told you in the fax, it's his only chance to live. I understand you probably needed time to think. I know how angry you must be with me, but—"

"Time to think?" He was roaring at her, and she involuntarily took a step back in fear. "You think that anger at you would make me hesitate about saving my son's life? Is this what you think of me?"

She was confused for a moment. "Are you saying you will do it?"

"Of course I will," he said without hesitation, and before he could go on, she was in his arms crying with relief and gratitude and trepidation worse than she'd ever known. His arms, remembering without reasoning, closed around her. He smelled her clean, fresh scent and recalled instantly the feeling of silkiness on his cheek when he used to bury his face in her hair. His heart felt as though it would explode, spewing equal parts love and rage on them both. She had stolen this from them, destroyed their prospects because she could not understand his politics.

"Oh, Diego," she sobbed. "I was so afraid that because of me . . . because of what happened . . . that you might not forgive me . . . ." She couldn't go on.

"I don't forgive you," he chided. "But Nico is my son. Did you think I would let him die?"

"No," she answered quietly, chastised, and knew

that it was true in spite of all her anxiety. Others had fed her doubts about Diego, but in her heart, she had always known that he would help.

"We need to talk, Melinda. About Nico. But about what you did also. You owe me that much."

"Yes," she said, "I do." And feeling already that her son was on his way back to health, she knew she owed her ex-husband more than she could ever repay.

"Sit down," he said, righting the chair that he had knocked over at her entrance. "First, tell me about our little boy. Do you have pictures?"

There was a small lamp on the table, and he turned it on as he took a chair beside her, waiting while she drew out the few snapshots that she carried in her wallet. Her heart melted as she watched him eagerly study the photos, and she remembered not only why, but how she had loved him. She saw him scowl and saw that he was looking at a picture of Nico held aloft between her and Jack, the three of them laughing. It was a captured moment that she treasured, not because it was so unusual, but because it was an everyday occurrence in her happy family life, the kind of existence she could never have had as the wife of Diego Roca. She ached for what she had lost, but she cherished what she had now, and she grasped viscerally how it was possible to love two men with every fiber of her being.

Patiently, she explained to him how they had discovered Nico's illness, how it had progressed, and everything the doctors had told her could be expected. Understanding the need for haste, Diego agreed that he would conclude his business in Israel on the following day, as he had anticipated, but instead of returning directly to San Domenico, he would detour through Washington. Since his journey would be for humanitarian purposes, he expected full cooperation from the American government in providing facilities for the procedure to be done quickly and for him to be returned as soon as possible to his own country. He would contact his ministers at home to explain the situation and hope that an additional brief absence would not further weaken his shaky cabinet.

Anger flared when they discussed the circumstances of her leaving and his attempts to prevent Nico from going with her. He accused her of betraying their country; she countered that he had betrayed their love. At one point, their recriminations grew so loud that the Mossad agents posted outside the door entered with drawn guns. But they assured them that the discussion, though heated, was not threatening, and the agents retreated while Melinda and Diego attempted to lower their voices and their expectations.

The lights of the city beneath them dimmed, to be replaced by the rising sun gleaming off the golden Dome of the Rock, warming the light Jerusalem stone to an orange glow. Still they didn't stop talking until David knocked discreetly on the door and suggested that soon the tourists would come, and this would not be a good place to continue a private conversation.

"I trust you can help me to complete my business today," Diego said to David.

"Of course," David responded. "This was a personal favor, but I don't forget business."

"Good. Then I can go with you tomorrow," he said to Melinda.

"Thank you, Diego," she said, touching his shoulder. Not thinking, he took her hand and put it to his lips. In the instant that followed, when the current passed between them, as surely as lightning splits a tree, they knew there was no resolving their differences, but there was no denying their bonds.

David brought her back to the King David, and after thanking him with all her heart, she went to her room, physically and emotionally drained. She called Jack to ask about Nico and tell him that her trip had paid off. She would be returning with Diego. She could hear both the relief and apprehension in his voice and knew exactly how he felt. When they told each other they loved each other before hanging up, there seemed to be an extra measure of fervor in their words.

Leaving the curtains open, she lay on the bed to watch the day break over Jerusalem. But her eyes closed of their own volition, and soon, she was dreaming. She was in her own home, in her own bed, with Jack beside her. Nico lay between them, but they both knew that there was somewhere they had to go, and, leaving the baby behind, they simply grasped arms and flew together out the window. As they wafted effortlessly on the breeze, like a couple in a Chagall painting, she looked down and saw below her the same configuration of city that she had seen from Mount Zion. Caressed by the wind, she felt herself becoming aroused and willed them both out of the sky and onto the ground. Now, they were naked in a grove of olive trees and, laughing together, certain they had alighted in the Garden of Eden. And though Jack told her it was forbidden, Melinda insisted they must make love. Touching him, tempting him, she felt his resistance give way and his desire rise to meet her own. She guided him with her hands and felt herself suffused with warmth as he entered her body.

"I love you, Jack," she said with a sigh, feeling her passion reach its peak.

"Mi amor," he whispered, and she opened her eyes and saw that it was Diego who was in her arms.

She groaned and turned away and then opened her eyes for real to find the sun high in the sky, streaming through the window, baking her in its glare. The pillow was soaked with her sweat, and she felt hot and uncomfortable, aroused and guilty. Hugging herself, she blocked out all thought and, needing release and forgetfulness, quickly finished what the dream had started.

By the time Samantha returned from her class at the Institute for Creative Epistemology, the household had retired for the night. She had started out by going to weekly group classes, but Luke urged her to start attending more often, volunteering his time for private tutorials. Their sessions left her feeling both exhausted and exhilarated. While she had her occasional doubts about the efficacy of Luke's teachings, she dismissed her misgivings simply because it made her feel better.

An eerie shadow was cast by the scaffolding still surrounding the east wing of the house where construction was under way to repair the damage from the fire, and, shuddering a little, she left her car in the circular driveway and hurried inside. A series of strategic lights had been left on for her benefit, and she followed them up the stairs to Moira's room, where she peeked in on the peacefully sleeping child. Tiptoeing in, she put the little girl's legs back under the coverlet and placed a feathery kiss on her brow. The knowledge that her sister was on a mission to save the life of her own son added fervor to her usual silent prayer of gratitude. Leaving the door ajar, she took one more appreciative backward glance before turning out the hall light and heading toward the master bedroom. A faint glow flickered beneath the door, and she supposed that Drew had gone to sleep and left a lamp on the night table burning so she could find her way. Wearily, she pushed open the door, then gasped with shock and delight when she saw that her assumptions had been mistaken.

A dozen votive candles formed an aisle to the bed, casting a romantic glow over the entire room. On the night table was a silver bucket containing a bottle of chilling champagne. Beside two crystal flutes stood a bowl of the most perfect ruby red strawberries she'd ever seen, their stems intact and glistening. And as the pièce de résistance, her handsome dark-haired, blue-eyed husband lay in the center of the bed, wearing the bottoms of a pair of silk pajamas she had given him for his birthday last year, with the top thoughtfully laid out for her.

"I thought you'd never get here," he sighed, putting down his book and looking at her, his eyes darkened by desire.

"You did this for me?" she asked rhetorically, her heart full.

In response, he pulled her to the bed and kissed her, moving his body under hers so she could feel him stirring. They had been spending less than their usual amount of time together lately. Since the fire, their tracks, so closely linked at home and at work, seemed to diverge. Pressure from Sarah's death had forced Drew to cut back production at DMC, and Sam's beloved experimental car design division had been forced into hiatus. As a result, he was spending many additional hours at the plant, whereas she wasn't bothering to go in at all. At home, they were focused on Moira and on the complexities of rebuilding their burned-out stately home. It had even occurred to her that she was enjoying her sessions with Luke mostly because an intense, though not entirely rational, young man was paying her undue attention, and with all the stress at home, it was just the sort of flattering distraction she needed. But now, in her husband's arms, responding to his touch with desire, she realized how much she had missed their closeness and that, in reality, nothing could take its place.

Except, suddenly, in the back of her mind, she remembered a discussion she had had with Luke that very evening and pulled back.

"Damn. We can't do it," she informed Drew.

"Why not?" he asked, his hands creeping under her blouse, unwilling to take her words seriously.

"It's sort of an experiment. Luke said—"

"Luke?" Drew interrupted, making no effort to hide his disdain. "What does that snake oil salesman have to do with our love life?"

"How can you call him that? You've never even met him."

"I don't have to. Obviously, he preys on troubled

people and inveigles his way into their lives. The bastard is after something," he said with utter certainty.

"That's not fair. He's never asked me for a thing," she protested, extricating herself from her husband's embrace.

"Does he know who you are?"

"Of course."

"Then don't worry. He will."

In truth, Sam had had these same thoughts herself, but now she felt compelled to defend Luke.

"You are being entirely unfair and narrow-minded."

"I don't think so. What's this guy done for you except tell you not to have sex with your husband?"

Uncomfortable, she stood up and started to pace. "It's nothing tangible. But I think he has something to say worth listening to."

"Really? Like don't have sex with your husband?"

"No," she objected, then corrected herself. "I mean, okay, he did say that, but it's not what it sounds like. He knows the reason I came to the institute in the first place is because I want to have another baby."

"Honey," Drew said, mildly teasing, "didn't anyone ever tell you? You can't do that by not having sex."

"I know," she conceded. "It sounds stupid. But even the doctor said that if you do it too much, try too hard, that also makes it difficult to get pregnant."

"And you think that's what our problem is?"

"No, not really. The real problem is, I don't know what our problem is, and it's making me crazy."

"Maybe because we don't have a problem. We're happy, right? Let nature take its course. If we have another baby, fine. If we don't, we've got Moira. And we always have each other. Why not just leave things alone?"

"I can't. I admit it's become about more than just the baby. All my life, whenever I've wanted something, I've figured out what I needed to do to get it and then done it. It's how I started designing cars. It's how I got you. I've always been able to control things."

"Really? Didn't I have anything to do with it?" he asked with mock offense.

"You know what I mean. Maybe it's because of everything that's been going on. What happened to Sarah. I feel so vulnerable suddenly. And her whole problem was triggered by trying to get pregnant, too."

"You're not comparing yourself to Sarah, are you? Her problems started long before she wanted a baby. Your case is nothing like hers."

"I know. But maybe, somewhere in the back of my feeble mind, there's a connection. I just don't feel like I even know myself anymore."

Drew shook his head. "And how long do you think all this is going to take?"

"I don't know. But Luke said he'd work with me privately."

"Oh, yeah, I bet."

"Drew, for heaven's sake." She looked at him, dismayed. "You can't be jealous."

"Why not? This guy is after something. If it's not your money, it's your body. Both are well worth having."

"I don't know if I should be flattered or insulted." She grinned, sitting back down on the bed beside him. "You trust me, don't you?"

"Yeah. It's him I don't trust. Has it ever occurred to you that he might have designs on you, with all his private lessons."

She considered lying, then decided against it. "Well, as a matter of fact, yes. But then I realized it could just be my baser instincts projecting themselves onto him."

"Or it could be your common sense trying to keep you out of trouble."

"Maybe you're right. But I have to follow it through. Just see what he has to offer. I promise you, if there is the least bit of hanky-panky, I'll be the first one out of there."

"Fine. But I reserve the right to say I told you so."

"Fine."

"Does that mean you don't want champagne and strawberries?"

She looked at the plump red fruit, at the condensation creating rivulets on the icy bottle. "I didn't say that," she lamented.

"Just no sex."

"Right."

"Okay, but if we have champagne and strawberries, I can't guarantee what will happen after. I'm not as spiritually evolved as you are, and I can't promise to stay in control."

"Pop the cork." She giggled. "I'll take my chances."

It wasn't until he started dipping the strawberries into the champagne and feeding them to her that she lost her resolve. "I think maybe I'll start separating tomorrow," she whispered as she tugged at the string of his pajama bottoms. She never even bothered to put the top on at all.

From the window in her office next to the headmaster's, Colette saw the black car stop at the gate to the school's grounds. As usual, when no one was expected, the gate was closed, and she watched as the driver got out to open the gate. A scowl came over her face when she recognized the pale woman with the platinum hair, and she almost spat, wondering how men could find that sort of cheap Hollywood imitation attractive, but knowing that they did. She peeked through the door joining her room to Ian's. He was peering at his computer, making changes on the new curriculum. His shutters were closed to keep the morning sun from glaring on his screen. *Good,* Colette thought, *he could not have seen.* She had time. With a brisk, stern walk guaranteeing that she would not be stopped by some student in the hallway, she hurried down the stairs and out the front door. She was pleased that at least the tart had stopped to close the gate behind her before driving to the school building, giving Colette just enough time to be standing at the entrance when the woman approached.

"Mademoiselle Simard," Daisy greeted her warmly. "Do you remember me? I'm Daisy Howard from the American embassy."

Colette smiled stiffly and nodded. She was surprised that the bitch had remembered her name. Usually these Americans were too self-centered to even notice her. "We were not expecting you," Colette said, her reproving tone unmistakable.

Daisy seemed not to notice. "I know," she said breezily. "But I decided to make the trip at the last minute, and the car phone doesn't work out here for some reason. Anyway, I've brought someone to meet Mr. Taylor."

Colette peered through the tinted windows and saw a girl, perhaps fifteen or sixteen, sitting in the passenger seat, eyeing the school eagerly. When she noticed Colette looking at her, she quickly lowered her gaze to her hands, folded neatly in her lap.

"I'm very sorry," Colette said, "But you should have called before you made the trip from Paris for nothing."

Daisy bit her lip in disappointment. "Oh. Is Mr. Taylor away from the school? I would have thought during the week—"

"He is here," Colette interjected quickly, unwilling to let a meddling official believe for even an instant that they weren't always on the job. "But he is busy. He can't see anyone."

"Surely, just for a minute, since I have come all this way—"

"I am sorry. But the curriculum must take precedence. Would you like to make an appointment for another time?"

"Shit," said Daisy deflated, seeing she wasn't going to get past Mlle. Simard without a major struggle and unwilling to create a scandal when she was about to ask for a favor. "Fine. I'll call from the city."

Colette watched with satisfaction as Daisy moved to the passenger side of the car and leaned into the open window, explaining to the girl.

In his office, Ian looked up from his work and tried

to hide his irritation as Ryan Jessup knocked on the door and entered.

"Mr. Corbett said I had to come see you."

It was not the first time Ryan had been sent to his office. Ryan's father was a Texas fast-food magnate who had brought his family to France while he organized the openings of a chain of Tex-Mex restaurants across Europe. Ryan, who was obviously spoiled and used to being kowtowed to because of his family's fortune at home, was having trouble adjusting to being just another rich kid in the company of people with more money and fancier lineage than his own. His response had been to become the class clown, and although it made him popular, his grades and his relationships with his teachers were suffering.

"Why are you here today?" Ian asked wearily.

Ryan handed him a sheet of paper. On it was a rather good, but distinctly unkind caricature of poor Mr. Corbett, the history teacher, looking fatuous and effeminate, wearing nothing but an American flag while he masturbated over a picture of Charles de Gaulle. As much as he disapproved of Ryan's handiwork, Ian had to admit to himself that it neatly summed up his own feelings about Corbett's unique combination of defensive chauvinism for the country he had chosen to leave twenty years ago and slavish veneration for his adopted home, with the added hint of style that marked him as possibly outside the heterosexual community. The drawing also showed that coupled with his impertinent insight, young Jessup had a certain degree of artistic skill. Giving himself a little time to formulate his reprimand, Ian went to open his shutters. Directly below his window, he was shocked to see Daisy Howard getting into her car and making a U-turn.

"Ryan," he said quickly, "you're on the track team, right?"

"Yeah," the boy responded laconically, hoping his punishment wouldn't involve his extracurricular activity, since he loved nothing more than to run.

"Okay. There's a woman in a black car, leaving the school. If you can stop her before she hits the street, you're free."

"You mean it?" the boy asked, unable to believe his good luck. "No detention or nothing?"

"Anything," corrected Ian. "But she's already turned around," he added, looking down. "You don't have a lot of time."

Ryan was out the office door before he finished speaking. Ian watched as seconds later, he reappeared, racing down the driveway. Realizing the kid must have leaped from the third-floor landing to the first, Ian laughed as he hit the save button on his computer and headed out the door. But being a lot more prudent and a little less athletic, he decided on the stairs for himself.

By the time Ian reached the entrance, the car was slowly making its way back, with Ryan trotting happily alongside. He saw Colette in front of him, watching the car's approach, as he was, but before he could speak, she marched briskly down the middle of the driveway and planted herself directly in the car's path about fifty feet from the school, forcing Daisy to brake to a halt and altogether confusing poor Ryan as she lashed into him.

"What do you think you are doing, young man?" Her face had turned red with fury.

"Mr. Taylor said—"

"Mr. Taylor is working," she interrupted, choking with anger. "He has no time for visitors."

"It's all right, Colette," Ian said quietly, coming up behind her. "I sent Ryan to bring Miss Howard back."

She jumped, startled, and with a last venomous look through the windshield recovered and turned to Ian. "I thought you needed to work on the curriculum. Mr. Kogan never allowed visitors without prior arrangement."

"That's fine as a general policy," said Ian gently, "but I think we can make exceptions on a case-by-case basis."

She shrugged and turned away as Ian opened the door for Daisy.

"I'm sorry," Daisy said, long shapely legs preceding her out of the car. "I didn't mean to start an incident. I guess I really should have called."

"Never mind," said Ian, surprised at how genuinely glad he was to see her. "Rules were made to be broken." He caught a glimpse of Ryan grinning on the other side of the car. "That doesn't go for you, Jessup. Get back to class. And no more rude drawings. Find a better use for your natural talent."

"Yes, sir," said the boy happily, but fascinated by the stunning woman he had stopped at the gate, he only moved a few steps toward the school, out of the headmaster's sight lines but well within observing distance.

"I've brought someone for you to meet," explained

Daisy. "I guess I purposely didn't call, because it's kind of complicated, and I didn't want you to have too much time to think before you met her."

"Sounds intriguing," said Ian, not unwilling to go along. Daisy motioned toward the car, and the girl emerged. Ian could see she was an incipient beauty, with black hair and huge, dark, almond-shaped eyes fringed with heavy lashes and set wide in a lovely, pale face. She was achingly shy and moved with awkward grace, loping between girlish embarrassment and womanly aplomb.

"This is Daniela. Her mother works in the American embassy in Paris as a cleaning woman. I found Daniela asleep in the embassy library one night. She told me she sneaks in there to read the books because the ones they give her at school are too boring."

"How's your English?" Ian asked the girl.

"Fine, thank you," she answered politely, making him smile.

"Her French, Spanish, and Italian are okay, too," offered Daisy. "She taught herself."

Ian raised an eyebrow. "Really? And what are you reading now, Daniela?"

"In English?" she asked.

He nodded, his interest piqued.

"Stephen Hawking's *A Brief History of Time,*" she said.

"How old are you?" he asked.

"Sixteen."

"Need I say more?" Daisy smiled. "You can probably guess why I'm here."

Ian nodded again. "We should talk. Let me get someone to show Daniela around."

"I'll do it" came a voice from behind them.

"Ryan, I thought I told you to go back to class."

The boy shrugged sheepishly.

Ian had to smile. He was definitely not a bad kid in spite of his overprivileged beginnings. "Okay. Daniela, would you mind going with Ryan? Stick to the beaten path, Ryan, if you know what I mean. Gym, classrooms, dorms, garden. Don't scare her off."

"Don't worry, Mr. Taylor. I wouldn't do that." He sounded so genuine that Ian looked at him in surprise and had to smother a grin as he realized that Ryan had become instantly smitten with the newcomer. Polite and obedient, Daniela stayed a few paces behind Ryan as he headed into the school, checking over his shoulder to make sure she was following.

When they'd disappeared inside the building, Ian turned back to Daisy. "Shall we go to my office?" he offered.

The day was warm for early spring, and a brilliant sun, after a week of rain, had forced a wall of forsythia hedges into yellow blossom. "It's so nice. Could we just sit on one of those benches and talk?" Daisy asked, not mentioning that she had caught a glimpse of the dour Colette Simard peering at them through a window.

"What a good idea," Ian said with surprise, as though she'd revealed something unknown to him before.

"The grounds are so beautiful here. I would think you'd spend as much time out-of-doors as you could."

"To tell you the truth," Ian admitted, "I hardly ever leave the school building. There's a lot of work. And I guess I just haven't been in the mood to appreciate its beauty."

"Being in mourning can make you want to close yourself off from the world I guess. But you have to come out some time. It helps."

He was taken aback by her candor. He had said nothing about his bereavement, and he'd found that even when people knew he had lost his wife, they avoided the topic like the plague. Yet, he felt that Daisy had understood the truth and appreciated her stating it. He took her arm and led her to one of the benches. A magnolia tree, planted by the school's founder to remind himself of his southern roots, was starting to bloom overhead. With satisfaction, Daisy realized that they could no longer be seen from Colette's window.

"So tell me about Daniela," Ian said, anxious to turn the subject away from himself. "I take it you want me to accept her into the school."

"I'm that transparent, am I?" she said, laughing.

"Or I'm that perceptive," he countered with a smile.

"She *is* exceptional. You can see that, can't you?"

"If what you say about her is true, she is. She's hardly said a word to me."

"She's very shy. It's her only defense. When I found her in the library, she was so terrified, she wouldn't even speak to me. I just assumed she'd been reading and fallen asleep and nobody had noticed. Her mother told me later that she'd been sneaking Daniela into the library at night because they were homeless. Her husband had taken all the money she'd been saving from work and run off, not even leaving her enough for the rent. They'd been evicted and were staying in a shelter. But one of the shelter supervisors had started making advances toward Daniela, and she was afraid to stay there."

"Did she notify someone or file a complaint?"

"Who? She knew they'd just get kicked out. She'd have even less chance of protecting Daniela if they were on the street."

Ian nodded, understanding. Daniela's appeal hadn't gone beyond him either.

"Believe me, Ian," Daisy appealed to him, "this girl is so smart, she's really one of a kind. Please. Will you take her in? If it's a matter of money—"

He waved the thought away. He was relatively new at the school, but he knew there was a procedure for this sort of admittance. It involved testing, financial investigation of the parents, assessment of the family character. He was certain that as a member of the school's board Daisy knew about it as well. But she'd chosen to come here instead and simply present him with the child and her need. For some reason, it touched him. Laughter interrupted his thoughts, and he saw that Ryan and Daniela were emerging from the school and bounding toward them. The solemnity was gone from Daniela's face, and for a moment, she looked like any other teenager. But drawing close to the adults, her guard went up again, and her eyes grew somber. How sad, Ian thought, to grow up so afraid.

"She likes it here," Ryan called to them, racing ahead. "She didn't even mind the dorm bathrooms, which really suck if you ask me."

"No one asked you, Ryan," Ian pointed out. "Would you like to stay here, Daniela?" he asked her.

He heard Daisy catch her breath in excitement and felt her body tense beside him. For an instant, he was inordinately pleased at having pleased her, then immediately, silently chastising himself, he refocused on the young girl in front of him. Daniela was looking at Daisy, her face an unguarded display of hope and apprehension. Daisy nodded at her, smiling encouragement.

"I would study very hard," Daniela promised.

"Yes!" said Ryan, pumping his fist in the air. Then embarrassed at giving away his feelings, he gruffly added, "The food sucks, too."

"Thank you, Ryan, that will do," Ian informed him. He turned back to Daisy. "When . . . ?" he began.

"Actually," she admitted a little sheepishly, "I've got her bag in my car. I didn't mean to assume, but she doesn't really have an option, and I thought the sooner the better."

"It's okay, don't apologize. You're right. Ryan, get Daniela's bag out of the car and take her to the junior girls' dorm room. We'll have a bed and locker set up for her."

"This is it?" said Ryan in disbelief, pulling out a small patched duffel bag from the backseat. "This is all your stuff?" A look of mortification crossed Daniela's face, as it hit her instantly just how humiliating her history would be in a place like this. But Ryan had already forgotten his dismay and was racing ahead, and Daniela, willing to swallow pride for protection, hurried to follow.

"I don't know how to thank you," Daisy said to

Ian, putting her arms around him to deliver a fervent kiss of gratitude.

"I'll probably end up having to thank you," he answered, amazed at how warm and pliant her lips felt upon his cheek. With Sarah's mental illness and then her death, he realized it had been almost a year since he had been this close to a woman who was not a relative. He had forgotten how good it could feel.

Daniela came back out to thank Daisy and hug her good-bye. Ian instructed Ryan to take her to his office where they would fill out the proper enrollment forms for her, then made the boy swear to go directly to his own classroom.

He walked Daisy to her car and opened the door for her. "Come back and check on her," he said, unwilling to admit the invitation was as much for himself as for Daniela.

From her office window, Colette Simard watched with pursed lips. She had let things go wrong with the last headmaster. She would have to see to it that she did not make the same mistake again.

5

"Do you want me to come to Washington?" Sam asked her sister. "If you do, just say so. Drew can stay with Moira and I can be there to help you."

"Thanks," said Melinda, appreciating, as she always did, the force of the Myles militia. "But I don't think so. At least not right now. Diego's in the house and I just think the added strain—"

"Whoa," Sam interrupted. "Back up a minute. Diego's in the house? Your house?"

"Well, yes."

"Isn't that pushing the hospitality thing a little too far?"

"Come on, Sam. He's going into the hospital tomorrow to give our son one of his kidneys. A little gratitude would be in order."

"Okay, you're right. And it's just a day. No big deal."

Melinda hesitated. "Uh . . . actually . . . it'll end up being a week or two. He's going to come back here after he gets out."

"Are you kidding?"

"No," said Melinda, starting to feel a little indignant at having to explain herself. "He'll be in intensive care for two days and then spend a couple more days in the hospital. But he won't be ready to fly home for at least another week. I mean, I can't very well send him to a hotel all alone after he's just had an operation."

Sam saw her point, but it still didn't feel like a comfortable decision. "What does Jack have to say about all this?"

"Not much," confessed Melinda. "He's just being the best husband in the world and telling me that whatever feels right to me, he'll go along with."

"He *is* the best husband in the world. I don't think mine would be so benign. He's making noise because I'm taking classes with Luke and he doesn't trust him, but that's a whole different story."

"Really? But I thought you said Luke was a spiritual teacher?"

"He is. But Drew still thinks he has designs on me."

"Does he?"

"Oh, I don't know. Anyway, it's all too stupid compared to what you're going to have to go through. How's the baby?"

"Nico's doing great. We checked him into the hospital yesterday because he has to spend a couple of

117

days before the operation in an antiseptic environment to make sure there's no infection. But one of us is always with him. We have to wear masks and gowns, and that scared him a little bit at first, but he's used to it now, and it's fine. Jack's at the hospital now."

"And where's Diego?"

"He's here. He goes to see Nico, too. But with me. Jack's been great, but just to be fair, I try to keep them apart as much as possible."

"And how do you feel about it?"

"I just want my baby to get through this and live a healthy, normal life."

"Of course, but that's not what I'm asking."

"I know. But it's all I can think about right now."

After more words of love and encouragement, the sisters hung up. Sam had made it perfectly clear that the minute Melinda wanted her there, she would drop everything and catch a shuttle to Washington. But at this point, Melinda had all the backup she needed. No one could take her place beside Nico's bed when he wanted his mommy. And nothing would ease the pressure on her heart until the operation had been performed and she had been told it was successful.

She looked at her watch and saw that she still had an hour and a half before she was due back at the hospital. Since she had spent the night in a chair beside Nico's bed, Jack had insisted she go home and lie down for a few hours when he came to relieve her. At first she had protested, but when he pointed out that she was going to need even more strength for after the operation, she realized he was right and promised she would try to get a little sleep. Instead, she'd used the time to call her parents and her sister to keep them apprised of the latest developments. Now, as she went to finally stretch out on the bed, there was a quiet knock on the door. Without thinking, she called, "Come in," then sat bolt upright as she saw Diego standing awkwardly at the threshold of her bedroom.

"You are resting," he said, making no move to enter. He had showered and changed out of the khaki officer's uniform that was his presidential garb and was wearing a pair of beige slacks and a white shirt with sleeves rolled up over arms as taut and muscular as she had remembered. His bronze skin gleamed against the clean, crisp cotton, and without his perpetual cap, she noticed his hair needed cutting, and his black curls, wet and unruly, were spilling over, leaving their damp imprint on his collar. She thought of Jack, her blond and beautiful husband, so full of light, and saw in Diego his dark and brooding opposite. Without even articulating it in her own mind, she knew that although Jack had opened her life to uncomplicated joy, whereas Diego had almost led her to unspeakable tragedy, both had the power to ignite in her unbridled passion. And for the moment, occupied with the fate of a small sick boy, fathered by one but nurtured by the other, neither one of them could offer her any consolation.

As he stood in her bedroom door, she saw he was as uncomfortable as she was. "It's all right. I couldn't sleep anyway. Let's go down and have tea."

He made some mild protest, but they both knew they needed to talk, and they could not do it in the room she shared with her current husband. Diego had spent the flight back from Israel speaking to his aides, planning for the time he would be gone from San Domenico. It was obviously no easy matter for a head of state to abandon his government for so long a period no matter how necessary or humanitarian the reason. By the time their discussions had ended, Melinda, exhausted from her emotional ordeal and the quick turnaround, had fallen asleep. Once on the ground, most of his attachés made a connecting flight to San Domenico, but one assistant and two bodyguards remained. The assistant had been dropped at a nearby hotel, but the bodyguards had posted themselves outside the house on Thirty-first Street, taking turns coming in to eat and sleep in the small maid's room off the kitchen. In effect, this was the first time that Diego and Melinda had been alone since she asked him to help Nico, and there was still much to say between them.

He waited in the living room, perched on the edge of her sofa while she made tea and brought it to him. He took the cup that she poured and placed it carefully on the edge of the coffee table. She realized he wouldn't drink it, but she hadn't had the strength to make the strong black espresso that he favored, and she knew that it was more ritual than need that compelled her to offer anything. When she'd poured her own tea, she looked up and saw that he was watching her. She could not be sure, but she thought it might be tears that made his eyes shine so brightly.

"What happened, *mi amor?*" he asked so softly that it made her heart break.

"You changed" was all she could say, knowing it was glaringly inadequate.

"No. I have always had a commitment to do what must be done for my country. You once understood that. So perhaps it was you who changed."

"What good does this do, Diego?"

"For me, it is necessary. I have not spoken your name in two years. But not a day goes by that I don't long for you. And for the son you stole from me."

Melinda felt a chill. She needed to defend herself, and what if she could not? Would he withdraw his offer? For a desperate minute, she considered what would be the most politic thing to say, the thing that would make him consent to do for Nico what he said he would do. Quickly, she decided her best protection was the truth. She had loved this man, known him heart and soul. He needed to see that she had lost as much as he had.

"He's my son, too. You called me a traitor. You kept us prisoner. I was afraid of what you might do. I only wanted to protect him."

"And I only wanted to keep you."

"Oh, Diego, don't you think I know that? But it wasn't enough. Not for me, and especially not for Nico."

"Instead, you brought him here, made another man his father, and see what happened."

"Don't. You can't blame his disease on America. That's too stupid for you. No one knows what causes nephrotic syndrome. And we both know that if he had had to be treated in San Domenico, with the way things are there now, he wouldn't have made it this far. But you are still his father. You're the one who can give him life again. Believe me, I wish I could do it, but I can't."

"Why? So you would not have to rely on me?"

"But I am relying on you. I came to you because I believed in your humanity. That's never changed. I watched you transform yourself from a loving man to a controlling one and I couldn't stand it. But in the end you couldn't kill the man who cared so deeply about every wrong and every pain. You buried him alive, but he's still there. I see him in your touch when you sit by Nico's bed and hold his hand. I see him in your eyes when you look at your baby boy."

"And what do you see when I look at you?"

"We can't go back, Diego. I'm married to someone else now, and I love him. Jack is a good man."

"I can see. Nico loves him. He doesn't even know me."

"That can change. If you will accept that I had to make a different life for myself to survive, there's no reason why Nico shouldn't spend part of his time with you, know you, learn to love you, too."

"He is all I have. I cannot love anymore. I cannot trust. You killed that in me," he added bitterly.

She believed him, and it hurt her. "I'm sorry. I was in the wrong place at the wrong time. I was foolish to think that I could be anything other than what I am, which is basically a simple American woman. You were right when we first met and you accused me of romanticizing the revolution. I didn't understand it then, but I see that now. The reality of living with its consequences was something that only a true native could do. And much as I loved you and loved your people, I was never a true native."

"I knew that," he admitted quietly. "From the

moment I held you in my arms, I knew you were not one of us and never really could be. You were a beautiful alien thing. It's what I loved when I possessed you and what I hated when I could not convert you."

"But even though we had to move in separate directions, we did have something very special," she offered. "And we still have Nico."

"Yes," he agreed. "We will always have Nico. And magnificent memories."

She saw then that regaining his son had reconciled him to losing her. Perhaps all would never be forgiven for either one of them, but a truce had been achieved.

She looked at her watch. "I should get back to the hospital."

"I will go with you if you don't mind. It will be my last chance to see him before the operation."

"Are you afraid, Diego?" she asked him suddenly.

He thought for a moment, considering her question seriously. "For myself, no. For the baby, of course. But it will be all right," he added quickly. "I feel it here." He pointed to his heart. "I think perhaps it was for him that you and I, who had no business ever being together, loved so deeply. If there is a purpose for everything, he was ours. He will survive. He must. He is our reason."

"Yes," she said, grateful, "I think so, too." And then they were in each other's arms, holding each other tightly, consoling each other for all they had suffered, comforting each other for all they had still to endure, and finally, in the end, allowing themselves to love each other in spite of everything.

"The process of separation is never an easy one," Luke was telling Samantha, "but that doesn't mean it's not valid or necessary."

She had admitted to him that she had not followed his advice and had, indeed, continued to sleep with her husband. Her original intention had been to simply not talk about it. After all, it wasn't exactly any of Luke's business. But he had begun their private session with the direct question put so plainly that she had automatically answered honestly. His response was neither condemnation nor disappointment, but still, she felt off balance. *I'm losing it,* she thought, *and I don't know why, and I don't like it.*

Luke saw he had confused her and was satisfied. It had been exactly his intention, and he was adept at his technique. He needed her to surrender her own reasoning to his, to accept what he said as right. Only then could he accomplish what he wanted. It was taking more effort with Sam than was usual. But she was smarter than his usual target, and looking at her lovely face, he was certain that the extra effort would be worth it.

"Let me give you another example." He made his voice gentle, heartening. "You have a child. Did she used to use a bottle at night?"

"Of course."

"But then there came a time when you took it away, right?"

"Right."

"Why?"

"Because the dentist said it was contributing to cavities. She was three. It seemed like a good time to stop."

"Was it hard for her?"

"You bet. The first night, it took her an hour to get to sleep. She was so miserable. I just felt awful."

"But you didn't give her back her bottle?"

"No. I would have just had to start over again the next night."

"If it had been up to her, she would have kept the bottle, don't you think?"

"Absolutely."

"But with your greater experience, you knew that the bottle wasn't good for her, so you kept her away from it until she got used to the idea and now she doesn't use a bottle."

"I see what you're getting at, Luke," Sam interjected. "But I don't exactly equate sleeping with your husband with sucking a bottle. It's not exactly a habit I'm trying to break."

"Neither is drinking milk. You weren't trying to get Moira to stop drinking her milk, you were just making her drink it in a different way."

Sam was silent. When she'd discussed Luke's theories with Drew, they had sounded far-fetched, more psycho-babble than real. But somehow, listening to Luke's soothing voice, it was all starting to make sense again. He was looking at her expectantly, obviously waiting for her to speak. She felt suddenly defenseless, her weakness exposed. She needed to think more clearly, but she couldn't, and it was making her desperate.

He took in her discomfort. "You've been trying to get pregnant for a while and haven't been able to. You sleep with your husband, you don't use protection, something should be happening. But it's not. So you must be doing something wrong. Maybe not physically, but psychologically. You stop doing it. You break the bad habits. When you start again, you've got a clean slate."

"If I don't know what the bad habits were, how do I know if I'm breaking them?"

"A habit is a habit whether you recognize it or not. You can deny smoking is addictive or harmful. But if you stop doing it, you stop needing it, and then after a while, you just don't do it anymore whether you recognize it as a problem or not."

She shook her head. Nothing made sense anymore. She wanted to leave, to go home and just sleep, but she felt rooted to the ground, unable to stop listening to him.

He looked at her sympathetically. "I'm going to suggest something." He looked at her, trying to assess if she was ready. She wasn't as easy to read as most of the others, but he felt reasonably sure he'd gotten to her.

"What?"

"Move into the institute. Just for a while. Until you can get this thing under control."

"No. Out of the question. Drew would be horrified. And what about Moira?"

He mentally kicked himself. He'd forgotten about the child, but he'd dealt with that sort of thing before. There were ways to seem accommodating while keeping interference with his strategies at a minimum. "You can bring her. We've got a wonderful system for child care. You'll have plenty of time to see her and be with her, but she'll be involved in a fabulous developmental program. The kids love it here. It's like camp, only better."

Sam *had* noticed the brightly painted rooms with children's artwork displayed all over the walls and windows. She'd seen troops of little ones singing songs and listening to stories told by cheerful, energetic young men and women. For a moment she thought how nice it would be for Moira to come home from school and have a whole household of kids to play with instead of a staff paid to be attentive to her needs. Sometimes, she knew, there were advantages in having less. But almost immediately she put the idea out of her head. Luke saw and intercepted her thoughts.

"Just think about it," he said. "You don't have to do anything you don't want or that doesn't make sense to you. But I suggest that you examine again what holds you back and what pushes you forward. Make your own analysis, your own choices, your own decisions. Not mine. Not Drew's. Your own. And we'll talk about it next time."

She realized she was being dismissed and, for a minute, felt a disappointment so sharp it surprised her. Luke saw her response and hid a smile. *Leave them wanting more,* he thought. It works in show business and it works here. At times, he actually thought of his mission as show business. Both areas provided an ideal opportunity to get money and girls. And when things were going well, as he expected they would with Samantha Myles Symington, it could be both lucrative and highly entertaining.

Feeling particularly off balance, Sam headed out of

the building still engaged in an internal dialogue about whether to trust Luke, Drew, or her own instincts, if she could just figure out what they were. She was interrupted by a loud and cheerful "Hi!" Startled, she forced herself out of her reverie and realized that the door had not magically opened for her, but was being held by a tall woman with frizzy dark hair, who was letting her pass.

"Oh, I'm sorry," she said. "I was lost in thought. How are you?" she added, not really interested, but trying to be polite.

"Great" came the reply, which did not surprise her, since most of the people associated with the institute always seemed particularly happy. It was a quality she envied but mistrusted even more. Samantha would have walked on, but the woman seemed intent on having a real conversation.

"I'm Gina. We've been in some of the same classes together."

"Of course. Gina," responded Sam, not actually remembering. "Well, have a nice day."

"Thanks. You're Sam, aren't you?"

Sam sighed. Gina wasn't going to give up. She nodded and smiled. "See you next time," she tried again.

"You're one of Luke's favorites. I've noticed that."

"Oh, I don't know," Sam said demurely, although she had noticed it herself and been quite flattered by it.

"Sure you are. Are you going to be moving into the institute like the others?"

An alarm bell, quiet but insistent, went off in Sam's

head. "The others? Do all his quote unquote favorites move into the institute?"

"A lot of them."

"Really? And what happens to them after that?"

"Actually, I don't know. It's a pretty big deal. You have to be invited; you can't just say you want to live in. I tried, but Luke would never let me."

"Why not?"

"Don't know. Guess I'm just not one of his favorites. So are you going to be moving in?"

Sam looked at her interlocutor. She had been so involved in her own evolution with the "master" that she had failed to notice the exclusionary game going on around her. Suddenly, it no longer seemed so laudable to be picked from the pack. She thought perhaps Gina was jealous, and she felt sad for her. With her angel hair and her loose dress worn with motorcycle boots and a jeans jacket, she had a kind of ditzy quality, but there was something about her eyes that looked smart. She deserved better than to hang around a self-styled guru waiting for him to place her among the chosen. "As a matter of fact," Sam said, "I was kind of thinking about it, but now I know for sure I'm not."

"Why not?"

"Because," replied Sam, realizing only as she said it that it was true, "I'm beginning to suspect it's a lot of bullshit." The words themselves were a relief.

"Does Luke know that?"

"I don't think so. I wasn't sure about it myself until just this minute."

"But you are now?"

Gina was studying her. Sam was surprised that for all her desire to be part of Luke's coterie, she didn't seem very shocked or disturbed by Sam's assessment. "Yeah, I guess so. I'm not exactly sure why, but something you said triggered something in my head, and I think maybe this guy is putting one over on us."

"Sam, can we go somewhere and talk?" And as Gina took her arm and resolutely led her out of the parking lot, Sam noticed that, suddenly, she didn't seem like a ditz at all.

Ian looked at his watch. He had told her to come at a quarter to two, and it was already almost three. His ostensible reason had been a performance by the children of an abridged version of *Julius Caesar,* with Daniela playing Portia to Ryan's Brutus. The two had been virtually inseparable since Daniela's arrival five weeks ago, and when the junior English class had begun to rehearse the play as a component of their Shakespeare studies, he had insisted that she audition for the part with him. It had been an amazing sight to see the painfully shy young girl emerge from her shell and blossom under her exuberant friend's tutelage. That Ryan and Daniela loved each other was obvious to anyone with an eye, but their relationship was also so clearly chaste and filled with innocent wonder that they managed to escape both the teasing of their fellow students and the scrutiny of their teachers that usually accompanied any such coupling. Academically, Daniela had easily been living up to her high promise, which Ian was sure would not surprise Daisy. But that she had evolved from the frightened creature she had been to this popular and evanescent thespian he was sure would interest her mentor. However, he realized, glancing at his watch again, if she didn't come soon, Daisy would miss the entire presentation.

He took a quick look over his shoulder, as he had been doing every ten minutes since the performance began, forcing himself not to turn his head more often lest the students get the idea that he was not interested in what they were doing. He was, in fact, delighted with it, with the perfect dramatic English rendered in a polyglot of accents, and proud to know that the students in his school were not only learning, but enjoying it. But he couldn't help wishing Daisy were there to share it, only because, he told himself, he was sure she would revel in it as much as he did, and it would be good for the school's relations with the board. Quickly, he scanned the back of the auditorium, knowing that if she were there, she would stand out. But through the sea of receptive grins and parental pride, there was no shock of platinum hair on perfect pale skin. He felt himself prodded and turned attentively to Colette, who whispered some unimportant observation in his ear.

"Were there any calls for me earlier this morning?" he whispered back, too preoccupied to reply directly to her comment.

"No," she hissed, perfectly aware of why he was asking. She had overheard him inviting the American tart to the play, even though it was school policy not to include board members in internal programming. It had been inappropriate, and she had taken care of it. She could not tolerate interference from the outside. She needed the headmaster to be completely reliant on her. She had made the mistake before of allowing outsiders a part in Paul Kogan's life, with the result that he had used her, passed over her, and moved on. This time, she would keep more control. She had no choice. For others, there was a life outside of the American School in St. Denis. But for Colette Simard, it was all she had. It was both work and life, and she had made it her mission to ensure that she would be there always. One way or another, she would make Ian Taylor see that she could be more than the efficient assistant and occasional bedmate she had been for his predecessor. So far, he had given her no encouragement. But he was a recent widower, and she had read that it took at least a year to get over the death of a spouse. Her task was to keep him isolated, out of harm's way, until he was ready. Then she would make herself a fixture in his life, whether as wife or as deputy almost didn't matter, as long as it was permanent and inviolable.

This time, he was nudging her, and she broke from her reverie to realize that everyone was clapping except her. "Didn't you like it?" he asked in disapproving amazement. "I thought it was wonderful. Those kids worked so hard. We have to show some support."

"Of course," she said, feeling herself flush as she vigorously brought her hands together. "Bravo!" she shouted, "Bravo!" intent on showing him just how much support she could be.

Afterward, there was socializing, and the students

whose parents had not been able to come milled around with those who had. Ian was not surprised to see Daniela hanging shyly back while Ryan tried to include her in his own exuberantly Texan family circle. He had not really expected Daniela's mother to make an appearance and wondered for a moment if she were disappointed or relieved. He saw Mrs. Jessup waving a brightly manicured hand in his direction and made his way to the group.

"Weren't these kids wonderful?" he said enthusiastically after they'd all exchanged greetings. "You should be very proud."

"Oh, we most certainly are," drawled Mrs. Jessup, adding several syllables to each word.

"Just don't turn him into a pansy actor," roared her husband.

"Oh, don't listen to him," Mrs. Jessup responded. "This is Shakespeare, Henry, not acting, for heaven's sake."

Ian saw that Daniela seemed a little overwhelmed. "You all right?" he asked her quietly. She nodded, although she didn't seem entirely certain.

"Your parents couldn't come, dear?" Mrs. Jessup asked, sounding a little more strident than concerned. Daniela simply shook her head. "Business keep them away?" Mrs. Jessup went on, clearly fishing. Daniela looked stricken.

"That's right." Ian came to the rescue. "Some folks have to work. Like our students. We'd better let them change out of their costumes. They aren't through with classes for the day yet. Say good-bye to your parents and run along, Ryan. You, too, Daniela."

Grateful, she was gone before he'd finished the sentence. And since Ryan couldn't bear to let her out of his sight unless he had to, the boy gave his mother a quick hug, shook hands with his father, and dashed after her.

"Ryan seems quite . . . uh . . . taken with that girl. Who is she?" asked Mrs. Jessup when they'd gone.

"A new student," responded Ian, knowing that was not what she was asking at all. "Her name is Daniela Lender. She's quite brilliant. I think she's been a good influence on Ryan. She makes him study more, and his grades have improved."

"Lender," mused Mrs. Jessup, seeming to have missed everything Ian said after that. "What kind of name is that?"

"Neither a borrower nor a lender be," cackled Mr. Jessup.

His wife gave him a dirty look. "We knew some Lenders in Texas. They weren't in our country club of course," she added with heavy meaning. "You don't suppose . . ."

Ian knew exactly what she was supposing and had no interest in examining it with her. "As far as I know, Daniela is not from Texas. Now, if you'll excuse me, I'm afraid I've got work to do as well. It's been wonderful seeing you. Until next time."

He hurried off, fully intending to go into his office and settle down to the pile of papers that kept growing in his incoming box, but the sight of Colette standing at the door, waiting for him, suddenly depressed him beyond all measure. For the first time, he understood why Paul Kogan had had trouble finding a replacement for himself. Loneliness was the most profound when it occurred in the midst of a teeming populace. *If I stay here now,* he thought, *I will either quit or shoot myself.* He had no desire to do either.

"Colette," he preempted her before she could catalog his tasks for the rest of the day, "I have to go into the city."

"But you have—" she began sternly.

He refused to listen. "I have an appointment in the city. I'm late already. I'm sure you'll have no problem supervising the day's end without me."

She set her lips. On the one hand, she wanted him to understand that she was fully capable of doing anything he did; on the other, she wanted to impress on him the necessity of his remaining. "There are parents—" she tried.

But he was ahead of her. "Without appointments," he reminded her. "You made that rule, and it's a good one. Anyone who wants to see me can make an appointment with you, and I'll be happy to meet with them anytime. Just not today."

And before she could answer, he was gone.

Exhilaration surging, he turned on the ignition of the Peugeot he had leased in St. Denis. It sputtered a few moments, then died. He felt a moment of panic. Since the school was quite a few kilometers from the town and not near anything else, he'd assumed he'd be needing a car and had acquired one two days after his arrival. But, in fact, he hadn't driven it once in the three months he'd been there. All his meals were eaten at the school, whether with students in the dining room, with faculty at meetings, or served to him in his private quarters, usually by Colette. Everything else he needed, from clean shirts to postcards to razor blades always seemed in plentiful supply. He supposed it was a credit to Colette's subtle management that he had never questioned how these things materialized for the asking. He had just fallen into the habit of mentioning a requirement to Colette and expecting it to appear, which it invariably did. He was always considerate in asking, always careful to thank her, just never conscious of what methods were used to acquire whatever it was he wanted. Since Colette was usually with him or where he could find her, he assumed that she must assign one of the handymen to drive into St. Denis and obtain his requisitions. It had never occurred to him to drive for recreation, and seeking entertainment outside of the books he read, which Colette supplied as well, held no interest for him. Until this moment, he had had no reason to go off the school grounds at all. But now, without knowing where he wanted to go or why he needed to get there, he felt that if he didn't leave this instant, he would choke and die on the very air he was breathing.

He turned the key again, slowly this time, mouthing a silent prayer. The engine chugged twice, turned over, and began to hum, coughed, then started to die. He held his breath while he delicately pumped the gas until the hum returned and grew more steady. He breathed a sigh of relief as he swung the car around and headed out of the gates, opened for the departure of parental traffic. Following the signs, he found the autoroute, pressed the pedal to the floor, and was on the outskirts of Paris in a little more than an hour.

He had come without an agenda, but as he'd grabbed his keys from his desk drawer, he'd also slipped a school directory in his briefcase, which he'd brought along to support the idea that he had some kind of appointment. Stopping at the side of the road, he pulled it out now and turned to the back pages. There, just as he had remembered, were the names and addresses of the school's board members. Twelve Rue de Seine, it said. He got the Avis-supplied map out of the glove compartment. Tracing his finger down the center of the map along the blue line that was the river, he found it easily. It was across the Pont D'Eveque from the Louvre Museum in the sixth arrondissement. He could be there in twenty minutes. He looked at his watch. It was close to six. She would probably be out. Still at work. Or meeting a friend for a drink. Or maybe not even in the city, which was why she hadn't come to the performance at the school. It was pointless to go there. He started the car again. With the rush hour traffic, it took him twice as long as he had estimated to get there and almost as long to find a place to park.

Walking around the corner to her street from where he'd parked on the Rue de Bac, he thought the quartier suited her perfectly. There was a café on every corner, with picture-perfect Frenchmen at every table, wearing scarves with no coats and sipping espresso while they looked disdainfully at passersby. The shops were small and charming, a combination of bakeries, art galleries, and fashionable boutiques. A flower vender's cart blocked the corner, and on the spur of the moment, he bought a small bouquet of violets, realizing only as he held his hand out for his change that he'd probably end up having to throw them away since she wouldn't be home. Arriving at the door of number twelve, he almost laughed out loud as he realized he wouldn't even have the chance to find out. Her building was a typical old-fashioned apartment, built around a courtyard, closed off by huge wooden doors that were locked against intruders. As in many multiple dwellings in Paris, the doors were opened by pushing numbered buttons on a security panel that when pressed in the proper combination of a preprogrammed code automatically released the door. There was no intercom, no way of reaching the residents inside without knowing the code.

He stood outside for a few minutes, leaning against the doors. It began to drizzle. Holding the flowers, he felt even more foolish, and when an elderly woman wearily scuffled by him, he bowed and offered her the bouquet. It pleased him that she accepted them wordlessly, almost gravely, as though it was her due, smiled engagingly, and went on her way. Perhaps, in Paris, things like that happened to her all the time. The rain was beginning to come down harder, and he turned to go. Suddenly, the wooden doors behind him opened, and he almost fell inside.

"'*Scusez-moi*," said the young man, stepping around him to open his umbrella.

"*Uh . . . merci*," mumbled Ian, stepping inside. Then realizing it was a fairly large building with no directory, he stuck his head outside again and asked, "*Connaissez-vous Mlle. Howard?*"

"Cinquième" came the reply.

Thanking the man, Ian let the door close behind him. He was in a large courtyard. There was a doorway on his left leading to a formidable wooden staircase covered in red carpet. He did not see an elevator.

"Five floors," he sighed as he started up, not sure why he was bothering. On the third landing, he almost turned back, but it seemed silly to come all this way and not even knock on her door. He took the other two flights two steps at a time. It was a strictly personal ordeal, but he wanted it to be over. Out of breath, he pounded on the door, then leaned against it, panting. No one came. He knocked again for good measure, then headed down the stairs. He wasn't surprised; he hadn't really expected her to be home, wasn't even sure any more if he wanted her to be. What would he have said if she'd asked why he had come. He had no answer.

He plodded heavily down the last flight, disappointment weighing on him like a wet coat. He passed through the courtyard and back onto the Rue de Seine. The doors clicked shut behind him, making sure he understood there was no going back. It was raining much harder now. He watched as Parisians hurried past him, umbrellas bent against the wind. The thought of going back to the school made him cringe. The thought of going to a café and sitting alone made him sad. He pulled his hat lower over his head, and a torrent of water fell from the brim into his face.

"Excusez-moi, monsieur," a voice said from under a floral umbrella that narrowly missed his eye.

He realized he was blocking the security panel and moved out of the way with an automatic, "Sorry."

"Ian?" The umbrella came down, and he saw it was Daisy. "What are you doing here?"

"I brought you some flowers, but I didn't think you'd be home, so I gave them away," he said as if that explained it all.

She looked at him and saw the ineffable melancholy in his face. She couldn't tell if the water on his cheeks was rain or tears. Had she asked, he would not have known himself.

"You're soaked" was all she said. "Come up." He followed her up the stairs silently. "Sorry, it's five flights."

They were both panting a little when they reached the top. She unlocked her door and held it open for him to enter. He stood in her small foyer, making a sizable puddle on the polished wood floor. Through the living room windows on his left, he could see the top of the Eiffel Tower surrounded in mist. He stared out the window but didn't budge, didn't speak. He felt paralyzed, as though he'd forgotten how to move. He couldn't even remember how he'd gotten there, not just to this charming garret on the Left Bank of Paris, but to this place in his life, so detached and desolate.

She put away her umbrella and her own coat, then seeing he had made no move to remove his, she took his hat and helped him off with his coat. She saw the rain had soaked through his coat, and his shirt was wet as well.

"Better take it off," she ordered as she went to a small linen closet and pulled out a large towel, throwing it at him. He caught it and wrapped it around his neck. He knew she was acting normal and he was not. He cleared his throat, aware it was his turn to say something.

"Daisy," he began, but his voice cracked, and he cleared his throat again. "I don't know why . . . I shouldn't have . . ." He stopped. It was not volitional; he simply could not speak any more. If she had not taken his shirt and hung it in the bathroom to dry, he would have grabbed his coat and fled.

"It's okay," she said and patted his shoulder. He could feel her hands on his bare skin. They were soft and dry and warm. "Go sit down. I'll make us some tea."

He found his way to the sofa, a large deco camelback in a deep green chenille. He sank into it, grateful for the down-filled cushions, and soothed by the quintessential view of Paris rooftops and landmarks, he let his head rest against the back. The room was stylish but comfortable, a mix of antique treasures, exotic artifacts, and utilitarian pieces chosen by a discriminating and well-traveled eye. He wanted to get up and examine some of the more interesting *objets:* a tanka from Tibet, a collection of Chinese snuff bottles, but he did not have the energy to rouse himself. He could hear her in the kitchen, which was up a twisting wrought-iron staircase off the foyer. The kettle whistled. Cups clinked on saucers. She'd be down soon. He was tired—of thinking, of feeling, of not thinking, of not feeling. Waiting for her to arrive with the tea, he closed his eyes for a second to clear his thoughts.

When he opened them again, the rain had stopped and the sky was black. The tip of the Eiffel Tower seemed to be pricking a full yellow moon. A halo of light emanated from the Gothic curves of Notre Dame. The orange glow of lamps shone from inside apartments where he could see people moving back and forth in front of their windows like a shadow play. Daisy was sitting in a chair opposite him in the dark, her feet folded under her, watching him. She was wearing an oversized T-shirt that came down to her thighs and a pair of heavy socks. Her hair had been carelessly brushed back from her face, which was bare of makeup. She looked like a fallen angel. He noticed that his shoes were off and he was stretched full on the couch, covered with a soft afghan.

"I'm sorry," he said.

"It's okay. I've always found grief exhausting myself."

He didn't deny it. "I don't know why it suddenly came over me today."

"I take it you haven't done a lot of public mourning."

"What would be the point?"

"Relief."

"I don't think there is any," he said, sounding more forlorn than he had intended. "Anyway," he added, trying to cover, "I've never been the sackcloth and ashes type."

She saw he was embarrassed and changed the subject. "Are you hungry?"

"What time is it?"

"Dinnertime."

"Then I'm hungry. Can I take you out some-where?" he offered, feeling he owed her at least that.

"Actually, I cooked while you were sleeping. Just a plain ragout, nothing to get excited about."

"I'm excited," he said, following her up the stairs. The kitchen was cozy with just room enough for a table for two. She'd set it with colorful china bowls and large crystal goblets. Candles waited to be lit in simple silver candlesticks. An open bottle of Bor-deaux breathed beside a long, unsliced baguette. The aroma coming from a pot on the stove was heady and delicious.

They ate with gusto and finished the bottle of wine. Where his power of speech had been immobilized before, now he could not deactivate it. She asked about Sarah, and he told her everything, from the horror of thinking she might be his sister to the triumph of learning they were not related and could marry. He spoke about how wonderful things had been and how terrible they had become. And finally, he talked about his pain at losing her so many times to her personal demons before he lost her at last to a force other than her own.

By the time he had finished speaking, the candles had started to sputter. Outside, the rain had begun again, accompanied by flashes of lightning that cracked through the night sky.

"I should go," he said, wishing he had drunk a little less of the wine.

"I don't think so," Daisy answered with the same thought in mind. "It would be treacherous enough without the addition of Chateau Lafitte. You'd better stay over. You can go back in the morning. I'll set up the sofa. You already know it's comfortable," she added, teasing.

He watched her while she brought out sheets and a pillow and threw them over the sofa. She was still in her T-shirt and socks, decidedly unglamorous but overwhelmingly delectable. Anyone else, in any other circumstances, he knew, would be maneuvering his way into the large bed with satin quilt that he had glimpsed though the open door of her airy bedroom. But he could not. He realized he had come here wanting to forget but had ended up only remembering more. After he had thanked her and they'd said good night, he lay on the sofa for many hours, watching the silhouette of the Paris skyline come into relief on a lightening sky. He could hear her even breathing in the other room and recalled what it was like to feel the soft sigh of a woman's breath on the back of his neck. His arms ached with an emptiness that seemed unfillable by anything in life. Finally, he fell asleep as the sky turned pink and dreamed of lying beside Sarah while she slowly disappeared, turning into a vaporous cloud that enveloped him and left him gasping for air.

When he awoke, he smelled coffee and, pulling on his pants, made his way upstairs to the little kitchen. Daisy was in a white silk kimono, freshly showered, with hair still wet. For someone who looked almost ethereal, she moved around the tiny space with surprising earthiness, pouring hot milk into huge cups half-filled with dark rich coffee, popping in toast, and slathering on butter and jam.

Suddenly remembering what had fomented his

journey in the first place, he asked between sips, "Why didn't you come to see the play?"

She looked at him as though he were crazy. "You told me not to."

He caught another piece of toast as it leaped, burning, out of the toaster. "No, I didn't. I waited for you. I almost missed half of it looking to see if you'd come in late."

She passed him the butter. "I'm sorry, Ian. But there was a message on my machine from your Mlle. Simard telling me that there was a change in plans and I was not to come. Considering what a scandal I almost caused the last time I showed up without an appointment, I figured I'd better stay away."

"Shit," he said as he handed her the toast and she accepted with a surprised smile. "I knew she had a problem, but I didn't think it was venal."

"A little territorial, would you say?" asked Daisy, getting the picture.

"Not any more," said Ian, finishing off his coffee. "The next time you come to see me, which I hope will be soon, with or without an appointment, that woman will either be different or gone."

Standing in the headmaster's bedroom at the American School in St. Denis, Colette Simard scowled at the empty bed and cursed under her breath. Ian had told her he did not need her to wake him up, to make his breakfast, to arrange his schedule. But she had insisted it was part of her duties as arranged by his predecessor. She did not tell him that she had also shared the very same bed with Paul Kogan that he now occupied. And it was only when she had pressured him to make good on his promise of marriage that, like the coward he was, he had fled, not even allowing her the official recognition of his post, which she had been directing from behind the scenes for two of the three years of his tenure in any event. She knew, of course, that she was not the most attractive of women, but she had learned that she could mute her brittle demeanor and that sufficient alcohol, candlelight, and loneliness could make what nature had hardened in her appear soft. She was also aware that Ian Taylor, unlike Paul Kogan, was not a man to grab at every opportunity to satisfy his lust. But isolated in St. Denis with only Colette to rely on, he might have come around to viewing her in a favorable light. But she would have to be careful not to let the intrusion of the blond American embassy whore derail her plans.

By the time Ian's rented car drove through the school gates, she had already formulated her strategy. She greeted him at the door of the school and did not even mention his absence the night before. With well-practiced outrage, she informed him that she had discovered someone, she presumed a student, many of whom, she knew, considered it amusing to imitate her fastidious manner, had called several of the invited guests to the junior class performance and notified them that the play had been canceled. She had learned of the ruse when one of the parents had called to find out if they were rescheduling. She suggested that Ian punish the entire class until the guilty party confessed.

Stifling a laugh and feeling a little guilty for thinking the worst of his assistant, Ian promised to take it under advisement.

"We'll straighten it out," he said kindly. "Don't worry." He put a comforting arm around her shoulder as they headed toward his office. Colette smiled to herself. She wasn't foolish enough to interpret his gesture for anything more than the pity it was meant to convey. But it was proof positive that she was still in the game.

6

Sam had known it would be a difficult sell, but somehow, she hadn't expected Drew's reaction to be so violent. "It's not like I'm going away forever," she emphasized. "Just a couple of weeks. I . . . uh . . . need some time off," she ended lamely.

"Time off from what? From me and Moira?"

She could hear how hurt he was, and she almost lost her resolve. But she had made a commitment. "No, that's not it at all. But we have a certain kind of life together, and it's put me in a rut that I feel I have to get out of."

"Is this about starting up your experimental division at DMC again? Because if you need another car to design—"

Even though she knew he had a right to be upset, it made her angry. "Don't patronize me. I don't design cars to combat PMS or something. I'm not a bored housewife looking for a hobby."

"What are you looking for?" he asked, exasperated.

It was a good question, and she hadn't prepared an answer. It took her a minute to think of one. "I need to resolve some internal issues. It's not about whether I love you and Moira. I do. It's about whether I love myself."

"This is all that jerk's bullshit," Drew spat out.

He was right, of course, but she had to find a way to assuage him. Trying to lower the degree of tension, she spoke softly. "Please, Drew, give me some credit. I'll admit that I'm abdicating my responsibility for a little while, but think of it as a two-week vacation from my full-time job. Is that too much to ask?"

He threw up his hands. "You explain it to Moira, because I sure as hell can't."

Moira had been easier to convince than her father, especially when Sam had promised to return with a set of Barbie dolls, which they had been resisting buying for her in spite of repeated requests. There was something about the rampant consumerism of this busty but anatomically incorrect doll that both Sam and Drew felt they should object to on principle. All the girls in Moira's first-grade class had at least one already, and Drew had tried to compensate with elaborate and sophisticated toys and games that they could play together. He had bought her a junior magic set and himself an autographed copy of a book pur portedly by Houdini, which he had found in a second-hand store. Father and daughter practiced for hours, putting on shows for Sam, where Moira would make coins disappear and Drew would escape from elaborate bonds that the little girl knotted around him. But after the performance, when Drew had asked her what trick they should learn next, Moira had impishly responded that she'd like to learn how to make a Barbie doll appear. Eventually, seeing the yearning in his daughter's eyes when she passed another child and her Barbie on the street, even Drew had relented.

When Sam told Moira she was leaving, the child asked only two questions. "Is Daddy going to stay with me?" and "You won't forget to bring the Barbies, will you?" And when Sam answered both questions satisfactorily, she was surprised at the alacrity with which Moira accepted her impending absence, kissed her good-bye, and wriggled off her lap.

Sam packed a small bag and went to say good-bye to Drew. She explained that she would not have her own phone at the institute, but she would call each day to speak to him and Moira. If he needed to reach her, he could leave a message with the switchboard and she would get back to him.

"Have you told your sister what you're doing?" he asked. Sam knew why Drew was asking. They had both spoken to Melinda that morning, and she had informed them that Nico was scheduled for transplant surgery the next day. Sam had offered to drop everything and come to Washington, but Melinda had insisted that she didn't need support yet. She might later when Nico came home, and then she'd want to call on Sam. But she didn't want to take Sam away from her own family longer than necessary. This was Drew's way of letting Sam know he didn't think her going to the institute constituted a necessary absence.

"Please, honey," she tried. "It's not as if we've

never been separated before. I'm just taking a little vacation."

"Do you think I'd mind if that's what it was? I'd be happy if you wanted to spend two weeks on the Riviera. Three weeks even. Just don't get more involved with that phony medicine man."

"You're jealous," she said, "but you don't need to be."

"You want to know the truth, baby. I'm not jealous, just disappointed. You used to be smarter than that." It was a zinger that went straight to her heart as he knew it would. She wanted to take him in her arms to try to explain. Instead, their good-bye kiss was perfunctory at best. She called Moira away from her toys and held the little girl close. "It's going to be okay, sweetheart," she whispered. "I really, really have to do this, but Mommy will be home soon. I promise."

"I know," said Moira, unperturbed, and hurried back to her play. Sam took a deep breath and told herself not to cry. She was doing this of her own volition. Almost.

Hoisting the bag over her shoulder, she walked out the front door, past the scaffolding that still enclosed the east wing, although the facade behind it had already changed from scorched and blackened hull to creamy new plaster, and down the drive. At the entrance to the estate, she pressed the electronic release button, and the gates slowly swung open. Walking onto the pavement, she stopped at the curb and looked around. A moment later, a small blue Honda pulled up. She got in.

"How'd it go?" Gina asked, taking her bag from her and tossing it onto the back seat.

"Ugh" was all Sam could say.

"He didn't take it well?"

"To say the least. He said he wouldn't mind if I wanted to go to the Riviera, but I'm an idiot for going to stay at the institute. He's hurt and disappointed that a smart girl like me could get taken in by a charlatan like Luke. Believe me, he couldn't feel worse about it than I do."

"You were vulnerable. Luke's an expert at preying on the defenseless."

"You're telling me. That's why I'm agreeing to this. If I can expose him, maybe I can redeem myself and get back some self-respect."

"Not to mention what you might be doing for the rest of the world. With crazies like Luke, it starts with spiritual claims and ends up with suicides and bombs. If you get him for us, Sam, you could end up saving a lot of lives."

"I know," Sam said gravely. "It would be easier on Drew if I could explain it to him."

"But you won't?"

Sam could hear the worry in Gina's voice. "No, Gina, I won't."

"I'm sorry, Sam. This is so important to us. I can't stress enough how crucial what you're doing is. If any one of us could have gotten to Luke ourselves, believe me, we would never have put you in this position. But he's got a sixth sense or something, because no operative we ever tried to put in there, including myself, could get into his inner circle. I've never seen anyone do it as fast as you did."

"Why do you think that is?" Sam wondered.

"He wants you," said Gina, disconcertingly straightforward.

"Thanks" came Sam's sardonic reply.

"It's going to make it trickier for you. But he wouldn't let you in on what he's doing if he didn't. You have to make him believe that you believe in him. That you'll do whatever he wants."

"What if he never tells me about this whole Armageddon Advance that you keep talking about? What if there are no hidden caches of weapons or nerve gas? What if he has no intention of blowing anybody up, and all he wants to do is me?"

Gina grinned. "Then we'll consider ourselves lucky."

"Gee," Sam said with a sigh, only mildly amused. "Is the FBI always so supportive of the civilians it recruits?"

"We wouldn't do it if we didn't think it mattered," Gina said, deadly serious again.

"I know that," Sam said. "Neither would I."

By the time they entered the institute, they were deeply engrossed in an animated dialogue about inner versus outer meditation. Since students were always meeting up with each other before and after the sessions, their appearance together would not cause suspicion or comment. As they headed into the classroom, Luke was already seated in front of the picture windows in a trancelike state of hyperfocus. But instantly, he noticed Sam's bag over her shoulder, and within a blink, he was by her side, drawing her into his private office.

"Gina," he directed over his shoulder, "why don't you lead the others in the meditation exercise?"

As he closed the door behind her, Sam could hear Gina beginning. "Okay, everybody, select an object, observe it closely, without criticism or comment, focus on the smallest detail, do not name it . . ."

Luke took Sam's bag from her hand and placed it on the floor behind him. "I hope this means that you've decided to stay," he said solicitously, as though she were checking into a rehab center to cure a serious drug habit.

"It seemed the right thing to do," Sam said truthfully.

"It is, absolutely," reiterated Luke, and for a minute, she wondered if he was gloating. But instantly, he was concerned about her. "What about your daughter? Didn't you bring her with you?"

Samantha shook her head. "It seemed right to come alone" was all she said. She couldn't tell him that the risks she took for herself she wouldn't dream of imposing on her child.

Luke was sympathetic. "It can't have been easy. Sometimes it's difficult to make other people understand why we have to do the things we do. They think we are being selfish. But it's not selfish to be fulfilled, to work at becoming the person you want to be, any more than it's selfish to eat or sleep or breathe."

"It's ironic," she said. "I came to the institute to free myself to get pregnant. But as long as I stay here, I'm making that impossible."

"When things are right, Samantha," he said, touching her cheek, "nothing is impossible. You're going to find that out."

"That's why I'm here," she said, hoping he hadn't noticed her shudder.

Although some of the institute's inhabitants shared rooms, Sam was given a room of her own on the top floor of the building. The other rooms on her floor were unoccupied. Her first few days were spent in meditation, in classes, in solitary walks on the grounds, and in a daily long, private session with Luke, listening to his soothing voice tell her that there were answers for all the world's ills if we only knew how to see them. She asked if he could show them to her. He said when she was ready, he would.

When he did, Sam was prepared to hear every word. Each morning, when she dressed, she carefully clipped the tiny microphone to her bra strap, let the wire fall to her waist, and taped the miniature recorder to her side as Gina had shown her. Each night, she carefully dewired herself and arranged the equipment under the bed as she had been instructed, assured that somewhere, not too far away, someone was hearing every word that was said and would be instantly aware and available if the need arose. Then she waited for Luke to make his move.

In requesting her appointment, Kathleen Jessup had made it clear that it was a matter of some urgency, so when she placed the letter on Ian's desk with a flourish, he expected that it must be some incendiary missive, even though he recognized Ryan Jessup's still somewhat childish handwriting.

"Read it!" she commanded, and he did as he was told. Glancing at her face that was contorted with rage, he realized he must have missed something in this simple request to include a friend in their holiday plans.

"I'm sorry, Mrs. Jessup," he said, handing her back the letter. "As far as I see, he's just asking if Daniela can spend the vacation with you. If that is objectionable to you, you need only tell your son no. I don't see what that has to do with me or the school."

"It is not that simple, Mr. Taylor." Her drawl had assumed an ugly edge with her anger. "Ryan is smitten. He is not willing to take no for an answer. You are the one who brought that dirt-poor Jew into the school. You are responsible."

Ian felt his spine stiffen. "I beg your pardon?" He struggled to maintain an air of politeness, assuming he had heard wrong, although he was sure he hadn't.

She knew he hadn't, as well. "You heard me. It is entirely inappropriate for a school like this to admit someone like that. That is not why people like us send our children here."

"Mrs. Jessup, this school is an academic haven for English-speaking children interested in an advanced education. If you send Ryan here for any other reason, you have made a grave mistake. As for Daniela Lender, she is an outstanding example of the type of student we aspire to."

"Don't give me that bullshit, Taylor. She's a nothing. And she doesn't belong. And I don't want her consorting with my son," she shouted, all trace of the genteel southern lady gone.

Ian struggled not to be sucked into her mire. "You will have to take up what your son does with your son. But as long as I'm in this school, we will judge the student by how they perform, not how much they're worth."

"Keep up that knee-jerk liberal crap, and you won't be here long, I'll guarantee it."

"Why, Mrs. Jessup" came the mellifluous greeting from the area of the door, "I thought I heard your voice."

Ian whirled and tried to keep the instantaneous joy he felt at the sound of her voice from overwhelming all reason.

"Miss Howard, I'm so glad you're here" came the honey-toned retort. "You are on the board, so you're just the person to settle this dispute. Isn't there some sort of policy on the books about who we let into this school?"

"Yes," Daisy replied evenly. She could see the welcome look in Ian's eye turn to dismay. "Our policy—on the books—is to let in any child who is academically qualified." She saw him relax. From the doorway, where she had been trying to stop Daisy's entrance, Colette sent daggers in her direction.

"Oh, fine, if you want to talk about the official line. We've all got to put up with that. But we're among friends here. And I know none of us wants to contaminate our standards. We have our children to consider. And I, for one, don't want my Ryan involved with some money-hungry, social-climbing Jew whose biggest dream would be to catch a nice, rich American boy to pull her out of the gutter."

Ian was not prepared for the rush of contempt that flooded through him. He had deliberately sought to maintain the high road, not engaging in name-calling or counter recrimination with someone as unenlightened as Mrs. Jessup. But now, he just lost it. "Okay, that's it, Mrs. Jessup. I've listened to all I'm going to take from you." He wasn't shouting, but the venom in his voice made it seem like he was talking very loud. "If you want to consider your child, the best thing that ever happened to Ryan was that he somehow managed to escape your ugly, small-minded way of thinking and become a pretty decent kid in spite of being the son of an ignorant bitch like you."

Beneath her peroxide blond big hair, Mrs. Jessup's face turned apoplectic. "How dare you—"

"No," Ian went on. "How dare *you!* There is nothing going on between your son and Daniela that isn't completely positive. She has helped him to become a serious student and made him a more responsible person. Because of her religion, which gives her a stronger moral fiber than you'll ever know, her relationship with Ryan is not only beneficial, I am utterly certain it is completely chaste. You can take Ryan out of the school, which would be a shame for him. But you won't ever talk about Daniela or, for that matter, anyone in that disgusting manner again. I have never hit a woman, but I will gladly flatten you if you make even one more of your repugnant comments in my presence."

Out of the corner of his eyes, Ian saw Colette's mouth open in shock. He couldn't be sure, but he thought Daisy was trying to hide a smile as Mrs. Jessup turned to her. "You're on the board, Miss Howard. You're my witness. I want to call a board meeting and have this man fired immediately."

"If anything, Mrs. Jessup," Daisy said sweetly, "I'd recommend him for a raise."

Mrs. Jessup was sputtering. "If people weren't waiting for me at Cap D'Antibes tomorrow, I would take my son out of this school right this very instant. As it is, you'll be hearing from me."

"I'm sure we will," said Ian with perfect equanimity as Mrs. Jessup stormed from the room. She pushed past Colette, who was clucking with unabated consternation. "Go with her, Colette," Ian said just to rid himself of her disapproving visage. "Make sure she leaves the kids alone."

He stood at the door and watched as the two women disappeared down the corridor. Balancing on the edge of his desk, Daisy waited, sucking in her breath. As he turned to her, she could hold herself back no longer and burst into laughter. "Did you see her face when you said you would flatten her?" she managed to choke out. "Did you see *my* face?"

His initial outrage dissipated, Ian, too, started to laugh. "I guess I kind of lost it."

"Kind of? You were great. She *is* an ignorant bitch."

"I said that, too, didn't I?" he said with such incredulity that it set off another paroxysm of hilarity.

"I love how principled she is. Like she'd pull her son out of school, except she's just got to go to the Riviera and she has nowhere else to park him."

"Poor Ryan," answered Ian, sobering.

"Yes," Daisy echoed, wiping the tears of laughter from her eyes, "poor Ryan."

They were silent for a moment, recovering from their hysteria, shaking their heads, mutely remembering, and knowing they were thinking the same thoughts, feeling the same feelings. And then, suddenly, Ian stopped thinking and went to her, where she was perched on the corner of his desk. His arms went around her, and his mouth was on hers, and neither one of them was laughing any more. Still kissing her, he drew her closer and her legs went around him. He picked her up and, carrying her, went to the door and kicked it shut, locking it behind them. Then he brought her back to the desk and poised her on the edge. With one hand, he reached beneath her skirt and pulled off the lace bikinis from under her skirt; with the other, he unencumbered himself. And then, standing in front of her, he lifted her legs around him again, drawing the two of them together. She caught her breath, surprised at the power with which he moved inside her. It had been a long time for both of them, and there was succor in remembering the sweetness of bodies joining. And by the time appetite had turned to ardor, they realized they were nurturing their souls as well.

Returning from seeing Mrs. Jessup roar off in her Rolls-Royce, Colette approached the headmaster's office, prepared to admonish him for speaking as he had to someone as influential as Mrs. Jessup. She would not condone Mrs. Jessup's bigotry, but she would point out that until Daniela Lender had been admitted, the school had, in fact, had no Jewish children. Formulating a stern but forgiving speech in her head, she turned the knob, but the door was stuck. She pushed against it, but it did not move. She thought she heard rustling inside. She knocked.

"I'm in a meeting, Colette," Ian called. "Come back later." Then she distinctly heard a female giggle.

Infuriated, she marched back down the corridor and out into the day, not stopping until she'd reached the road outside the school grounds. She would not be made a fool of, she thought to herself, seething. She stood in the middle of the road and flagged down a truck, forcing it to stop at the barrier of her body.

"I need a ride to St. Denis," she said, getting into the cab without even asking.

"Sure," said the driver, and they exchanged no more words until he had deposited her at the town center. Boiling with anger, she sat down in the town's one café and ordered a *citron pressé*. While she waited for her drink, she glanced around her. Only one other table was occupied. She studied the brown-haired woman, distinctly American, reading the *Herald Tribune*. Pretty, but without the glamour of the whore who was debauching the headmaster at the school at that very moment. She signaled the waiter, wanting to know where her drink was, but the American called him, and naturally, he detoured to her first. It infuriated her how Americans always took it for granted that they could get whatever they wanted, do whatever they pleased. But she would not let that happen, not this time. She would find a way to stop Daisy Howard from getting a man she had no right to claim.

The operation was described as almost routine. Throughout the ordeal, Melinda and Jack repeated the statistics to each other like a litany. Mortality from surgery is extremely rare. Over ninety percent of children with kidney transplants are living five years or more after receiving a new kidney. Still, when the four-hour surgery was over and the doctor came out to tell them that it had gone extremely well for both donor and recipient, they held each other and cried.

For Nico, the effects of the transplant were immediate. The symptoms of his disease began to wane, his puffiness disappeared, and the drugs he was being given to induce immunosuppression were starting to kick in. After the first groggy day, he was already sitting up in bed, laughing and playing with his parents and winning the hearts of the nursing staff who would stop in to see him just to cheer themselves up.

The discomfort for Diego, as with most donors, was greater. Emerging from the fog of anesthesia, his first conscious thought was an awareness of the pain. His second was that Melinda was standing by his bed. She saw him open his eyes, and as he waited for his vision to clear, she came closer and took his hand.

"Hi," she said quietly, smiling. "How are you feeling?" She squeezed his hand and seemed, with the pressure of her fingers, to lessen his distress.

He tried his voice, not sure what would emerge. "I'm okay," he croaked, realizing as he said it that it must be true. "The baby?"

"Nico's doing great," she beamed. "The doctors say he came through it like a trouper. The kidney started to work immediately. He woke up before you did. Jack's with him. I didn't want you to be alone when you came to."

"Thank you, *mi amor,*" he said, then promptly fell asleep again.

He slept on and off for the next two days. Sometimes, when he opened his eyes, she was there. Sometimes, he just dreamed of her. By the third day, he was out of his bed, sore and slow, but walking. He asked for and received permission to hobble down the corridor and visit his son. He was not expected, and he stood in the doorway of Nico's room, watching with an ache in his heart that far surpassed the pain in his side. Melinda and Jack leaned over on either side of Nico's crib, reaching in to the toddler, who held fast to one finger from each of their hands in his chubby little fists. Every nerve in Diego's body screamed that he should be the one at Nico's side. *"This is the child of our love,"* he wanted to shout at Melinda, *"born of our passion. No matter what I do, I can never forget that. No matter whom you marry, you can never change it."* But even as the giver of life, he was the outsider here, the intruder. And, somewhere, he understood and regretted that he had put himself in that position.

Jack saw him first, and in the second that it took him to acknowledge the appearance of Melinda's ex-husband, Diego was able to identify the turmoil with which his presence was regarded. That Jack loved Nico was obvious. That he wanted Nico to live was indisputable. That he would tolerate anything if it meant saving the child had been demonstrated. That he appreciated with all his heart what Diego had done could not be questioned. All these things had been spoken of and established. But no one had mentioned the fear in Jack's heart that Diego had read on his face. That as much as he loved Melinda, he knew that Diego cared as deeply. That though she shared history with Jack, she shared adventure with Diego. That no matter how certain Jack was of his wife's feeling for him, he could never know what feeling she still had for her first husband. And though Jack recognized that they would always owe Diego for Nico's life, he wished to hell he'd disappear. But none of this had been, or would be, stated, and adopting an air of nonchalant concern, Jack came toward him with an outstretched hand.

"Diego, good to see you up and about," he said, sounding a little too hearty even to his own ears.

Diego hobbled to the side of the crib and grinned at the clapping baby, his heart full. Seeing his joy and sharing it, Melinda took his hand. Diego saw Jack take note but say nothing, only putting his own arm around Melinda as if to protect her from the San Domenican's aura.

"The doctor tells me I can be released in two days," Diego told them after they'd discussed the baby and his condition.

"You'll come to our house," Melinda said without hesitation.

Diego looked at Jack. "Perhaps it will be too difficult for you. Nico will still be in the hospital for at least another ten days after me. It will be a strain."

"Stop, Diego," Melinda insisted. "It's already been decided. You won't be in any shape to travel home for the next two weeks, and I'm not going to let you spend them in a hotel alone." She turned expectantly to Jack.

"Of course," Jack said obediently. "It's all been arranged."

"Well," Diego said, "if you're sure."

"We are," Melinda reiterated. Diego noticed that Jack did not reply.

Three days later, Diego was ensconced in the cheerful guest room where he had spent the night before his operation. The baby had to remain in the hospital under observation for another couple of weeks, but his recovery was progressing, and, like a normal child, he slept through most nights. They were told that these first few weeks were a grace period and that at some point the functioning of Nico's new kidney was bound to diminish, but usually all that was required was a readjustment of medication. But while things were going well, they were advised to try to reestablish their normal lives, catch up on their sleep or their work, and prepare for the possibility of increased attentiveness later on. During the day, while the baby was awake, either one or both of them was at his bedside. Although his movement was restricted, Diego, too, came to spend some time with Nico, being certain to arrive when Melinda had a shift alone and to leave when Jack came to relieve her. But when Nico closed his eyes for the night, Melinda went home, and Jack, who hadn't been to his office since a week before the operation, decided to spend a few hours at the State Department to assess how punishing his workload would be when he returned full-time.

Relishing the comfort of her own bed after so many nights on the lumpy hospital cot, Melinda tried to sleep. But her mind was still tuned to danger, and her ears, used to listening to the labored breathing of her child, could not get used to the utter stillness. Certain she heard sounds coming from the nursery, she sat up in bed to listen, then remembered that Nico was still in the hospital. Still, the feeling that someone was in

Nico's room would not go away, and finally, chiding herself for her restless imagination, she got up to peek in and satisfy herself that it was empty. But it was not.

"Diego?" she called softly. He was standing over the baby's crib in the dark, silhouetted by a street light outside the nursery window.

"I'm sorry. I disturbed you," he apologized.

"No, I couldn't sleep either. I heard noise so I came to investigate."

"Your . . . Jack is not home?" He would not refer to that man as her husband. Illogical as it was, he thought of that post as his.

"He missed so much work with Nico in the hospital. He's trying to catch up." She joined him by the crib, studying him for a moment. "What are you doing in here?"

"Imagining," he admitted. She didn't need to ask what. "I miss him. I miss you," he went on, unable to stop himself. "I remember—"

She put her hand to his lips. "Diego," she whispered, stopping him in midsentence. He could feel her breath on his cheek. "Please don't do this."

"I can't help it. It's breaking my heart."

"I'm sorry," she said, and he could hear that she meant it. "What you did for Nico was so wonderful, you don't deserve to suffer. But I don't know how to stop it." He thought she might be crying, but he could not see in the dark. He wanted to grab her, pull her to him, wrap himself around her. That would ease the pain. He remembered the softness of her breasts, the warmth of her thighs, the way she felt when he entered her.

"Melinda, *mi amor*," he said hoarsely and buried his face in her neck. She tried to pull away from him, but he would not let her go, and she did not try too hard. "I know why you left," he was able to admit, now that he could breathe her scent. "But things could change . . ."

This time she did wrench herself out of his grasp. "Things *have* changed, Diego. I am married to another man."

"Do you love him?" he asked, not believing that she could.

"Yes," she said simply. "I loved him even before I knew you. We have been tied together for a long time. He has always been there for me."

"And I have not." He articulated what she was suggesting.

"This time, you were," she said, acknowledging but not excusing. "And it was the most important time. But not in the past. Not always."

"And because of that, you stopped loving me?"

"No." She needed to be honest for her own sake as well as his. "I never stopped loving you. But I started to hate you."

"Do you hate me now?"

"How could I? After what you've done. But we can't go back."

He barked a bitter laugh. "Remember what Barbara Walters said about us? That our story was a fairy-tale romance? In a way, it still is. Except I started out a prince and turned into a frog. Do you think if you kissed me, I could change back again?"

"Diego, don't." She was backing away from him,

but he saw that it was not fear of him, but of herself that propelled her out of his reach. He started to move toward her, but in the dark, he miscalculated the distance between them and banged into the corner of the crib. He let out a yelp of pain, and instantly she was by his side. "Oh, my God, Diego. Are you all right?"

"I will be," he gasped, his face contorted with the effort to remain upright.

"Here, let me help you." She put his arm over her shoulder and, with her hand around his waist, made him lean on her as she inched them out of the nursery and down the stairs into the room they had made his recovery room. By the time she laid him on the bed, he was sweating with the effort. She sat beside him and stroked his brow while he closed his eyes and took deep breaths, waiting for the agony to subside. In a few minutes, the pain began to ease, and as the dizziness passed, he opened his eyes again. She was watching him with such love and concern that it brought a knot to his throat, and the ache that had been in his side moved to his heart. Seeing his body relax, she saw that the crisis was over, but still, she needed to be certain that no damage had been done.

"I'm just going to make sure you didn't break any stitches or something," she said quietly. With gentle hands, she lifted his shirt and lowered the drawstring pants that were loosely tied around his waist, until she could see the white patch of bandage just above his pelvic bone. Trying to ignore the hardness of his body and the softness of his skin (which she remembered with a clarity that both shocked and embarrassed her), she felt around his wound with feather fingers, making sure it was secure and dry, that no bleeding had occurred. And though the pain was gone and her touch was light, each brush of her hand burned its imprint not only on his body, but on his soul.

He caught her hand with his, intending to hold it away from him, but instead, he clasped it to his chest. She could feel his heart beating, and it seemed strangely intimate, as though his body were telling her secrets she did not ask to know. "What we had, Melinda," he said, speaking so quietly that she had to lean toward him to hear, "does not go away. Ever. No matter what. We cannot forget."

"I know that," she whispered, so close that a tear from her eye fell on his cheek. Slowly, he pulled her to him, savoring the awareness that in a moment her lips would be on his.

"Melinda? Are you downstairs?" came the voice, and suddenly, the thread was broken.

"I'm here, honey," she called out, jumping away as though she'd touched an exposed wire.

Seconds later, Jack's face was in the door, inscrutable, his eyes surveying, looking for clues to what his mind had already imagined.

"Diego was walking around in the dark and banged himself, and I was just making sure that he hadn't done any damage, like popped his stitches or anything. But he's not bleeding, and his dressing looks like its still in place, so I guess there was no harm done after all. But after an operation like that, you can't be too careful."

She was talking too much, and they all knew it. She stopped abruptly, embarrassed. Diego and Jack looked at each other. There was no need to explain. Jack would forever owe a debt of gratitude to this man, but he would gladly have seen him dead.

"Let's go to bed," Melinda said evenly, aware that the daggers from their eyes alone could have fought a lethal duel. "Good night, Diego," she added softly. "Sleep well." And then before the two men who loved her could exchange a word, she took her current husband by the hand and led him out of the room, leaving her former husband lying in his lonely bed, cursing the fates that had twisted her out of his grasp.

Lying beside Jack, his back to her, Melinda could feel the waves of tension that emanated from his body like an electromagnetic field. She knew what he must be feeling, and she ached for him, for them both. Molding her body around him, she twined her arm through his. "Don't be afraid," she said.

"Aren't you?" he asked, turning to face her, so close to her on the pillow that even in the dark she could see the apprehension in his eyes. In response, she kissed him, a lush and lingering kiss meant to arouse and reassure and make him forget that she had not answered his question. Her touch ignited his desire, and, inflamed by his need for comfort and hers for peace, they made love, stoking the fires of passion in order to consume whatever disquieting thoughts smoldered beneath the surface. He put his hands under her bottom and lifted her to meet the force of his drive, almost savage in its demand. She opened her legs and closed her eyes and suddenly saw Diego's face. Then, quickly, she opened her eyes and registered Jack and closed her legs around him. And finally, no longer in control, unable to resist or reason, she allowed desire to overwhelm her and didn't try to decide who or what it was she wanted beyond release and respite.

ℳ7℘

After the first time, in his office in the school, Ian didn't speak to Daisy for two weeks. He couldn't put a label on what had happened. The word *ravish* came to mind, for even though she had been willing, he felt it had been a surprise attack, that he had swooped down on her from his position on the metaphorical high ground. When their encounter had ended, she had left rapidly, and he hadn't tried to stop her, both of them fearing a return of Colette Simard and wanting to avoid an embarrassed attempt at explanation. He wondered if Daisy thought he was rude, not calling or sending flowers or whatever it is one did after these intimate, yet strangely disconnected, moments. Or whether it had just been a momentary indulgence to her, a carnal celebration over prejudice, which had amused her and was already forgotten. He had thought to call her many times but somehow couldn't formulate what he would say after hello. It seemed too late to be blasé, too soon to be anything but. And now, on a Sunday afternoon, with affairs at the school in relative good order as far as he could see, he had driven into Paris and was, once again, walking up the five flights to her little apartment on the Rue de Seine.

He knocked on the door, half hoping she would not be home, his heart beating from the climb and the apprehension. She opened the door without asking who it was. "Oh" was all she said when she saw him, and she stepped aside for him to enter.

"I waited outside until someone was coming in and then walked in behind them," he said even though she hadn't asked for an explanation.

"If you had called, I could have given you the code." He realized it was simply a statement, not a reprimand.

"We seem to like to drop in on each other," he smiled.

He had brought her a bag of cherries from the greengrocer around the corner on the Rue de Buci. They sat in the living room, eating them, silent but not uncomfortable. He was grateful that she didn't see the need for small talk any more than he did. He watched her, her long frame folded in a chair, hair falling in her face as she bent over the table to spit the pits into a small ceramic bowl. It was warm in her sunny apartment, and she was wearing leggings and a cutoff stretch top that revealed an expanse of snow-white midriff. She was completely natural and utterly sensual, all the more for being unaware of it. He had an urge to grab one of her bare feet and kiss her toes, each one separately. He had no idea how such a gesture would be received.

"Listen," he began after clearing his throat to break the silence, "I'm sorry it took me so long to get in touch with you after . . . last time," he ended lamely, still at a loss as to what to call their encounter.

"Why?" she asked.

"I guess I should have called or something," he said, taken aback.

"I could have called you," she answered, and he saw that her expectations were not what he assumed.

"Why didn't you?" he asked, curious now.

"Because I figured you were troubled by what happened, even though it was really quite wonderful, and you didn't know how to deal with it. And when you wanted to, you'd come to me."

He looked at her a little awestruck. She had told him what he was thinking far more succinctly than he had been thinking it. She saw she'd impressed him without even trying and laughed. He laughed, too, and got down on his knees in front of her, holding her feet in his lap. She was so different, so secure and knowledgeable, so unafraid. It was beyond his experience and understanding. "How did you get that way?" he asked and knew she would know what he was asking.

"No one ever told me I had to be different," she replied, and he saw she understood what a gift that was.

"When Sarah died . . ." he hesitated and looked at her, wondering if perhaps she would be uncomfortable at the mention of his late wife. He should have known better. She touched his hair, encouraging, sympathetic. It was the moment that he realized there were things in this life still to cherish. Strength and kindness in an untroubled soul. "I cried," he went on. "Because she was gone and I loved her and missed her. Because of how she had died. But more, because of how she had lived. From the moment I met her, I wanted to protect her; I knew she needed protection. It was so obvious, so clearly written on her face. But I couldn't help her, really."

"I think you must have helped her a great deal," Daisy interjected softly.

"Yes, of course, you're right. She'd never had unconditional love, and I gave her that. But in the end it wasn't enough. She got better for a while. And she tried so hard. Every day was a real struggle. I loved her, and I felt sorry for her. But it made me tired, too, you know. And I think, toward the end, she sensed that, and it was making her come apart again. We never talked about it. And of course, I never said anything to anybody else. And especially after the fire, what would have been the point. She was gone. Why shouldn't her family think that things were going great for her right up until the very end? At least they had that. They could believe that she was at peace when she died." He stopped. "I'm sorry. I didn't come here intending to deliver a morbid monologue. I don't know why I'm saying all this to you now."

"Because you need to," Daisy said simply and got down on the floor beside him. "It's hard to be the keeper of the flame."

"I think it's why I got as far away as I could as soon as possible. They thought it was because it would hurt me too much to stay at Belvedere. It did hurt. But I was more afraid of hurting them. Of saying something to destroy the myth. Because there was a point when I thought"—he took a deep breath, this was hard to say—"I thought, if she falls apart again, if she starts having blackouts and doing things she would never do as herself, she's going to end up in an institution. And if that happened, maybe she'd be better off dead. And then, when the fire . . ." His voice cracked.

She put her arms around him. "Thinking something doesn't make it happen, Ian. You are not responsible."

"I know here," he said, pointing to his head. "But not here." He touched his heart.

"They're not separate," she scoffed gently. "It's all you, mind and body. If I kiss you here"—she put her lips to his—"don't you feel it here?" She put her hand between his legs. "If I touch you here"—she left her hand where it was, but pressed it against him—"doesn't it tell you something here?" She placed her forehead next to his. "You know what you know. Accept it and let it go. Then move on to what you need to do next."

Suddenly, there was no question in Ian's mind or body about what he needed to do next. He put his hands around the bare skin of her torso, almost completely circling her narrow waist. She raised her arms and let him undress her, pulling up her top, releasing her breasts, full and round, into his hands, enticing him with their surprising voluptuousness on her narrow frame. Then he brought his hands down and took the rest of her clothes with them, and when she stepped out of them, he did what he had imagined doing, kissing each one of her toes while she lay back and sighed with delight. Then she undressed him, and they stood facing each other, aware that though they had made love before it was the first time that they had seen each other's bodies, and it was clear that they took pleasure in what they saw. Urgent and hurried as their union had been before, this time it was compellingly slow as they touched and kissed, ventured and caressed, leaving no area unexplored, no sensation unenhanced. And finally, when his tongue had paved the way and brought her nearly, but not quite, to the end of the road, she guided him inside her, and together, they finished the journey. Afterward, he lay on her breast, looking out at the Paris skyline, not speaking.

Again, she understood. "You have nothing to feel guilty for, you know. Not for loving her or tiring of her problems or crying for her or going on after her." She held his face in her hands and kissed him gently on the eyes, the nose, the mouth. And then he knew why he had come. He had come for absolution, and in the grace of her body and the goodness of her heart he had found it.

"Are you hungry?" he asked, suddenly feeling ravenous himself.

"Always," she said with a laugh. "But I have nothing in the house."

"I'll get something and cook for you."

"You cook?"

"Really well."

"What a bonus. Unfortunately, it's Sunday. The market's already closed. And the stores don't open."

"Come to my place. I'll make you veal with truffles."

"You're kidding! I adore truffles. How come you have truffles?"

"I told you. I like to cook."

They were dressed, in his car, and on the highway in half an hour. They spent the drive singing American oldies but goodies, going through the Presley oeuvre before starting in on Motown. Somewhere in the middle of "Stop! in the Name of Love," they arrived in St. Denis.

"We have to stop in town," he told Daisy. "I don't think I have enough olive oil."

"Isn't everything closed?"

"Stores, yes. But there's a café on the town square that I always go to, and I've gotten to know the owners. I'm sure they'll lend me some."

He pulled up in front of the café and ran inside while Daisy waited in the car. Most of the tables set out in front of the café were empty, and she paid no attention, humming the Supremes while drumming her fingers on the dashboard. A woman came and sat at one of the tables, waiting for service, but Daisy, watching for Ian's return, hardly noticed her. He came out of the café, carrying a bottle half filled with olive oil, and gave her a smile and a thumbs-up. He looked around him more from force of habit than interest, and suddenly, he stopped, and the bottle slipped from his hands and went crashing to the sidewalk, splashing its greasy contents. Daisy groaned and jumped out of the car to join the staff of the restaurant who had come running, concerned, offering assistance, napkins, commiseration.

"What happened?" Daisy asked, looking at Ian's

pale face as he accepted a napkin and sopped up some oil from his pants.

"I don't know . . . I thought . . . I . . ." He stood up and looked around. The tables were empty again. He seemed baffled.

"Are you okay?" Daisy studied him, troubled.

"Yeah," he said, shaking himself out of it. "I'm fine. The bottle was slippery, that's all."

The owner appeared with another bottle, this time plastic. They exchanged apologies and drove off.

Back in his cottage at the school, Daisy sensed there had been a sea change. Something had happened, but she couldn't figure out what. Ian wasn't talking. He said it was because he had to concentrate on his cooking, but she knew that wasn't true. She could see his mind was nowhere near his frying pan. Dinner was a delicious but desultory affair, and by the time it was over, Daisy had assessed the situation.

"Do you want to talk about it?" It was a simple query, not a demand.

"No," he answered, and it pleased her that he had the grace to be direct. She could tolerate anything except pretense. "I'm sorry," he went on. "It's not you, it's me. But I can't talk about it yet." He had seen an apparition. Perhaps it had been caused by guilt, perhaps by fear. But he didn't want to give it substance by discussing it.

"Can I borrow your car?"

"What?"

"I'd like to go back to Paris."

"You don't have to do that," he said guiltily.

"I know that. I want to. Obviously, something is

179

going on with you and you have to deal with it yourself. I can live with that. So can I borrow your car?"

"Of course," he said, not up to making a pretense of protest. "I don't need it during the school week. Bring it back on the weekend, and we'll go somewhere." He gave her the keys. "I'm sorry," he said softly into her hair.

"Don't be." She shrugged. "Just figure it out and call me."

Easier said than done, Ian thought, closing the door behind her. He went to the night table by his bed and opened the drawer. From under the letters, the magazines, the paperback books, he pulled a bulging manila envelope and turned it upside down, shaking the contents free. Photographs spilled out onto his bed, snapshots of him and Sarah and the family taken over the years they had known each other, a short lifetime of love and pain. Picking them up at random, he sifted through them, unleashing the memories that he'd been keeping so tightly tethered. He tried to make sense of what he had seen, tried to explain to himself the workings of an imagination fueled by guilt. But still, she had seemed so real, and she had looked at him so accusingly that he had felt immediate contrition—for believing her dead, for living himself. Weighted with sorrow and regret, he pushed the pictures aside and stretched out on the bed, exhausted. He closed his eyes, and Sarah's image flickered before him. He thought of Daisy's words: "Accept it and let go," and finally, as the vision faded into sleep, he resolved to do just that.

In the morning, coming to wake him, Colette found him lying fully clothed, photographs scattered around him. In the face of her insistence that her job description included rousing the headmaster, he had given up trying to convince her that an alarm clock could accomplish the same thing. He had, at least, managed to limit her intrusions to school days. She shook her head in disgust, taking in the untidy mess. She assumed this was the influence of the American whore. Before he had taken up with her, doing their dirty business behind locked doors, he had been an exemplary headmaster, fastidious and capable. She had seen a lot of potential there, for the school and for herself. Now everything was threatened.

She reached out a hand to shake him awake, and then her eye caught on one of the photographs. Carefully, not disturbing him, she lifted it for a closer look. It was Ian and a woman whom she'd never met but who looked vaguely familiar. She reached for another picture and then another, all with this woman, sometimes with Ian, sometimes alone. From the configuration of the couple in the photos, she understood that this was Ian's late wife, which would make it impossible for Colette to have seen her. Yet something was troubling her, something about the face, so open and American. And then it came to her, and she understood why she thought she knew this woman, where she had appeared before. And as she gently shook the headmaster awake, her spirits lifted. The tide had turned in her favor. If things continued to go her way, she could guarantee that Daisy Howard had paid her last visit to the American School at St. Denis.

"So, are you finding yourself?" Drew asked his wife on the phone, aware that he must sound like a petulant child.

"I think I'm making progress," Sam responded, not exactly lying. "Kiss Moira for me, and I'll keep you posted." She hung up before she could blurt out something that might give her away. She was hurting her husband and she hated it. She was pretending she needed time away from him when what she really wanted was to be in his arms.

In fact, she'd been there a week already, and she wasn't any closer to finding out Luke's secrets, if he had any, than the day she arrived. They had spent countless hours in private sessions, and even though his logic had become more convoluted and his lectures more contrived as time went on, Sam had indicated nothing but admiration bordering on awe, which she hoped was not overdoing it. The more reverential she appeared, the more Luke seemed to revel in her company, but still, he made no mention of hidden arsenals or secret agendas. The level gaze that he directed into her eyes, which at first had seemed so meaningful, now struck her as vaguely creepy, and she wished with all her might if he was going to make a move, he would make it soon, so she could give Gina whatever information they needed to put him out of commission and get on with her life. She had even tried backing out, insisting to Gina during one of their stolen moments that even if the Institute for Cognitive Epistemology was in fact a front for some neo-Nazi movement, Luke was never going to share their program with her. But Gina had refused to let her off the hook. "Think about Oklahoma City," she reminded her. "Remember those horrible images of children being carried out of a bombed-out building. It could happen again. And it could happen here."

It was enough to make Sam drop her arguments. "But I'm only giving it one more week," she had informed her. "As much as I want to do my duty as a citizen, I've got a duty to my family as well. My husband is really suffering."

"He'll get over it when he finds out what you've done," said Gina. "You're going to be a hero."

"He may also just slug me for lying to him and putting myself in danger."

"You're not in danger," Gina maintained. "We're tracking you wherever you go. We won't let anything happen to you. Just don't give up."

Be careful what you wish for, Sam thought as she heard a knock on her door and Luke identified himself. She looked at the clock beside her bed. It was past nine. Although they'd been meeting together nearly all day every day, it was the first time he'd come to her after dinner. Her heart started beating faster as she went to the door. She had said she wanted him to make his move, but in fact, she'd never really thought about what that move might constitute. And now that it was about to happen, she was scared to death.

"Am I disturbing you?" he asked as she let him in.

"Not at all," she answered, hoping her voice didn't sound shaky. "I was just reading over my notes from the past few days. I can't tell you how much you've helped me, Luke. I'm really starting to see things in a new way." She knew she was being unctuous, but she'd learned Luke not only appreciated adulation, he expected it.

"I'm glad to hear it," he responded, genuinely pleased by any agreement with his ideas or methods. "That's why I came by. I thought maybe now that you'd had time to digest what we've been doing, you might need to talk about it."

"You're absolutely right," she cooed. If she was going to get things rolling, she might as well go for broke. "I understand everything you're saying about separation, and I see how my past is holding me back. My problem is I'm just not sure what direction I should take for the future."

His eyes gleamed, and she saw that she had made the right choice, pushed the right buttons. "I can help you there, Sam," he said, taking her hands and leading her to the small sofa that constituted the conversation area of her room. Not letting go of her, he sat down, forcing her to take a position beside him. "I think you have it in yourself to be very special," he told her, leaning close enough for her to feel his breath on her face.

Her instinct was to recoil, but she forced herself to smile and stay where she was. She hoped that somewhere Gina was listening and that she'd hear whatever it was she needed to hear, then burst in and get Luke the hell away from her. She also realized the sooner she got Luke to reveal himself to her, the sooner she'd be free of him.

"It means so much for me to hear you say that," Sam said, sighing. "Because I really feel like if I'm going to develop in the future, it's got to be with the institute—and with you."

"Yes, I feel that way, too," Luke responded. He reached out to touch her. She caught his hand in hers as if moved to hold it, figuring it would be safer in her palm than roaming free.

"I feel like there's so much more for me to know, Luke." She hoped she wasn't leading too much, but if there was something to find out, she wanted to get it over with. "You're so . . ."—she searched for a word—"evolved." She hoped that didn't sound stupid. "I wish I could just share your knowledge, your beliefs."

"You can," he said fervently. "I can introduce you to a truth you never even suspected. Part of the institute is for everyone, but not everyone in the institute can be part of the greater plan."

"I'd like to be, if you'll let me," she intoned solemnly.

"Sam," he whispered her name in assent. He moved more quickly than she expected, catching her off guard. With his body draped over hers, she was pinned to the sofa with his weight. She wanted to shove him off, but instead, she merely wrenched her head out of his line of fire, so his lips ended up falling somewhere in the vicinity of her hair and the cushions. She tried to look tempted and terrified at the same time. Only the first was feigned. This would be a good time for Gina to appear, she thought, but then admitted to herself that it would be premature.

"I feel so committed to you." Sam wriggled free. "But at the same time, I'm so wary. You have so many people who adore you. I don't want to be just another . . ." She trailed off, certain he'd get the message.

"How could you think that, Sam? You are not just anyone. You are special to me. I told you that. And I'm going to prove it to you. I have something to tell you, to show you . . ."

She leaned forward eagerly, encouraging, "Yes?"

For a minute, he didn't answer, and she waited, anticipating. But then, she saw he was no longer gazing intensely into her eyes. His head was cocked, and his focus appeared elsewhere. It took her another second before she heard it, too. She marveled at how finely his instincts were honed. His ideas might be crap, but his meditation exercise worked. The clamor was stopping outside her door, and suddenly it changed from indiscriminate noise to very specific voices. With horror, Sam realized that one of the voices belonged to her husband and he was shouting about her.

"I don't give a shit what your regulations are," Drew screamed. "She's my wife and I want to see her."

"If you had only called, sir . . ." A woman was trying to placate him.

"I did call. I left a message with your switchboard. She didn't get back to me, so I came to get her."

By now, Luke was off her, standing a few feet away, watching, waiting for her reaction. She didn't like it, but she knew what she had to do. Flinging open the door, she attacked.

"What the hell are you doing here?" she accosted her husband.

Seeing her, he instantly quieted. "We need to talk, Sam."

"I talked to you this morning." She steeled herself.

"Barely," he answered accurately. "We're not communicating, and you know it as well as I do. We can't go on this way."

"You have no right to come in here and demand—"

"I'm not demanding," he interrupted, his voice low but strong. "I'm beseeching."

Sam looked at his blue eyes and almost melted, ready to give up everything she had gained. He was her husband, and this was not her problem. Then she caught a glimpse of Gina peeking around the corner of the corridor. From the look on her face, Sam knew that whatever Gina's methods, she had been privy to what had taken place with Luke, and she was desperate not to lose ground. Without a word, she was pleading with Sam not to blow it for them. Sam looked at Luke, thought about Oklahoma City, and knew without a doubt that he was capable of something equally maniacal. She swallowed hard and turned back to Drew, venom in her voice. "I am sick and tired of your pressuring me to do what you want me to do and be what you want me to be. It has no meaning for me anymore, don't you understand that?"

Drew reeled as if he'd been physically hit. "What the hell are you talking about?"

"I'm talking about your selfish, petty, bourgeois life and how much I hate it."

"And Moira?" It was such a quiet, simple question, she almost burst into tears. She forced herself not to react.

"This is not about Moira," she said, ice in her tone. "This is about the fact that I don't want you interfering in my life anymore. I'm at the institute because that's where I need to be right now. I don't want you coming after me or trying to force me to come back with you. Because I'm not going to let you do it."

"Jesus Christ, you've been brainwashed." He was aghast.

"Not at all, Mr. Symington." Luke stepped in smoothly, putting a protective arm around Sam. "Sam is just discovering a part of herself that she didn't know before. She's learning things that are important to her. You can't stop enlightenment once it has begun."

"You did this," Drew accused. "You've done something to her."

"Please, give her some credit. She's too smart to be bamboozled. If you don't know that about her by now, then you don't know her at all."

Sam wanted to punch him for his sickening presumptions and his patronizing tone. Instead, she smiled at him and took his hand. "Please go, Drew," she said. "I'll call you when I want to see you."

Drew looked at her, baffled. He *did* know his wife better than he knew anyone in the world. He knew her with his heart and soul, not only with his mind. And this was not the woman he knew. Something was definitely wrong, and it wasn't that she had decided she didn't want to be bourgeois. But looking at Luke's smug face and Sam's blank eyes, he knew he wasn't going to figure out what was going on by talking to them. Without another word, he turned on his heel and walked away. Sam wanted to call him back, to run into his arms and let him take her out of this place. Out of the corner of her eye, Sam saw Gina tensely poised. She said nothing as the elevator closed and Drew was gone. Gina sighed with relief and disappeared around the corner again. Luke hugged Sam. He was smart enough not to gloat. "I know how hard this must have been for you," he said, all unctuous empathy, "but you did the right thing. Get some rest. Tomorrow, your life is going to change." He kissed her before she could avoid it, making no attempt to hide his excitement.

I've done it, thought Sam as she closed the door behind him and double locked it. *Tomorrow, Luke will tell me his secret, and Gina will have what she needs to put him away. So if I'm such a success, why do I feel so lousy?* And she lay down on her bed and cried herself to sleep.

Guillermo Valdes sat in the presidente's office, his feet on the presidente's desk, and painstakingly deciphered the English words in the current issue of *Newsweek* magazine. The item appeared on the page labeled "Newsmakers" under the heading Transitions. "Recovering" it began in bold type, then went on, "In Washington, D.C., President Diego Roca of San Domenico. From surgery after donating a kidney to his two-year-old son who lives in the capital with Roca's ex-wife, movie star Melinda Myles, and her current husband, State Department attorney Jack Bader. Although both father and son are said to be doing well, Roca is expected to remain in the D.C. area for at least two weeks before doctors give him permission to return home to San Domenico."

Moving his lips while he read, Valdes chuckled to

himself. He had been formulating his plan ever since Manuel Noriega had been indicted in the United States for drug smuggling. The more recent scandal involving upper echelons in the Colombian government and their suspected connections to the Medellin cartel had only served to set the stage more effectively. Over the past two years, he had developed his own alliances, delivering leads to a contact in the U.S. State Department named Mort Freeman, whom Valdes had met while Freeman was writing a position paper on San Domenico's complicated relationship to democracy. Valdes had even on occasion sacrificed his own men and profits, signaling Mort to tip off the Drug Enforcement Agency as to the time and place of a drop in the States, never too big of course, while loudly and publicly decrying any suggestion that officials in San Domenico would, in any way, condone trafficking in cocaine.

By now, through Freeman's gullibility, he had positioned himself in the State Department as a trusted American ally, vocally opposed to the drug trade. At the same time, Valdes had seen to it that Diego Roca, with his own ideas of what constituted San Domenican independence, had remained an enigma to the Americans, vulnerable to hostile interpretations of his policies and, therefore, an obvious target for negative assumptions. He had laid the groundwork carefully and had been patient, knowing that none of it would work if his timing wasn't impeccable. But never, in his wildest dreams, had he anticipated that fate would deliver such a prime opportunity for action to his doorstep.

With the *Newsweek* article on the desk in front of

him, he placed the call to the private number that connected directly to his old friend Mort.

"Freeman here" came the immediate response after half a ring. It was a number Mort gave only to sources on the highest level. When that phone rang, he knew it was big news.

"Mort, my friend, it is Guillermo Valdes."

"Guillermo! Good to hear from you. So your *el presidente* went under the knife. He's going to get himself an image of good samaritan if he isn't careful."

"I wish that were so," Valdes sighed wistfully, making certain it sounded like he was saying less than he knew.

"What?" Mort had the instincts of a barracuda. "What? You know something? You got another tip for me?" Mort liked the San Domenican's little handouts. They were making him very popular at the DEA and giving him plenty of clout right here at State.

"I'm afraid it's more than that," said Valdes gravely.

Mort was smelling blood. "I'm listening, Valdes."

"We intercepted a Piper Cub taking off from a field in San Domenico. It was loaded with cocaine. We estimate a street value of maybe twenty million."

"Pretty hefty package. Any idea who was sending it?"

"Unfortunately, yes. We interrogated the pilot and another man who was with him. They told us they were under direct orders from Diego Roca."

Mort let out a low whistle. "The big cheese himself, eh? How do you know it's true?"

"Let me put it this way. Civil liberties in San

Domenico are interpreted differently than in your country. They were well aware of the consequences of lying here and were not prepared to face them."

"Used a little muscle, eh? Would their testimony stand up in an American court?"

"I can only say, again unfortunately, the evidence was most convincing," Valdes affirmed with complete confidence since he had manufactured every thread of it himself. The pilot and his friend were being well paid for their statements, their families taken care of. Valdes had compiled quite a list of their previous infractions, which he had told them he was prepared to destroy as long as they cooperated. The alternative, he made clear, would make any atrocities they had heard about from previous "dirty wars" seem tame. Valdes was certain these men would never recant.

"Could we extradite them if necessary?" Freeman asked, already calculating the rewards of such a coup.

"As long as *el presidente* is absent and I am in charge, I can guarantee it. If Roca returns to San Domenico, who knows?"

Freeman got the message. "Okay. Fax me affidavits, signed statements, depositions, anything you've got. I'll hand deliver to the DEA. If the information is solid enough, I think they'll take action."

"I am sorry to have to do this, but I see no other way. I would be betraying both my country and my conscience to ignore such a heinous crime."

"Yeah, sure," said Freeman, not doubting for a moment that Valdes's motives had more to do with his ambition than his morality. He couldn't care less. "Just send the stuff."

At seven P.M. that night, Melinda and Jack left Nico

sleeping peacefully at the hospital and headed for home. The evening was balmy, and the cherry trees had begun to bloom along the Potomac. Parking the car in the garage when they arrived, they decided to postpone entering the house they now shared with their recovering guest and take a walk over to Dumbarton Oaks. The nineteenth-century mansion and its gardens officially closed at six, but in previous explorations, they had found an unsanctioned entrance through a wisteria-covered arbor into the orangery. In response to a light spring breeze, a grove of cherry trees shed its petals like snowy confetti, while the magnolias released their perfume into the sunwarmed air. They strolled, arms around each other's waists, savoring the serenity of the park and the peace of mind that came with knowing that soon their son would be home and Diego Roca would be gone.

For Melinda, it had been a time of ambivalence. Watching Diego with Nico, talking to him about the past, planning with him for the future, had reminded her of the man she had once loved so desperately she would have given her life for him. And even though she knew that in all likelihood he could only be so kind and vulnerable away from the pressures of the country he ruled, it was a redemption to know that for the brief triumph of their life together, she had not been wrong. At the same time, she was never more aware of Jack's solid and loving presence and of the fact that *he* had almost given his life for *her* and would do so again if necessary. But too much love could cause as much distress as too little, and Melinda knew that her heart would ease greatly when Diego Roca had left her home and returned to his own.

"I'll be glad when he leaves," Jack said as if reading her mind. For him, Diego's presence had been less equivocal, more a simple thorn in his side. While Jack shared Melinda's gratitude at Diego's sacrifice for his son and was forced to acknowledge that, though Jack was the one Nico called Daddy, Diego had given him life, he was and always would be uncomfortable at the passion they obviously shared for the same woman. He had no problem with Nico developing a relationship with his biological father; there couldn't be too much love in a child's life. But there could be too many lovers in a woman's life, and though he trusted Melinda with all his heart and knew she loved him with all her soul, he was not one to ignore the allure of temptation.

"I'm glad he came. I'm glad he stayed. But me, too," agreed Melinda, as aware as her husband that no matter how strong their commitment, it could never be taken for granted.

They walked for a while in comfortable silence, then left the park and headed home down Thirty-first Street. By the time they got to Avon Lane, they could already see the cars double-parked near the corner of Q Street.

"Is somebody having a party on our street?" Melinda wondered.

But Jack had recognized the dark sedans as government vehicles. "It's not a party." He quickened his pace, and Melinda followed, realizing, as he did, that the activity seemed to be centered around their own house. The door was ajar, and they walked in, astounded to see Diego facing a cadre of five men.

"Mort!" Jack said, surprised to recognize his

colleague among their uninvited visitors. "What's going on?"

"Sorry, Jack. I couldn't warn you. This is Frank Kurasik and George Hellstrom. They're from DEA." Jack noticed Mort hadn't bothered to present the other two burly men, who hovered near Diego as though awaiting orders.

"What are you guys doing here?" Jack asked, not even bothering to acknowledge the introduction.

One of the DEA men answered; Jack didn't know which one. He hadn't really bothered to get their names straight. "We have a warrant for the arrest of Diego Roca."

Melinda gasped. Roca, who had said nothing up till now, nearly spat. "This is a violation of international law. I am here as a guest of the American government on a humanitarian mission."

"Is this some kind of joke?" Jack asked.

"I'm afraid not." Mort was talking for the group.

"What's he charged with?"

"Drug traffic violation."

"This is absolute rubbish," shouted Diego. "I have never—"

"Don't say anything, Roca," Jack interrupted. "As your counsel I advise you to keep silent."

"My counsel?"

"Yes," Melinda pressed, relieved that Jack had automatically assumed the role. "Let Jack handle it, Diego. He knows what he's doing. Just do what he says."

"Let me see the warrant," said Jack, practically grabbing it out of the DEA agent's hands. Mort looked on smugly as Jack perused it. His eyes strayed to Melinda, who had paled and was standing with her hand on Roca's arm. He'd met her a few times at State functions, but like everyone else, he was always blown away by how gorgeous she was in person. He wondered if there had been anything kinky going on in the house with the three of them together. "Shit," said Jack, shoving the warrant back at them.

"He's going to have to come with us," said Frank or George.

"I will not—" Diego began, but Jack signaled so forcefully for him to be silent that he complied.

"He comes with me in my car. No cuffs, no agents. I don't care if you have to wake one up, but you get a judge, and I'll bring him down. This is a bullshit warrant, and I'll get it straightened out. But you can't expect my client to sit around waiting in line with a bunch of criminals."

"Where do you come off . . . ?" one of the DEA men began, but Jack just ignored him.

Pointing his finger in Mort's chest, he warned, "This is an international incident, Mort, and you're obviously in it up to your neck. If you're right, sure, it's a big coup. But if you're not, you're looking at a new career. So if I were you, I'd hedge my bets."

Mort looked a little uncomfortable. Finally, he turned to his henchmen. "It's okay. Bader's in State. He'll bring him down. Let it go."

They could see that Frank and George were not happy with the decision. They had come to make a collar and didn't like returning empty-handed. But even if Roca got downtown on his own steam, they'd still get credit.

196

"One hour," threatened Frank or maybe George. "He better show up or your ass is grass."

"Don't take it so personally, buddy," said Mort as they headed out. "It happens with a lot of piña colada presidents."

"You're supposed to be a diplomat, Mort. Learn to shut up," Jack said, slamming the door behind him. He went back into the living room, where Diego was pacing, while Melinda sat white-faced on the couch. "Do you have any idea what this is about?" Jack asked him.

"An idea, that's all," answered Diego.

"There's no truth in this, is there?"

"Jack!" burst out Melinda as though he'd said something impolite.

"I've got to ask." Jack made no apology.

"I don't know what you've heard or what assumptions you have made about me. You can choose to believe what you want. But never would I involve myself in the filth of drugs. Never!"

"That's what I choose to believe," said Jack. "Okay, put on your most official uniform. We've only got one hour. You can tell me what you think is going on while we're driving."

"It can't be true, Jack," Melinda said when Diego had gone. "I'd be the first to say he's done awful things. But it's always been out of some belief in a greater cause. Drug dealing doesn't fit into that category."

"Maybe he just got greedy," Jack conjectured.

"Uh-uh. Power is his aphrodisiac, not money. I know him." Jack gave her a look and she found herself blushing. "I didn't mean . . ." She didn't bother to go on. There was no way to reconcile her two lives and these two men. It was enough that Jack was helping her former husband, as Diego had helped her son. She didn't expect any more. And she could only pray that both their efforts paid off.

8

Fourteen hours after Jack had driven Diego to police headquarters, he brought him home again. He had called Melinda around midnight to tell her that he was doing what he could and that she should go to sleep, but worrying about them both, she had only managed an hour or two of fitful dozing. In the morning, she called the hospital to check on Nico, and, hearing that he was doing great and that he was happily playing with a candy striper, she told the nurse that for the first time since her child had been checked in, she'd be coming in late. Then she waited. When she finally heard the car pulling into the driveway, she ran to the door, opening it before Jack could use his key. She was relieved to see that he was not alone but noted that both men looked worn and haggard.

"It can't have been easy," she greeted them quietly. "But at least you're back. Both of you."

The two men followed her into the living room and, taking an easy chair each, plopped down in exhaustion. She offered food and drink, which they both declined, and waited for someone to tell her what happened. No one spoke. She realized they needed prompting.

"Is it over at least?" she asked hopefully.

"It seems," said Diego wearily, "it is only beginning. I am under arrest."

"What?" she asked, confused. She assumed that since they had come home together, the authorities had realized they were making a mistake and withdrawn their ridiculous charges.

"They had evidence," explained Jack. "No doubt manufactured. But they didn't want to hear about that. They caught two guys coming from San Domenico in a plane loaded with cocaine who said that they were under orders from Diego. They've got the plane, the drugs, sworn statements. It's all circumstantial, but it's enough to give them a case."

Melinda looked at Diego. "Melinda, please," he said before she could even ask. "You know me better than that." He was right; she did. "I know who is behind it. Guillermo Valdes, the minister of agriculture. He was angry because I ordered him to burn the coca fields." He laughed derisively. "He certainly got back at me."

"Did you tell them that?"

"Of course I did," Diego said.

"Of course he did," Jack echoed. "They interrogated him all night. I stayed with him so they couldn't pin anything on him. But by morning we weren't any closer to resolving it than the night before. At least I got him arraigned with the first docket."

"But if he's still under arrest, why . . . ?" The words seemed ungracious, so she just trailed off.

"Why am I here?" Diego finished for her. "Thanks to Jack."

"He's under house arrest," Jack explained, not daring to look at his wife. "Under my recognizance. He has to stay here until there's a break of some sort or the case comes up for trial."

Melinda tried not to let her dismay show. "How long will that be?"

"Months," Jack answered a little sheepishly. "But I wasn't going to let them put him in jail."

"Of course not," Melinda said quickly. "You did the right thing."

"I'm very grateful," Diego said quietly. "To you both."

"We owe you," said Jack, "for Nico."

"He's my son, too," answered Diego. "You owe me nothing."

"Well, I owe you both an apology," Melinda said, lightening the mood, "for keeping you here talking when what you need is a bath and a bed."

Agreeing, Jack and Diego rose heavily and faced each other. Jack put out his hand, and gripping it, Diego pulled him into a hug. Melinda watched, moved at the sight of the two men clapping each other on the back, bonded by adversity and by their love of her. They were extraordinarily different: one dark, one fair; one volatile, the other steadfast. But they were both men of honor, and she counted herself lucky to carry them both in her heart.

She went to the bedroom with Jack, while Diego retired to his guest room. Too tired to even shower, Jack managed only to pull off his clothes before falling into a dead sleep on top of the covers. She found a quilt and spread it gently over him, then, leaving a note so he would not worry when he woke up, she headed toward the hospital. But as she was going out the front door, she thought she heard a noise in the back. A little nervous, she went to investigate and was relieved to see Diego leaning against the banister on the small back porch that looked out onto the patch of green that passed for their back yard.

"Don't you want to sleep?" she asked quietly, coming up beside him.

"I will soon. When I went into the room and closed the door, it suddenly hit me that I wasn't free. I came out here to breathe."

"Poor Diego. I know what that must do to you."

"Are you thinking this is justice? You left me because you accused me of denying my enemies their freedom. Now it is denied me."

"I admit there were times I hated you and wanted to see you fall. But I am sorry this has happened."

"I was never able to make you understand. I interpreted the law. I never broke it. Everything I did was from conviction, never greed. Because of my principles, I lost more than I gained. I lost you and Nico."

"You retained your power. That was more important to you than love."

"And how important was love to you? Not more important than politics. Or American ideology. *You* left *me,* not because I didn't love you or I betrayed you, but because I didn't govern the way you thought I should govern. So which one of us forgot the value of the heart?"

She was silent for a moment, chastised. "You're right," she said at last. "My love lacked courage. I could have stayed and fought harder for your soul. Do you think it would have made a difference?"

He smiled ruefully. "Who knows? If it had, I wouldn't be in the predicament I'm in now. I showed Valdes how to be ruthless. He has turned his hand against the master. Perhaps it is what I deserve." He sat on the steps, his shoulders sagging with defeat. She sat down beside him, looking up at the sun, teasing the day as it peeked demurely through the clouds. She remembered lying with Diego by the lagoon in the jungle, watching the sun rise in the sky, heating her eyelids with purple stars. He had been so full of zeal and hope, so dedicated to righting the wrongs of his people. Something had happened along the way, but he did not deserve to be dragged through the mud with the false accusations of a jealous, greedy criminal. She put an arm across his shoulder and felt him tense with dread or desire, she could not tell.

"You'll get through this, Diego. Jack will help get you out of it."

"Jack. He's a good man. He works to save me even though he knows that if I could, I would take his wife from him."

"But you can't," she said. His only answer was to look in her eyes, probing for a truth she did not know and would not reveal if she did. Her face was hidden by a veil of chestnut hair falling over her eyes. He smoothed it back and let his hand linger on the back of her head, then used it to draw her closer. She could see the light reflected in the gold of his eyes, which proffered an invitation she could not refuse. Their lips touched, lightly at first and then, with the instant recall of years of ardor, pressed together, demanding what had been denied for so long. Melinda broke away, breathless. "Diego, please. We can't . . . I can't . . . Don't . . ."

"Sshhh," he soothed. "You are right to move away. Once I gave you adventure. Then I gave you passion. But I could never give you peace. And now all I offer you is confusion."

"You must be tired," she said, not knowing how else to answer. He had defined the situation for both of them. No more needed to be said. "I'm going to the hospital. Why don't you come inside?"

"Go ahead. Kiss Nico for me. I'll stay out here a little longer and pretend for just a little while that I'm not a prisoner."

Afraid that the magnetic force of their love had not yet lost its power and might somehow draw her into the circle of his heart, Melinda did not dare to approach Diego. Instead, she gave a little wave from her post near the door and then was gone. Feeling as alone as he had ever felt, Diego sat gazing at the heavens, wishing he remembered how to pray.

By the time Ian had a chance to think, the school day was almost over. He had been embarrassed to be awakened by Colette, lying amidst the evidence of his earlier distress. He had gotten up quickly, shoving the pictures back into their envelope, mumbling some excuse for falling asleep with his clothes on, and insisting that he did not want breakfast and he would see her in the school office. When he arrived an hour later, showered, shaved, and changed, she didn't mention the state in which she'd found him, but Ian found her presence more unbearable than usual. Trying not to be harsh, he had told her that he didn't care what she had done for Paul Kogan, he had no expectations from her on the personal front himself. In fact, quite the contrary. He had to insist that she no longer come into his private quarters for any reason at any time unless she was invited.

"We'll see," was all she said, and he resolved that if she did it again, he would simply fire her. By now, he knew enough of the school's routine to train someone else, and he had no intention of allowing her to infringe on his privacy just because that's the way she'd always done things.

It wasn't until after Colette had gone to do an errand in St. Denis and he had made his rounds of classes, done his paperwork, and reprimanded some recalcitrant students that he'd allowed himself to go over the events of the day before. He had been the victim of his own overactive imagination, and it wasn't difficult to fathom the cause. Clearly, guilt over the possibility of his own happiness had made him conjure the image of his dead wife, as though to remind him that since he could not save Sarah, he had no right to salvation himself. Considering the situation in the light of day, he saw how foolish it would be for him to sabotage his own future and how cruel to retaliate against Daisy. He had loved Sarah, deeply and truly, through crisis and tragedy and heart-wrenching ordeal. He needed to grant himself permission to start again, to love again, and maybe, this time, it wouldn't all have to be so hard.

When Daisy got home from her work at the American embassy, there was a message on her answering machine. She smiled as she heard Ian's apologetic tone. "Hi, it's me. I'm an idiot. You were right. Something did happen. I decided I was falling in love with you and then I spooked myself. This is probably not the way I should have told you this. I'm sorry. I really am an idiot." She laughed out loud and picked up the phone.

"You're not an idiot," she told him the minute she heard his voice. "You're a wonderful, sweet man who's been through a lot of tragedy and isn't quite sure how to go about accepting happiness."

"That's what I meant to say," he joked. "You're not mad at me, are you?"

"How could I be when I'm kind of feeling the same way myself?"

"Spooked?"

"No. Falling in love."

"Does it scare you?"

"Not really."

"Does anything scare you?"

"Living without love."

"Daisy Howard," he sighed, "you're an absolute joy. I've never met anyone like you. But you're going to have to be patient with me. I've never experienced a healthy, uncomplicated relationship before."

"I'm looking forward to showing you the ropes."
She laughed, realizing that she really was. "How
about if I bring the car back next Friday, and we
immediately take it to Deauville. I know a wonderful
inn there, right near the beach. It'll be too cold to
swim, but we can take long walks."

"Sounds wonderful. See you Friday, but I'll talk to
you before then."

He hung up the phone just as Colette entered his
office, back from her errand in St. Denis. "Monsieur
Taylor," she said, addressing him formally, "since
you insist that I do not appear in your apartment
uninvited, I am asking to come this evening. Shall we
say seven?"

Ian tried to cover his irritation. On the one hand, he
could see she was insulted by the morning's admonition. On the other, she was still trying to intrude on
his life. Much as he didn't want to create ill will
between them, he felt if they were ever to arrive at a
decent working relationship, he had to set the bound-
aries now. "I'm sorry, Colette." He tried to sound
cordial to counteract what he had to say. "I had a very
difficult night last night and I'm rather tired. Perhaps
another time."

"But there is someone you must meet. I have
arranged to bring her with me."

This time, he didn't even bother to hide his annoy-
ance. "Really, Colette, you have to stop doing that.
You cannot invite people to my place any time you
choose. You cannot make appointments without consulting me first. You cannot decide who I need to see.
How do I get this across to you? Because if I can't,
we're going to have a lot of problems."

She bristled, hearing the implied threat. But she

held her ground. "I wouldn't have scheduled it if it weren't important. This cannot wait, I assure you."

He sighed. There was no point in arguing now, since she'd obviously already committed him. He decided to turn it into an ultimatum. "Fine. You may bring this person I absolutely must meet at seven," he said, too exasperated to care that his tone was condescending. "But I'm warning you, if you ever do anything like this again, you can't continue to work with me."

She walked out without a word, and he worried that he might have been too harsh. After all, he was certain that she only meant well, and she was totally devoted to the school. She didn't seem to have much of a life beyond it. Outside his door, Colette leaned against the wall, a self-righteous smile playing on her face as she thought about how the high and mighty Ian Taylor would change his tune by nightfall.

Although he had recovered from his vision of the day before, Ian avoided the café in St. Denis and prepared a simple dinner for himself at home. He ate early and waited impatiently for Colette to arrive so that he could be rid of her quickly and call Daisy before settling down with a good book for the remainder of the evening. He purposely did not prepare coffee or refreshments; he didn't want to encourage them to stay beyond whatever time was necessary for Colette to conduct her business with him. Promptly at seven, there was a knock on the door. At least she hadn't used her key. She seemed to be taking his warning to heart. He opened the door, grateful for once for her punctuality. His greeting froze on his lips. He blinked twice to make sure that the woman standing beside Colette was real and not just some figment of an addled imagination. "Sarah?!" he finally croaked out.

"Not bloody likely," the woman said, pushing past him into the apartment. He followed her, not seeing the smile playing on Colette's lips.

"Who are you?" he asked, baffled, thinking perhaps she was a doppelgänger for his late wife. And then, remembering Colette, he became outraged. "Where did you find this person? Is this some kind of a sick joke?"

"No, Ian, it is very serious," she responded, the formality of the morning forgotten.

"Don't blame her," the woman chimed in. There was a mocking inflection to her voice that Ian found vaguely familiar. "It was nice of her to come and find me, but I would have probably gotten in touch with you sooner or later myself. Although after the reaction you had when you saw me at the café, I was starting to reconsider. You're still such a wimp."

And then, even though he couldn't see how it was possible, he knew without a doubt who she was. "Sunny!" he said, the horror in his voice undisguised.

"Give the man a prize," she taunted. He was studying her, his eyes probing. "Go ahead. You can touch me if you want. I'm real."

"But you're dead," he gasped. "I saw your body."

"No," she corrected. "You saw *a* body. A burned body, as a matter of fact, wearing dear departed Sarah's clothes."

"Who was it?" he asked, his dread growing.

"I believe her name was Jane Doe," she cackled. "I met a guy who worked in the morgue in a bar. We made a trade if you know what I mean."

"Are you telling me you set that fire at Belvedere on purpose? That you staged your own death?" She smiled smugly. His head was spinning. He sat down, afraid he was going to be sick. "Why? Why would you do something so horrible?"

"You should know. She already tried to destroy me once. I wasn't going to let her do it again." With a shudder, Ian remembered those last few weeks at Belvedere. Sarah's blackouts had started to return. There were moments when she didn't seem herself. He had wanted her to go back to Dr. Horvath, but afraid, she had resisted, insisting that the problem was only in his imagination. They hid it from the outside world, but it caused a terrible strain between them. In the end, she had agreed to go back into therapy. The fire had happened before they had a chance to even discuss it with the family. Afterward, Ian had held back the truth, not wanting to destroy their image of Sarah, finally at peace.

"Where is Sarah now?" he asked her quietly, yearning to talk to the woman he had loved.

"Sleeping."

"Can you wake her up, let her talk to me?"

"Not any time soon," Sunny spat at him. "She just didn't get it. She thought she could just squash us all together and everything would be hunky-dory. Living with you nearly bored me to death. But I paid her back. Frankly, she may never wake up."

He forced himself to remember that this obnoxious

woman was just an aspect of his injured wife. "You're sick, Sunny. You need help. All of you."

"All I need is money. Tell you what. Stake me to a small claim, say ten thousand dollars, and I'll disappear again. You won't have to say anything to anybody, and you won't ever have to see me again."

For a minute, Ian felt himself sorely tempted. In the corner of the room, from where she had been observing the proceedings, Ian saw Colette vigorously shake her head no. In the turmoil, he had forgotten about her. He wondered what her part in all this had been, but he knew that she was right. He couldn't just pay this woman off and pretend she didn't exist. "How did you get here without money?"

"Beats me. Little Sarah-poo must have gotten control when I was drunk or something and come running to find her hubby-wubby. All I know is I wake up in a shabby room in a country where I can't understand a damn word they're saying. I've got a one-way ticket that's used up and fifty bucks and that's it. I don't know where I am or what I'm doing there. If I hadn't seen you drop that glop all over yourself the other night, I probably still wouldn't have figured it out."

Ian put his aching head in his hands. He desperately wanted this to be nothing more than a bad dream, but he knew there was no way of waking up from this nightmare. He needed time to think, to figure out what to do. Obviously, he would have to take her back to the States, get her the help she needed. But he also had his responsibilities at the school. There were sixty-two kids who were counting on him. He felt a hand on his arm and jumped out of his seat. It was Colette. Sunny had lit up a cigarette and was flicking the ashes into his plant.

"I have a suggestion," Colette told him quietly.

He had no idea why she should even be involved or what business it was of hers to make the meeting happen, but he was far too weary to argue the point now. Except for a morass of confusion, dread, and loathing, his own mind was a blank. It was doubtful that he could come up with any reasonable solution himself right now, so he'd better consider any interim advice. She didn't even wait for him to answer. "The top floor of the school is empty."

"I thought it was used for storage."

"It is. But it used to be servants' quarters when the school was still a chateau. I cleared one out."

He looked at her sharply. "When did you do this?"

She saw his dismay and realized she'd better offer an explanation. "She was asking about you in the village. When I spoke to her, I sensed there was . . . a problem . . . that you might have to deal with." In fact, she was aware that she hadn't quite understood the extent of the problem, but she saw that her guess had been correct and that Ian's wife coming back to life was not an unmitigated joy for him. He had also confirmed what she had suspected from the beginning: that this woman could cause trouble for Ian, and he would need all the help he could get to avoid it. She went on as if she had answered his question. "The room is quite comfortable, really. And it locks," she added with emphasis.

"What are you two plotting?" Sunny had turned her attention back to them after finishing her cigarette and stubbing it out in the flower pot. "She really suits you better than I do, you know, Ian. She's got that churchmouse quality you like so much."

Colette wasn't sure whether to bristle at the insult or be pleased that someone else recognized that she was a fitting companion for the headmaster.

"So what's it to be?" Sunny ambled over to Ian, swiveling her hips in front of him. "Are you going to give me some money? Or am I going to have to make it on my back? Although I have to admit that with the energy level of this town, it could take a long time to screw my way out of here."

It was what Ian needed to convince him. "Sure, I can give you some money." He tried to sound affable. "But not until tomorrow, when the banks are open. Meanwhile, you can stay here for the night, since you don't have money for a hotel."

"Well, aren't you a good sport? Maybe I underestimated you, Ian. You're smarter than I thought. You're never going to get your sweet little Sarah back. And you and I are both better off without each other."

"Colette will show you to a room. We'll figure out the rest tomorrow."

"Come with me, please." Colette led the way.

"Don't mind if I do," said Sunny. "I could use a place to crash. And if you start having second thoughts, Ian, don't bother. I've made your life hell before; I can do it again." She followed Colette, who gave Ian a significant look and surreptitiously wiggled a key at him from inside her pocket to assure him that she knew what needed to be done.

When they'd gone, he closed the door behind him, took a few deep breaths, and poured himself a glass of brandy, which he downed in one gulp. He placed a call to the States and asked Robert to have Drew call him back. He left no other message. He thought perhaps he should have gone with Colette, but experience told him that Sunny would be more difficult to handle if he were around. He didn't understand or like Colette's involvement, but he had to grant that she was efficient. At least for now, Sunny would be off the streets and safe. He tried to conjure a semblance of joy at his wife's resurrection, no matter how maliciously contrived the circumstances. But all he could think was how miserable Sunny had made them in the past and how wretched she could make their future. Of course, they would try to bring Sarah back. But even if they did, Ian knew that the rest of their lives would be a struggle to keep her. There was also the legal factor to face. Sunny had committed arson, for all he knew maybe even murder. Even if the courts accepted that Sarah was not in control of her actions, she could end up institutionalized. As willing as he was to accept the burden of caring for someone he loved deeply, he knew that the road ahead for both of them would be filled with pain. And for just a moment, alone where no one could see, he thought about Daisy and what might have been, and let himself drown in a flood of regret.

The ringing of the telephone broke in on his ruminations and forced him to pull himself together. He answered, heard Drew's voice, and almost lost it again. He knew that his brother-in-law would have just as hard a time as he did accepting that Sarah was alive but, nonetheless, still lost to them. There was no gentle way to break the news.

"Are you sitting down?" Ian started.

"Lying down," said Drew. "I've had a rough day."

"It's about to get worse," said Ian. Quickly giving all the details of the encounter, but none of his own emotional response, Ian told Drew what had happened. Hearing Drew's gasps, he left no space for comment, rushing along with his narrative, needing to get the words said before the fears they engendered overwhelmed him. When he'd finished, there was a long silence. Imagining Drew struggling to get his bearings, Ian didn't try to fill it.

"Ian," Drew finally said, and Ian could hear the conflict in his voice, "I know I should probably get on a plane and come help you work this out, but I'm having a problem at home myself right now."

"What's wrong?" asked Ian, as concerned for Drew as for himself.

"It's Sam. She's . . . uh . . . How do I put this? . . . She's gotten herself involved with this guru or whatever he is."

"You mean like a cult?" Ian couldn't believe this. It was so unlike Sam.

"I guess it is. She's moved out of the house and into his compound. The guy's really freaky, and I'm kind of afraid for her. I don't think I can leave until I get her out of there."

"Jesus, Drew. Of course not." Ian was almost as shocked by Drew's news as his own. "Look, take care of that first. I don't want anything to happen to Sam. I can keep a handle on Sarah, I mean Sunny, for a while. In fact, it might be better for me to keep her here for the time being. If we come back to the States, there will be all sorts of legal ramifications, and I don't think that's going to help her mental state. It's quiet here. I have someone who will help me look after her. I can keep her confined. Maybe I can even get Sarah or one of the more cooperative alters, like Susan, to come out. Then, when school's out, I can bring her back and see about getting her some professional help."

"It's a big burden for you," said Drew.

"She's my wife," said Ian. "You've got your own to worry about."

They promised to keep in touch and hung up, their fears and concerns no less compelling for being shared. Drew slept fitfully, unable later to remember his dreams, only aware that they had covered him with a blanket of sadness that threatened to suffocate him awake or asleep. In the morning, Halsey brought in Moira, who happily nestled in her father's arms while the nanny went down to arrange for breakfast.

Drew nuzzled his daughter's downy neck. "You are so warm and toasty in the morning, I think I'll have to eat *you.*"

She giggled and let him nibble for a while, then abruptly pushed away. "Where's Mommy?" she demanded.

"You know," he told her as he did every morning. "She had to go away for a little while, but she'll be back soon. Hey, let's do some magic," he suggested to distract her.

"Okay," said Moira, grabbing her father's Houdini book from the night table where he'd been keeping it for nocturnal practice sessions on the sleepless nights that had come when Sam had gone.

"I learned a new escape. Want to see?" She nodded, but he could see tiny tears forming in her eyes. "Aw, Pumpkin, are you crying? What's wrong?"

"I miss Mommy."

He took her in his arms and rocked her. "Me, too, baby. Me, too. But she'll be back soon," he said, trying to comfort her.

"Why don't you go and get her and bring her home?" Moira charged her father.

"I don't think she's quite ready to come home yet, sweetheart," he tried explaining.

She didn't buy it. "When I go to Katy's house, you make me come home with you even if I say I'm not ready. Go get her today and tell her it's time for her to come home right now."

Drew laughed at her child's logic, then suddenly thought, *Out of the mouths of babes.* "You know what, pumpkin? I think I'm going to do just that." Under normal circumstances, he took for granted that Sam had her own timetable. But Luke's appearance on the scene had made for bizarre conditions and perhaps Drew was making a mistake in acting as though Sam were still in control. People held in thrall of charismatic leaders often had to be kidnapped and deprogrammed. If he couldn't get Sam to come home willingly, he'd get her home any way he could.

"You mean it? You're going to bring Mommy home? Today?"

"Yes, I am," he said confidently to his child as she threw her arms around his neck, believing that her daddy could do anything he said. Drew just wished he had as much faith in his powers as she did.

This time he knew better than to walk into the lobby of the institute and demand an audience with his wife.

He was surprised at how little she struggled. He had expected a screaming battle, was braced for the kicking and scratching, had even prepared an explanation should the police be called in. Instead, she had uttered some words of protest and, while not exactly pliant, hadn't seemed entirely resistent when he pushed her into the car.

"I'm kidnapping you," he announced as he sped away with a screech of tires. He had mapped his route, making sure he wouldn't be passing through any intersections where he might have to stop for a red light and allow her the opportunity to escape.

"You shouldn't be doing this, Drew," she complained. He was anticipating screams, flailing arms, something akin to what he had received when he had confronted her with Luke. But here, alone, her protest seemed almost mild. She kept looking over her shoulder. He couldn't tell if she was afraid they might be followed or hoping for it.

Just in case, he stepped on the gas, made a few surprising turns, and headed past the city limits onto the highway.

"Where are we going?" she asked.

He realized until that moment he had not known himself. But suddenly it was very clear. He didn't answer, but he knew in a few moments she would know herself. He heard the catch in her breath and understood that she had divined his destination. He wondered why she didn't object, thinking perhaps she was saving her strength for a major assault once he had stopped the car. But he doubted there would be anyone to hear her if she did begin to scream. Not many people knew about the Millpond, let alone frequented it. They hadn't been there themselves for years. In this meadow by the lake, their bonds had been forged. Today, it might become the place where they were broken.

He pulled up to the edge of the water, hoping the nostalgia they shared for the place would temper her mood and incline her to talk. But the minute he braked, she jumped out of the car, running toward the tree where he had first spotted her naked, hiding after being caught skinny-dipping in the lake. He leaped out himself, chasing after her, ready for the fight that he knew would follow. He caught up with her at the tree and threw his arms around her, bringing them both to the ground.

"What the hell do you think you're doing?" she shouted at him, struggling to get up from under him.

"I'm sorry, Sam," he said, not letting her up. "You may not believe this now, but it's for your own good."

"What? Breaking my ribs?"

"I didn't mean to come down on you so hard. But I couldn't let you get away."

"For God's sake, Drew. I was just going to look at the tree. Get off me. I can't breathe."

He didn't know whether to believe her. He had heard that people in cults were adapt at disarming their pursuers until they could get away. He couldn't take that chance.

"I'm taking you home, Sam, if I have to knock you

unconscious to do it. We're going to get a deprogrammer or whatever it takes. But I'm not letting that fake Luke get his hands on you."

"A deprogrammer? Are you crazy?" she yelled, outraged. Now the rage he had expected appeared. "I don't believe you, Drew. I told you I needed to stay at the institute for a couple of weeks. That's all I asked. To be left alone for two weeks. And you immediately assume that I've been brainwashed and I need to be overpowered. Is that what you think of me? Is that how much you trust me?"

"It's not a matter of trust," he began, a little confused. She sounded so rational, it was, indeed, hard to believe that she wasn't in control. "Luke is a criminal fraud—"

"You think I don't know that?" she interrupted before she could stop herself, then bit her tongue, hoping Drew was so incensed that he wouldn't even hear what she was saying.

As usual, he listened. "You do?" he asked, baffled. "Then why are you staying there?"

"Get off me, okay?" she said quietly this time. He did as she requested. They sat on the ground facing each other. She knew she was going to have to explain. She thought about making something up, but she knew it was no use. She had been able to fool him once; she could never do it a second time. "Luke's being watched by the FBI. They think, under the guise of his pseudopsychotherapy, he's really running a right-wing militarist organization. They think he's got a hidden cache of weapons, bombs, and nerve gas hidden away and that there's the potential for another huge disaster, worse than Waco, Texas, or as bad as Oklahoma City."

"Why am I not surprised?" said Drew, feeling vindicated. "But what does this have to do with you?"

"I was recruited to help them find it." She waited for his reaction. It was worse than she anticipated.

"What?" he asked first as though he couldn't possibly have heard right. "What?" She didn't bother to answer. He'd heard. "No." His whole body was shaking. "No! No! No! You are a businesswoman. You are a mother. You are a wife. But you are not a goddamn spy. And they have no right to put you in danger with a maniac. Come on. We're going home right now." He got up and started to drag her with him.

"Wait, Drew. Stop," she protested, holding him back. "I made a commitment and I'm really close."

"Are you nuts? Close to what? Close to getting him to blow you up so the FBI can make its case? No, I'm sorry. Not my wife." He started to move again, taking her along, but she dug her heels into the ground.

"Listen to me," she said in a voice so unyielding it stopped him in his tracks. "I am your wife. But that does not make me a person who cannot make her own choices. I am perfectly aware of my responsibilities to both you and Moira. And I am taking all the precautions I possibly can. But if I didn't believe with all my heart that it was important for me to do this, I wouldn't do it. I love you, Drew. And I respect you enough to let you make your own choices. I expect you to do the same for me."

He was quiet for a moment, at war with himself,

even though he knew she couldn't be different. But he was still baffled. "Why, Sam? Why did they pick you? And why would you do it?"

"They picked me because there was no one else. Luke has a very small inner circle, and they couldn't penetrate it. Apparently he likes me more than he's liked anyone in a long time."

Drew snorted.

"I know," Sam went on, correctly interpreting his derision. "I'm very aware he's using all this wonderful-life crap to get into my pants. But I can handle it. It's just another reason for me to want to help the authorities nail him. And I'm very, very close to getting what they need to do it."

"Fine," he conceded, "I can see why they came to you. I have a feeling that when it comes to doing what it wants, the government isn't really all that concerned about a citizen's private interests. But I still don't see why you'd agree. This has nothing to do with you."

"Yes, it does. We don't know who the crazies are out there or where they're going to strike. We're all vulnerable. And I couldn't bear the thought that if I didn't help, then maybe they'd never catch Luke. And maybe he'd be responsible for the next bomb or the next shooting, and some other mother would be crying, 'Why me, why my baby?' I couldn't live with myself if that happened, Drew."

She looked at him, her eyes begging for understanding. With a will of their own, his arms went around her, and he pulled her to him. "I understand, sweetheart. And I'm sorry. You're right, I should have trusted you. And of course, you want to do what you can. But I can't help it. I'm afraid. I'm not willing to risk you for any cause. Call me selfish, but that's the way it is. I couldn't live without you . . ."

"Sshh." She put her hand to his lips. "You're not going to have to. I swear to you, it's almost over. I've got a contact right in the institute. She's nearby all the time. I don't even see the others, but I know they hear me, see what I'm doing. And Luke has promised me tonight he's going to share his life with me. If I back out now, who knows how long it will be before they get someone else on the inside? And who knows what Luke will do before then? I have to do it, Drew. Please, try to understand."

He held her, his heart beating. He *did* understand. He knew that if she didn't insist on doing this, she wouldn't be the woman he loved. "What do I do with you?" he sighed.

"Just kiss me," she answered. "Kiss me, and then let me go."

He did kiss her. But it was harder to let her go. His fingers wound themselves into her burnished hair as he buried his face in her neck.

"Do you remember?" she whispered. He didn't have to ask what she was referring to.

"You were so beautiful," he said, "I thought you were a water nymph."

"I was so embarrassed," she laughed. "But then when you brought me my clothes and never let on to your fiendish fiancée that I was hiding behind the tree, I think that's when I knew you were a man I could love. You can keep a secret."

"Actually, I know how to keep a good thing to myself. And this, my darling, is a very good thing."

The day was warm, and when Drew put his hands under the light sweater that Sam was wearing, her skin felt like heated silk. He let his fingers trace each ridge of bone, each crevice of flesh, journeying where he had been so many times before but each time found a new adventure. Counting days, it hadn't been so long since they'd been together, but in heartbeats it felt like eternity. Between the sun and the warmth of his hands, Sam felt herself melting, and, unable to stay upright, she let herself sink onto the grass, drawing him with her.

"I love this place," she whispered.

"I love you," he said and put his lips on hers, exploring the sweetness of her mouth with his tongue. Making a small concession to the open air, they took off only what needed to be taken off and, feeling each other's excitement, joined together, flesh upon flesh, unencumbered at the point of passion.

Afterward, he didn't even try to convince her not to go back to the institute. But he did insist that she inform her contact that she had told her husband what she was doing and that the contact get in touch with him and explain exactly what precautions were being taken.

"And it's not open for debate," he added. "If I don't hear from someone and I'm not satisfied that you are going to be safe, I'm marching in there at sunset with a dozen cops or whatever it takes and I'm carrying you out of there. Do I make myself clear?"

"Very," she responded, thinking it was a fair solution. "I'll pass that on. In fact, I'm glad you know what's going on. I feel safer."

They got back into the car and drove back to Oakdale. They didn't notice the nondescript sedan behind them or hear the driver place a call on his mobile phone.

"Where the hell have you been?" Luke shouted to his henchman over the static.

"You told me to follow her. I did. We were out of range."

"Where?"

"At that place called the Millpond."

Luke was livid. He'd seen his residents kidnapped by their meddling family members before. That's why he had secretly instituted the practice of having his inner circle, the people who counted for him, followed on the outside. Not wanting to spook anyone, he kept it strictly confidential. As long as he knew where they were, he could always find a way to get them back.

"Did he have a deprogrammer there or something?"

"Not exactly."

"What then? What did he do to her?"

"Well, it's an open field, so I couldn't get that close, because I didn't want them to see me. But it kind of looked like he was humping her on the ground."

"What? I just saw her blow him off yesterday. And when you phoned in before, you said he'd grabbed her."

"I know. That's what it looked like. Like I said, I can't be positive. But the way they were moving, I'm pretty sure they were doing the nasty out there under the open sky."

Luke felt his blood start boiling. He didn't like having to entertain the possibility that he was being made a fool of. "Where are they now?"

"They're a couple of blocks from the institute. He's letting her out. Looks like she's going to walk the rest of the way."

"Shit," he said, "I think I'm being double-crossed."

"Want me to take care of her?"

"No, him. But don't kill him. Not yet."

Drew stayed parked at the side of the street for a few minutes, watching Sam disappear in the rearview mirror. He figured he'd give her two hours. If he hadn't heard anything by then, he'd go storming in with whatever power he could get and the hell with her investigation. He'd contribute to saving the world only if it didn't involve endangering his wife. When he could no longer see her, he started the car and rolled slowly around the corner, heading back toward Woodland Cliffs. He braked quickly, as he saw a car stalled across the middle of the narrow intersection, leaving no room to pass on either side. The driver had the hood up and was peering inside. Sighing, he pulled over to the side and got out, thinking more about getting the car out of the way so he could go home than about being a good Samaritan.

"What's the problem?" he called to the stranger.

"I'm not really sure. Do you know anything about cars?"

Drew smiled. "Oh, a little bit. Want me to have a look?"

"Would you please? I'd be very grateful."

Drew reached under the hood, figuring he'd check

the oil and water first. It was his last conscious thought except for the searing, blinding pain on the side of his head. He slumped, feeling the still warm engine press against his face as he fell. But by the time he was lifted bodily and thrown into the backseat of the car, he was out cold.

❧ 9 ❧

"It's a bogus charge, Mort, you know that," Jack was yelling at his colleague in the State Department offices. After spending an entire night observing Diego Roca being interrogated, he had only had a few hours' sleep, and his temper was short.

"I do not know that," argued Mort. "And even if I did," he contradicted himself, "what the hell do you care? The guy was married to your wife and probably wouldn't mind getting into her pants again. So why don't you just turn him over to the authorities and wash your hands of it?"

"Because," said Jack, overenunciating as if he were speaking to the mentally challenged, "it is a bogus charge."

"We got proof," Mort insisted.

"From Guillermo Valdes, a Roca adversary, who set you up so he could get rid of Roca and take over."

"Bullshit."

"Why do you think Valdes has been giving you all those tips?"

"How'd you know about that?" Mort asked. He thought he'd been keeping his source a secret. He should have known better. Sooner or later in Washington, everyone knew about everything.

Jack didn't even bother to answer. "Why didn't Valdes go straight to the drug enforcement people? Because the DEA investigates. The State Department doesn't. He needed a patsy. You were it."

Mort squirmed. More than once when Valdes had called him with a tip, he'd wondered himself why he'd been chosen to be the recipient of Valdes's largesse. Hearing Jack say it made it feel uncomfortably like the truth. But he wasn't about to admit that.

"It's out of my hands, Bader. The two guys who were caught with the plane are being extradited to the States even as we speak. They're talking to the grand jury tomorrow."

Jack grabbed Mort and kissed him.

"Hey, get off," Mort complained.

"You just told me what I needed to know," Jack crowed. "Where are they going to be?"

"Under wraps. I can't say."

"Mort, if you don't want me to make you look like a fool, and you know I can, set up a meeting for me."

"I can't do that. I gave Valdes my word. It's my responsibility—"

"That's just my point," Jack interrupted. "You're

shilling for Valdes and when the secretary of state finds out, you're going to be looking for a new career."

"Don't threaten me," Mort said.

But Jack could see he had him scared. "Just let me talk to them, that's all I ask. Before the grand jury. No matter what happens after that, I'll cover for you. I swear it."

"No matter what?" Mort asked nervously, and Jack knew that he had won.

He found Melinda at the hospital, keeping watch over a peacefully sleeping Nico, and told her that he might have a break in Diego's case.

She took his face in her hands and kissed him. "Thank you for doing this for him, Jack. Whatever he's done, he doesn't deserve to be ruined like this."

"There are still no guarantees," he warned her. "But I have to do something. I know you'd hate me if I let him go to prison, and I can't live with him under our roof for much longer."

"Don't be jealous," she cajoled.

"I'm not jealous," he told her honestly. "I'm scared. I see how the two of you look at each other, and I know how connected you are through Nico. And I can see that this experience is changing him. He's becoming the man you fell in love with again, isn't he?"

"I'm connected to you, too," she insisted, not answering his question. "Before Diego."

"Yes," Jack lamented, "but you've always been able to leave me. With much less justification. I couldn't live through it happening again."

She put her arms around him and held him close

and let the beating of her heart against his speak for her.

"One way or another," Jack said, his voice muffled in her hair, "it's going to be over soon. I'll see to it."

On the train, all the way to Paris, Ian thought about his alternatives. His first commitment was to Sarah, he had no doubt of that. Even if she had turned into a creature he loathed, she was still his wife, and he would have to be responsible for her. He knew he could tell Daisy the truth, and she would understand. But he also knew Daisy well enough to be aware that she would never abandon him if she thought he was in trouble. If he allowed it, she would stay with him for support and solace. But that would be both disloyal to Sarah and disheartening for Daisy. Aching, he thought about the unrestricted joy he had felt with Daisy, the promise of the love beginning to flower between them. Conducting an internal monologue of self-persuasion, he told himself it would be easier to nip the bud at this early stage than to allow it to blossom and have to rip it out by the roots. He drew a small jeweler's box out of his pocket and opened it. A beautiful cloisonné ring, a pattern of delicate daisies twining around its band, nestled in the center. He had found it in an antique shop in St. Denis and bought it to give to her in Deauville. He wondered if he gave it to her now, would it seem too much like a consolation prize? But he wanted her to have it, as a memorial to what might have been.

He climbed the five flights on the Rue de Seine, and Daisy threw open the door at the sound of his voice.

Her delight was undisguised, and before his defenses were up, she had attacked him with kisses. Her lips brushed his face, floating and landing like gentle feathers of affection, and he almost lost his resolve.

"Did you come because you missed me?" she asked between caresses. "I've been dying for you. I'm so glad you're here."

"Actually," he said, forcing himself to pull away, "I came for my car."

"Really? I thought you weren't going to need it during the week." She took hold of his hand, still unaware of his carefully cultivated metamorphosis.

"I don't," he said tersely, not trusting himself to speak in longer sentences for fear he'd give himself away with the tremor in his voice.

"Then why did you bother? I told you I'd come and pick you up on Friday on the way to Deauville."

"I can't go to Deauville with you," Ian said. It came out like a bark. She stepped back as if she'd been assaulted.

"This Friday, or ever?" she asked, quietly as usual, cutting right to the chase.

"Ever."

"Why?"

He took a deep breath in preparation for the big lie. "Because I don't think it's going to work out for us, and I don't want to waste either of our time. I'm not saying I don't like you or I didn't have fun with you. But it hasn't been that long since my wife died, and I don't think I'm in a fit state to start a new relationship."

"You seemed fit enough the last time we were together." She was looking at him suspiciously. He would have to come on stronger to have an effect. Kindness was not going to kill this affair.

"Hey, it was great," he said enthusiastically. "And that's what made me realize what a high it is to be with a new person. It's been a long time since I had a chance to play the field. I'm not ready to tie myself down to one partner. And I don't think you're the type of person who'd get off on being a sometime thing."

"Ian, what is going on? This does not sound like you."

He took another breath, like a diver who comes up for air only to plunge down again into the deep. He hated acting like a heel even though he knew that, ultimately, it was to her benefit. "That's just the point. You don't really know me that well. We've had some fun times, some great sex. But that's about it. I don't want to be put in the position of having to explain myself just because I wanted to get laid. I had a tough few years with Sarah, and I think I deserve some time off." He turned away, unable to meet her eyes, unwilling to see the contempt. He heard her move away and turned to see what she was doing. She came toward him, his car keys and a ticket from a parking garage in her outstretched hand. She dropped them into his palm.

"I don't know what you're doing or why you're doing it. All I know is that you're full of shit, and that alone is enough to make me wash my hands of you."

"Hey, good luck, and have a good life," he said nonchalantly, disguising the fact that he meant it from the bottom of his heart. He walked out the door and down the stairs without turning back. He left the building and walked straight to La Palette, where he ordered a double espresso and drank it down, hot and bitter, in one gulp. Then, checking the address of the garage on the ticket, he found his car and drove back to the school in St. Denis, aching from head to foot, as though he'd been pummeled by an opponent far worthier than he. Not until he was walking the dark path to his private quarters did he realize he'd forgotten to give her the daisy ring.

Colette was waiting for him in his cottage when he returned. He no longer questioned her sudden uninvited appearances. It was the least of his concerns. He had left her to supervise the end of the school day, and she reported that all had gone routinely well. "And how is she?" he finally asked.

"I brought her dinner," Colette told him. "She was nasty. But I can handle her. I saved your dinner for you—"

"I'm not hungry," he interrupted, wishing she wouldn't try so hard to take care of him, then relenting, added, "But thank you anyway. I should go see her."

"No," she said quickly. "She told me she doesn't want to see you. She was very rude about it. I was shocked."

"I'm not. She hates me."

"But she's your wife."

"No, Colette, she's not. She's an aspect of my wife. But she's not the woman I married. Not by a long shot."

"Anyway, I think it's better if you stay away. There's no point in getting her more upset. I'll spend time with her, talk to her. Maybe I can get her to calm down, then you go see her."

Ian sank into the sofa. "I've got to figure out what to do about her. I'm going to have to take her back to the States."

Alarmed, Colette hastily reminded him of his duty to the students. She saw him rubbing his temples, and, moving in back of the sofa, she stood behind him and began to massage his neck and shoulders. He started to object, but her hands, in fact, were skilled, and the pain was enormous. She smiled, conscious of the fact that he was already giving in to her ministrations, allowing her to share his secrets, counting on her for support. Keeping her fingers on the pressure points, she silently noted that the end of the semester was months away. With his blond whore out of his life and his crazy wife locked away, she had time to make herself indispensable before then.

"We're going to get into trouble for being up here," Daniela told Ryan as she let him pull her along the deserted corridor.

"No, we're not. Because nobody's going to know. No one ever comes up here," Ryan replied.

The two had remained inseparable, even after Ryan's mother had attempted to keep them apart with threats and insults. Ryan had gone to the headmaster, afraid that his mother might somehow manage to have Daniela expelled, but Ian had assured him that as long as he was in charge, the school would not buckle under to prejudice. For that, they had pledged him their lifelong loyalty, but he had laughed and told them that getting good grades would be sufficient.

Having finished their studying after dinner, they had left the other kids assembled in the recreation room and sneaked off together.

"We shouldn't be here," Daniela reiterated without making any attempt to leave.

"Look," he said, opening a door onto a room stacked high with textbooks. "It's just used for storage." To maximize his point, he tried another door. Finding it locked, he ran ahead, turning a third knob and stopping at the threshold of the room he had scouted before—and his purpose for bringing Daniela. She came up beside him, and saw what had brought them there: row upon row of beds, mattresses intact, waiting for a growing student body to call them out of reserve and put them to use. "Come on," he said and ran inside, diving onto one bed and then springing to another. She hesitated at the threshold, giggling. She knew it was wrong, but it looked like so much fun, and in the end, forgoing her usual maturity, she let the mischievous child in her take over and bounced up beside him. Holding hands, they jumped from mattress to mattress until, breathless, they fell on their backsides in a paroxysm of laughter. They lay on their backs for a few moments, catching their breath, then, supporting himself on one elbow, Ryan leaned over Daniela and gave her a small, solemn kiss.

"I love you, Daniela Lender," he declared somberly. "And some day, I'm going to marry you."

She knew he was serious, and though they were the same age, she suddenly felt years older. "You can't," she told him simply. "Your mother wouldn't let you. You heard what she said about me."

They had been outside the headmaster's door when Mrs. Jessup had gone to complain about their friendship. They hadn't meant to eavesdrop, but it had been impossible not to hear her abusive shouts, and Ryan had been profoundly embarrassed. He had been ready to barge in himself when the lady from the school board, Daisy Howard, had arrived and, assessing the situation, advised them to let her handle it. Listening from the hall, they had both agreed that Miss Howard and Mr. Taylor had managed his mother much better than he could, but even though Daniela had felt duly defended, she had been bruised by Mrs. Jessup's harsh and ugly words.

"Forget about my mother," Ryan insisted, stroking her hair.

"I don't know how we can," Daniela sighed, his caress causing sensations somewhere inside her that she didn't know existed. "If it hadn't been for Miss Howard, she would have gotten Mr. Taylor fired or pulled you out of school. She still could."

"If she does, we'll run away together," Ryan answered her, kissing her sweetly. She didn't care if it wasn't true. For now, it was enough to pretend and to be kissed again.

She turned her face up to him and then froze. "What's that?"

He heard it, too, a banging that seemed to come from the room next door. Tiptoeing into the hall, they went to investigate, then rushed back into the room as they heard Colette Simard approach the locked door. Peeking into the corridor, they saw her open the door and begin to chide, "You're wasting your energy. No one can hear you. I'm your only contact with the outside world, and if you continue to annoy me, I won't come back, either."

"You lousy bitch," came the blunt response. "What do you think you're going to accomplish by keeping me locked up in here? You think you're going to screw my husband? It's not worth it, believe me."

"My relationship with the headmaster is none of your concern," Colette advised her curtly. "But you'd do well to remember I am the one in control here and watch your tongue."

The teenagers looked at each other, embarrassed but fascinated by the frankness of the conversation.

"What's she talking about?" Daniela whispered to Ryan.

"I'm not sure. It sounds like the lady locked up is Mr. Taylor's wife."

"But I heard she was dead!"

"I know. This is weird. What do you think we should do?"

"Tell someone," said Daniela. "Maybe we should talk to Mr. Taylor."

"What if he knows about it? What if he's keeping his wife locked up here?" asked Ryan.

"Like Rochester in *Jane Eyre*," sighed Daniela. She loved that book. She had read it three times, and it always made her cry. "Rochester's wife was crazy. That woman sounds crazy, too, doesn't she?"

"Yeah, but this is real life, not a book. I mean, I don't want to get Mr. Taylor into trouble or anything, but I don't think you can just ignore somebody locked up against her will, whether she's crazy or not."

"What about Miss Howard? She helped us before. She'll know what to do."

Making sure that the coast was clear, they snuck out of the room and back down the stairs. Since they knew Colette was otherwise engaged, they hurried to her office, where they had no trouble finding the contact list for the school's board of directors. Ryan read out the numbers and kept a lookout for Colette's return as Daniela dialed. "Miss Howard?" he heard her say. "This is Daniela Lender from the American School. Something weird is going on here, and we didn't know who else to tell about it. Can we talk to you?"

Sam caught sight of herself in the mirror and realized she had to change her clothes. Anticipating Luke's arrival, she had dressed for protection: turtleneck, tights, leggings, boots, big shirt over everything. Outside, it was spring, yet she looked like she would be at home in the Alaskan tundra. She hadn't thought about her wardrobe; it had been an unconscious move to layer herself into security. But studying her image, she knew she was sending off a warning light as surely as if she'd had a blinking red bulb on top of her head. Quickly, she pulled off her après ski gear and replaced it with a simple flowing dress in a fabric of spring flowers on a muted green background that set off her hair and fired up her eyes. Demure but not dowdy, she appraised herself. For the tenth time in as many minutes, she looked at the clock on the nightstand and shook it to make sure it was still running. She wondered what Gina and Drew had said to each other, assuming that they had met and concurred or Drew would have shown up long before to drag her home. She was a little disconcerted that neither one of them had bothered to get in touch with her to confirm that all was well, but she understood that, at this stage of the game, it might not be worth risking nonessential communication. But it helped to know that Drew was aware of what she was doing, and between him and Gina and whatever forces were put at their disposal, Sam was confident they wouldn't let anything happen to her.

Still, when the knock finally came on her door, her heartbeat instantly doubled. "Who is it?" she asked to give herself a few extra seconds to compose herself.

"It's Luke," he announced. "You're not sleeping, are you?" His voice was at its most alluring, sedately seductive.

"I was waiting for you," she declared as she opened the door, deciding that honesty, whenever possible, would assist in her deceit.

He came in and studied her carefully, making no attempt to disguise the appreciation on his face. "You are looking exceptionally beautiful," he told her. "All the more reason for this night to be special."

She was glad she had changed her clothes but a little surprised at how blatant Luke's craving had become. Until now, he had always hidden any carnal interest behind a barrage of psychospiritual double-talk. On the one hand, his transparency made her uncomfortable. On the other, a rapid escalation of the situation was exactly what she needed. She didn't want to waste time on subtlety if she could get him to get to the ending she was looking for without too much prologue. With that in mind, she decided to turn up the heat a couple of notches.

"Oh, Luke," she sighed, imagining Gina laughing as she listened somewhere in a not-too-distant location, "I can't tell you how important this is to me. How important you are," she added for good measure, hoping she wasn't overdoing it.

Apparently, she wasn't. He took her hand and drew her to him. "You have progressed so quickly, Sam. You're the best student I ever had. I will be proud to initiate you into the inner circle."

"What exactly does that involve?" she asked, trying to sound enthusiastic and not nervous.

"As your spiritual guide, Samantha, I am going to bring you to a higher plane by making mind and body one."

You're telling me you're going to screw me, thought Sam, but only said, "That sounds wonderful." She wondered how she was going to put him off until after he had revealed the secrets that Gina was so certain he was harboring. She couldn't very well just come right out and ask him what was this thing called the Armageddon Advance and where was he hiding the weapons to enact it. To her utter amazement, he brought it up himself.

"Our relationship can only be consecrated in the institute's inner sanctum. It is there that we store the instruments that will break through the defenses of the materialistic world and bring about a future based on our teachings. Come with me. When you see, you will understand everything we stand for."

Bingo, thought Sam. *Did you hear that, Gina?* she queried mutely, then added a fervent silent plea, *You better be following me. Because I have no intention of consecrating anything with this creep.* Aloud, she said, "That's what I want, Luke." She could have kicked herself for sounding so inane; she should have been better prepared with appropriate dialogue. But Luke didn't seem to notice. He had taken her hand and was leading her out the door.

They took the elevator down to the basement. She followed him through the unfinished hallway and stopped when he did, in front of a concrete wall. She looked at him, baffled, and then her mouth dropped open as the wall slowly opened in front of him. *Shit,* she thought, *even if they're listening, how are they going to find this.* "My goodness," she said pointedly. "This is amazing. How did you get the concrete wall to open like that?"

He was surprisingly cooperative, pointing out the mechanism, barely visible on the floor, that operated the door, and explaining exactly how it worked.

This is so easy, she thought, allowing herself to gloat just a little now that she was certain that Gina could find her. The door closed behind her. There was a sudden eerie silence, and they were surrounded by utter black. She realized the walls had to be at least three feet thick. Luke threw a switch and a single bare bulb cast an ugly circle of light in the center of the room. She could see the room was close and dank, like a bunker. Against one wall were piled boxes and crates. Some of them were open, and she could see they were loaded with a wide assortment of rifles, guns, and grenades. She shuddered. And then she shrieked. In a corner next to the ammunition, gagged and bound to a sustaining column, was Drew. Without thinking, she started to run to him. But suddenly, her arm was wrenched back behind her so that she screamed in pain, unable to move. She started to cry. "What are you doing, Luke? Drew has nothing to do with this."

"How can you say that, Sam? You two are married. You took vows. For better or for worse, till death do you part. I'd have to say this is worse, but I thought after this afternoon, you'd want to go together."

She was horrified. "You know about this afternoon?"

"I know everything, Sam. That's why I'm the spiritual leader," he mocked her. She tried to control her panic, telling herself Gina could hear every word she said. She was probably getting backup at this very moment. They would probably be breaking into the room any second now. Unless . . . She didn't have time to formulate the thought. With a vicious swipe, Luke had ripped off the top of her dress. From the corner of her eyes, she could see Drew straining at his bonds. She thought she saw tears in his eyes, though it could have been sweat. The gag prevented him from uttering a sound. *Now, Gina,* she thought. *Come now.*

"What have we here?" Luke was smiling, toying with her as he plucked the tiny microphone from her bra strap and ripped the box from her body, making her scream again as the tape came away, taking her skin with it. He didn't seem particularly upset.

Sam tried to sound forceful. "That's right. Every word we've said has been recorded. The FBI is going to be breaking in here any second, and you don't stand a chance. It'll go better for you if you just surrender and don't make things any worse."

Luke laughed. "You sound like a bad cop-show script. If you're expecting Gina and her pals, I'm afraid you'll be waiting a long time."

Sam felt her stomach sink. "Gina?" she said stupidly, hoping he might be bluffing and not wanting to give away the game.

"Oh, yeah. I should mention your little lovefest at the Millpond made me think that maybe I couldn't trust you as much as I thought. So I sent out a few of my real loyalists on a search-and-destroy mission. We found Gina and her equipment and her cohorts. They can still hear you, but being in a similar position to your husband over there, I'm afraid they can't do anything about it. So your little rescue scenario is just a fantasy."

Now she realized why it had all seemed so easy, why Luke hadn't questioned anything she said, why he had shown her exactly how the secret door worked. He knew that he was safe. No one was left to help her. She stopped trying to pretend she wasn't afraid. "What are you going to do?"

"Just what I said. I'm a man of my word. I told you I'd bring you to our inner sanctum, and I have. Now, all that's left is the consecration." He grabbed a corner of her dress that she had been holding up, trying to cover herself, and ripped it from her.

She tried to run from him, but there was nowhere to go. He caught her at the wall and jerked her to him, yanking off her underwear, so she stood naked, cowering in his grip. With all his emphasis on serenity and internal focus, she had never realized what a strong man he was. She felt the relentless hardness of his body as she struggled against him and realized he didn't get that way through meditation. He had not only collected his arsenal, he had physically prepared himself for warfare. Thinking about Drew, helpless in his ropes, she forced herself not to scream.

But Luke, too, had remembered Drew. "Let us sanctify our union," he intoned, mimicking his spiritual voice, "before the congregation." Laughing, he lifted her easily and carried her flailing body to a stack of boxes, positioned in front of Drew.

When she saw her husband, eyes filled with pain, body slumped with defeat, Sam began to sob. "Don't do this, Luke. It's too cruel. Think about your own teachings."

"You reap what you sow," he said, his voice icy as he threw her facedown onto the boxes. Splinters of wood scratched into her breasts. She looked at Drew. His eyes were closed. He seemed to be willing himself somewhere else. She couldn't blame him. Luke noticed as well. "Open your eyes, Symington. Focus. Let your eyes see every detail. Without naming or defining." He laughed maniacally, and Sam saw Drew open his eyes. And for a split second, when his eyes met hers, she saw something. She knew her husband, could read his looks, and she was certain that in that point of stormy blue was not fear or dread, but power. For a moment, she was confused, and then she understood. For as Luke bent over her, rubbing her body with his own, intent on achieving her submission, Drew moved his hand.

Gathering all her strength, Sam pushed herself upright. Caught unaware, Luke was about to shove her down again, but she grabbed his hand and placed it on her bosom, kneading it into her breast and moaning with desire. For a minute, Luke was too taken aback to budge, but as she writhed against him, panting, she felt his excitement grow. He gave a deep-throated laugh. "You like this, don't you, baby? It's more exciting when someone watches."

"Oh, Luke. The other stuff never mattered to me. I always wanted you. You knew that, didn't you?" she breathed, counting on his ego being greater than his reason. Feeling the response between her legs, she knew she had guessed right. "Go slow, Luke. Let's not do it yet. Let's make it take a long time." Turning around to face him, she pressed herself into him, and acting as though she were in the throes of sexual ecstasy, she kissed him, thrusting her tongue deep into his throat while her arms encircled his head, locking him to her. She felt a wave of repulsion as his arms came around her and his hands cupped her buttocks, squeezing her closer. She felt herself choking and wondered how long she would have to endure. And then, in seconds, it was over. Concentrating on keeping Luke centered on her, she couldn't see what happened next. But she heard the crack of the rifle butt as it hit him on the back of the head. He slumped on her, and she moved away in disgust, letting him collapse on the floor.

"Houdini lives!" Drew gasped as he threw Sam the remnants of her dress. "And you thought I was wasting my time." She remembered mocking her husband and his efforts to master the escapist routines in his secondhand magic book signed by Houdini. She had been certain the autograph and probably the book as well were fake and had teased him mercilessly. Now she was ready to eat her words.

Trying to cover herself with her shredded clothing, Sam started to laugh and cry at the same time.

"Don't," Drew said, holding her tightly in his arms to stop her shaking. "We don't have time. We've got to find a way to get out of here." She realized he was right. Luke had told her how to get into the room but not how to get out. And unless they could figure it out themselves, they would be stuck in a bunker with a maniac and enough ammunition to blow up a small metropolis.

❧ 10 ❧

"Wake up," Drew said, holding the unconscious Luke up by his collar and slapping him lightly on the cheek. "Come on, let's go." He dragged the man to his feet, forcing him to move.

Luke coughed, then slowly opened his eyes. Sam was standing in front of him with a rifle, obviously selected from one of the open crates, pointed at him. Luke gingerly touched the spot on his head from which a blinding pain emanated. He looked at his hand and saw that it was red with his own blood.

"Don't worry, you'll live," said Drew. "Tell us how to get out of here."

Luke gave his head a shake, trying to clear the blur in his vision. "Or what?" he asked, his tone full of scorn. "She'll shoot me?"

"No," said Drew evenly, letting Luke go and taking the gun from Sam. "I will."

"Go ahead," challenged Luke. "Do you think it matters to me? Don't you think I'm prepared for death?"

"Well, we're not," said Drew, poking the muzzle into Luke's middle for effect. "What's the trick to open sesame?"

Taking a step back from the rifle, Luke dropped to the floor. Without a word, he crossed his legs and fixed his eyes on a distant spot on the wall.

Drew looked at Sam. "He's meditating," she said.

"Oh, for chrissake . . . ," Drew said, exasperated. He had no idea how to deal with this. Still, he kept his weapon trained on Luke. He wasn't taking any chances on the creep getting his hands back on Sam.

"Here's the problem," Sam said. "Luke's like Jim Jones in Guyana or David Koresh in Waco. To him, death is just the ultimate fulfillment of a greater destiny."

"You think he really believes the shit he spouts?" Drew wondered.

"To a certain extent, absolutely. He's not above using it to get girls or take people's money. But, yes, he thinks he is a superior being, and if he dies a martyr, he will be revered by his disciples forever. Unfortunately, he's probably right about that part." Drew tried not to let Sam see his concern growing, but her own fear was palpable. "He's not going to come around, Drew," she went on, and he could hear the rising hysteria in her voice. "He'll watch us die or die himself before he'd let us go. He is so convinced that he's got all the answers."

Drew eyed Luke. He hadn't moved a muscle since they had begun their conversation. He was placidly focused on the space in front of him, listening to every sound and feeling the air move around him. "Maybe he'll change his mind when the air gets thin," Drew tried hopefully.

"You don't know him." Sam was glum.

"Okay." Drew was assessing the situation. "We'll have to figure it out ourselves. He showed you how to get in. Try doing the same thing to get out. And if that doesn't work, try something else. I'll keep my eyes on the Buddha here."

Standing in what she believed to be the vicinity of the door, although there were no visible breaks in the wall, Sam played with the foot-tapping, hand-pressing configuration that Luke had employed to get them in. But it was rapidly clear that she was getting nowhere. "There's got to be a trigger point that activates the mechanism, and I'm obviously not getting it. I don't even know if I'm near it."

"Here," Drew said. "You hold the gun on him and I'll try. If he even blinks, call me." Handing her the rifle, he started moving along the wall through which they'd entered, touching, feeling, kicking. To no avail.

"Drew," Sam called, and he rushed to her side.

"Did he make a move?"

"No, he's still meditating. But it's given me an idea."

Drew took the gun from her and trained it back on Luke. "Go for it, whatever it is. Anything is worth a try." She dropped to the ground beside Luke, assuming the same position. Drew looked at her, baffled. "What are you doing?"

"I'm going to meditate, too."

"Are you nuts? Now? You can't still believe that garbage he was feeding you. Can you?" he added, a little uncertain. She gave him a look that told him she was insulted that he even asked.

"I never believed it," she told him "Well, not after the very beginning anyway. But even if Luke's teachings were just a lot of pseudo–new wave double-talk, his techniques were not entirely without merit. I mean, this meditation exercise really works whether you think that Luke is a god or a jerk."

"Okay, fine. It works. I just don't think now is exactly an appropriate time to get mellow. We've got to really concentrate on what we're doing here, or we won't be doing it very much longer."

"I agree. The meditation they teach at the institute has to do with turning outward, bringing your surroundings more completely into focus, not blocking them out. The way it works is—"

"Honey," Drew interrupted, "it's not that I don't believe you. I just think we should keep looking for a way to open the door."

She looked at Luke. He was still meditating, but she thought she noticed a flicker in his eye. He was definitely listening, too. She got up and stood on the other side of Drew, speaking quietly so that only he could hear.

"That's exactly what I want to do," she said to Drew in a fierce whisper. "If I focus and I just look—I don't mean search for something specific, I mean let my eyes see everything without trying to label it—and if I relax and clear my head of all the extraneous noise, like wondering if only I had done this or that or panicking because I'm afraid we'll never get out, then maybe the answer will just pop into my head. Maybe there was something that Luke said or did when we were coming in that registered but I just can't get to now because there's so much else going on in my brain. That happens sometimes."

Drew looked at her skeptically.

"Got a better idea?" she asked.

He shook his head, thinking at the very least it might calm her down. "Try it your way," he said and turned his attention back to Luke.

Getting down on the floor again, Sam arranged herself in a comfortable position, cleared her mind, and started to repeat the litany to herself. *Choose a point of focus,* she told herself. *Look at it. Absorb every detail without trying to name or define it.* She felt her senses sharpen. She could hear Luke's breathing and Drew shifting from one foot to another. She stared at the wall in front of her, not looking for anything in particular, just concentrating on what was there. She saw the rough surface of the concrete, the irregularity of the grain. There was a web of tiny fine lines, a hairline crack in the veneer. There were pockmarks and bubbles frozen into the solid material. And then she spotted it. A smoothness at waist level that stood out from the coarser substance of the wall around it. The color was slightly different as well, still gray but darker, oilier, as if hands had rested there too often and left a subtle stain.

That's all there is to it, she thought as she slowly rose from her lotus position. *It's so simple. One only has to look to see.*

"What is it?" asked Drew. "Did you find something?"

She moved to the wall. She turned and looked at Luke. "You're not a stupid man, Luke. And you're an excellent teacher. Too bad you're out of your mind." She saw his eyes surrender their previous point of focus and register on her. She smiled. He only glared in response. Then she reached out and placed her palm against the smooth, worn spot. She didn't even have to press hard. A section of the wall began its slow and steady move, bringing in a rush of air that she swallowed with her first yelp of joy.

"You're a genius," Drew said, laughing. "I love you."

"I love you, too," Sam agreed, "but can we get out of here now?"

"You, too, Luke. Move it," Drew ordered his prisoner. Luke stood heavily, and Drew prodded him toward the door. For a moment, Drew raised his face to drink in the light and the cool air of the outside, and in that instant, Luke had ducked out from under the barrel of the rifle and rolled to the far side of the room.

"What the hell do you think you're doing?" swore Drew, more exasperated than afraid. "Even if you manage to get yourself a gun, you're not going to get it loaded before I shoot you, so what's the point?" He started moving toward him slowly, carefully, always keeping him in his sight. He was surprised that Luke made no move to reach for a weapon, seemed almost to be waiting for Drew to approach. And then Drew suddenly understood exactly what Luke's point was.

He was standing over the ammunition, and in his hand, raised high above his head, was a pocket lighter. Drew forced himself to stay calm. "Don't be an idiot, Luke. This isn't a cause you need to die for."

"It's not my death you're worried about," Luke scoffed. "It's your own."

"Fine, I'll grant you that," Drew intoned evenly, assuming that panic wouldn't help him now, although he didn't know what would. "But your situation could still be salvageable if you don't do anything stupid."

"Drew," Sam called, coming back in from the corridor, "come on. What's taking—"

"Get out of here, Sam," he shouted, interrupting her.

"What?" she asked, confused, coming toward him instead of moving away. "Aren't you coming, too?"

"Just go," he shouted. "Run!"

"Why?" She didn't understand what he was getting excited about. She heard the click at the same time Drew did and turned and saw Luke standing over the stockpile, the lighter above his head, burning a small blue-gold flame. "Oh, shit," she whispered and stood stock still.

"So." Luke was grinning now. "It looks like we're back where we started. First thing, I think you should put that gun down, Drew."

"You're not going to blow us up, Luke. You'd be the first to go, and I don't care what crap you put out about there being a better place you go to, I don't believe you're ready to die just to get the better of us."

"Do you dare to put it to the test?" challenged Luke.

"I think you should believe him," whispered Sam hoarsely.

Drew looked at Luke. Even in the dim half-light, his eyes glinted with madness. "Okay," said Drew. "I'm putting the gun down. Close your lighter."

"Kick it over here," Luke instructed, keeping the fire alive.

Drew did as he was told. It landed in front of the ammunition, a few feet away from Luke. He stepped around to retrieve it, still bearing his flame aloft, not taking any chances. By the time he saw the corner of the box sticking out into his path, it was too late.

"Oh, my God," shrieked Sam as Luke tripped and went flying, the lighter, wedged open, blazing a fiery trail through the gloom and landing in the box. It started as a *pop-pop-pop,* like firecrackers going off in rapid escalation.

"Run!" screamed Drew as he grabbed his wife's hand and half carried, half dragged her to the still-open door. Behind them, they heard a boom and then another. "Get down! Cover your head!" Drew shouted as he pushed the door closed and then jumped on top of her, blanketing her body with his own. And at that instant, it began: a series of explosions, each one greater than the last, rocking them where they lay, the ground shaking beneath them as all around them the walls collapsed in huge chunks of debris.

They could not tell how long the eruptions lasted. An eternity seemed to pass between the first blast and the final awful silence that settled around them. It was dark, and the air was filled with a thick haze of dust. Sam coughed.

"Are you okay?" Drew asked quietly, trying to shift his body off her.

"I don't know. Can you get off me?"

"I don't know. There isn't a lot of room to maneuver. We seem to be pinned under something." He turned his body sideways, still partly resting on her, and waited for the particles to settle and his eyes to adjust. "It looks like a couple of slabs fell on either side of us first and kept the one on top from landing on our bodies. We're kind of in an accidental cave."

"At least we're alive," Sam said, coughing again. Her leg ached, and she tried to move it from under Drew's body and then she felt it—warm and oozing. "Drew, I think I'm bleeding. Something must have happened to my leg. It hurts."

"Okay, don't panic," he said, talking as much to himself as to her. "I'm going to try to lift myself up a little, and you pull out." She heard him grunt, but the pressure on her didn't ease. "I can't seem to pull myself up. Maybe there's something pushing down on us there. I can't see."

She maneuvered her hands beneath him and pushed against him, trying to dislodge him. A scream forced its way past his constricted throat. "What?" she asked, alarmed and bewildered. "What happened?" She could feel the sweat beading off him as his face blanched with pain. Then she understood. "Oh, God, Drew, I'm not hurt, you are. My leg's just sore because you were lying on it, but I think yours might be broken."

He nodded, unable to speak, pain still ripping through him to the point of nausea. He was afraid he might pass out, but he refused to allow it. He would not leave his wife alone in this tomb with his inert body. He fought to regain his equilibrium, and gradually, his agony subsided. "Let's not do that again, okay?" he joked when he could finally speak.

"My poor darling," she said, reaching up and wiping his brow with her hand. He rested against her. They were crammed together in a space the size of a coffin, with barely a foot of headroom above them and not even enough width to lie side by side without overlapping. But they were not crushed. "At least we're alive," she repeated and wondered how long those words would be her mantra in the dark.

"I don't think we're going to be able to dig ourselves out of this," Drew said quietly.

"Then we'll just have to wait for someone to find us," Sam answered matter-of-factly. "It's not like they could have missed the explosion. I'm sure there are mobs outside right now with firetrucks and digging equipment and whatever it takes to pull people out of disasters like this. They'll find us."

Drew rested his head beside his wife's, only a breath away, and echoed her words, "At least we're alive."

"Damn you, Bader," Mort Freeman shouted at Jack. "You swore to me that you would cover my ass no matter what." They were sitting in Jack's car, illegally stopped in front of the State Department building on C Street.

"I lied," said Jack.

"I set you up with Valdes's witnesses. All you have

to do is go over to the Holiday Inn on Fourteenth Street and talk to them. That's what you said you wanted. I got it for you. The grand jury hearing isn't until tomorrow. So I kept my part of the bargain; now you keep yours. Lay off me."

"I'm sorry, Mort. I can't. I just can't figure out any other way to get them to change their story about Roca being the front man for their drug deals."

"So who cares? Why is it your business anyway? Those *chulos* want to kill each other off, let them. Don't get involved."

"I am involved," Jack reminded him.

"Oh, yeah." Mort hit his forehead in mock forget-fulness. "You've got to compete with him for your wife. You think if you clear him, this is going to make her love you more? Don't count on it. You could be doing yourself in by getting him off. If he's in jail, no matter how horny she gets, she's only got you."

Jack would have liked to punch him in the face, but he needed him too much. "This has nothing to do with my wife," he said evenly, although he knew that was a lie, too. "You tried to get away with something; I caught on. Now, I'm willing to let it pass if you make a deal."

"I *made* a deal," Mort reminded him shrilly. "You're breaking it."

"No, I'm just escalating it a little."

"I'm not doing it. It's just going to be your word against mine."

"Okay, your choice. If you want to go through that and you can afford the scrutiny on the rest of your record—because you know once I point out a misde-meanor, they're going to go over your whole career with a fine-tooth comb. How far are you from retirement? It'll be too bad about that pension if it goes down the drain." Jack was bluffing. He didn't know if Mort had any other indiscretions in his files that needed to be hidden. He was just betting his entire stake that he did.

"Valdes finds out I turned on him, I could get a letter bomb," Mort said, and Jack saw he was home free.

"Just don't open your own mail, Mort," he said and started the car.

The two men were waiting in the double room they were sharing at the Holiday Inn, just as Mort had said. There were the remnants of several McDonald's meals scattered around the room. It smelled of grease and stale cigarette smoke. The pilot did all the talking, since the other one didn't know English. They were being watched by a guard in street clothes so Jack couldn't figure out if he was FBI, CIA, DEA, or just plain cop. He knew Mort wasn't violent, but he was reckless, and Jack knew nothing about his San Domenican friends. He liked having a neutral party in the room with him, especially a big guy with a gun. Mort looked at Jack, who gave him an almost imperceptible nod of encouragement. He introduced him to the pilot, whose name was Carlos. Jack didn't catch his last name, but didn't think it mattered.

"This guy's the lawyer," Mort announced, pointing at Jack. It wasn't exactly a lie. Jack was a lawyer. He just didn't happen to be the court-appointed lawyer who would be defending them and was arriving to speak with them later in the day.

"Good," said Carlos. "We have the plea bargain.

Right? We testify against Roca. We get sent home. Right?"

Jack looked solemn. "I don't think so."

Carlos jumped up knocking his chair over. The burly guard put his hand on the butt of his revolver. "What does this mean? You don't think so? The deal has been made. Valdes swore to us—"

"Well, I'm afraid that Mr. Valdes is not a member of the judiciary in this country. He has no say here."

"But he *arranged* it. He is taking care of everything." Carlos looked to Mort for affirmation.

"That's what I thought, too." Mort shrugged. That wasn't a lie either. In fact, Mort had been instrumental in putting Valdes in touch with the attorney general to get the deal made. He wondered if he could help Jack pull this off without ever actually telling a lie. Mort liked games, and this was turning out to be a fun challenge. In the end, he didn't care who got stuck with egg on his face as long as it wasn't him. "Do you want me to call him?"

"Yes, yes." Carlos's response was immediate and vigorous. He turned to Jack as if explaining everything. "Mort will call Valdes. He'll tell you. There's a deal. No deal, we don't have anything to say."

Mort went over to the nightstand and picked up the phone, studying the procedure for making a long-distance call. In a moment, Jack was at his side, extracting something from his briefcase.

"What's this?" asked Mort as Jack handed him a telephone.

"It's got a speaker," Jack explained as he unplugged the hotel unit and replaced it with his own.

"You think of everything, don't you?" Mort said almost admiringly as he started to dial.

Carlos was speaking rapid Spanish to his colleague, who was parroting his every nod and gesture. "Yes, yes," the second man proclaimed in his limited English. "Call Valdes. No deal, no talk."

Mort looked at him with more grimace than smile and switched the phone to speaker. They could hear the ringing. "This is Valdes's private line. So everybody shut up."

"¡Hola!"

"Hey, Valdes. It's Mort Freeman here. It looks like we've got a little problem."

"What?" He was nothing if not terse.

"It's possible that deal that you made with the AG for those two guys testifying against Roca won't hold." *Unlikely,* Mort thought to himself, *but possible.* He was still within the range of the truth.

"Why?"

"Up here they don't usually let drug dealers go free even if they turn state's evidence. Some states even have mandatory sentencing. Your guys could be facing heavy time in prison." *Just a statement of fact,* Mort thought smugly to himself.

Carlos was watching the telephone intently as if he could bore through it and see the person on the other end. Jack was watching Carlos. There was a long silence before Valdes spoke again.

"Fuck them."

"I'm sorry?" Mort said, taken aback. It wasn't the response he'd expected. He looked at Jack, who was already starting to gloat.

"Those men are nothing to me," Valdes mused. "I don't care if they go to prison. So long as you get Roca. You can still guarantee that, can't you?"

Jack was pumping his fist in the air as though he'd just hit a touchdown.

Forgetting he'd been forbidden to speak, Carlos let out a stream of invective in Spanish, while his cohort demanded to know what was going on.

"What's that?" Valdes inquired, instantly wary.

"Interference on the line," said Mort. "I'd better go." He hung up quickly. "Damn," he said, "that was my only lie."

"In the end," Jack laughed, "you're a good man, Mort."

They waited half an hour for the district attorney to arrive with a stenographer. With Carlos translating for his friend, it took them less than an hour to recant their testimony against Diego Roca and to explain that they'd been put up to it by Guillermo Valdes. Then they immediately requested asylum on the basis of being political refugees.

Driving Mort back to his car in the State Department garage, Jack was already on the phone. "Don't tell me it can't be done. Diego Roca is the president of San Domenico. He was wrongly accused, and now the charges have been dropped. Unless you want a goddamn international incident on your hands, get that goddamn monitor off his ankle now." He slammed the phone down. He saw Mort looking at him. "What?" he shouted at him. "What?"

"I just wanted to say I'm sorry about this," Mort said quietly. "I know you think I was just looking for glory, which I was, but I also really thought it could be true."

"Well, it wasn't."

"Yeah, you proved that. So what are you so mad about now?"

"I'm not mad," said Jack, sounding pretty irate. "I just want to make it possible for Diego Roca to go home as soon as possible. Which is now!"

By the next day, the cuff was gone, and deepest apologies had been proffered. The secretary of state begged Roca to be the guest of honor at an official State luncheon the next day to formalize the mea culpas and erase any vestige of ill will. As befit a head of state, he was offered the hospitality of the presidential suite at the Watergate for the rest of his visit.

"I have you to thank for this," Diego said to Jack, shaking his hand warmly.

"I couldn't let you stay here any longer," Jack confessed, only half joking. "I trust my wife, but I'm not a gambling man."

Diego turned to Melinda. *"Mi amor,"* he said and folded her in his arms. And although it was what he had always called her and he placed his good-bye kiss firmly on her lips, she knew that something had changed forever between them. He had been her hero and her lover. He had become her adversary and her jailer. But up until now, he had never been her friend.

It took Daisy less than an hour to make the ninety-minute drive from Paris to St. Denis. Daniela and Ryan were waiting for her at the gate to the school, as she had asked.

"You got here fast," Ryan said, impressed. She told them to get into the car and listened while Ryan told her again exactly what they had heard in the upstairs storage room.

"You've got to help Mr. Taylor," Daniela added. "I don't want the same thing to happen to him that happened to Rochester."

Daisy smiled. She didn't really see herself in the role of Jane Eyre. But from the little she'd learned from the children, it did seem possible that she'd somehow stepped into a Gothic romance. "I'll see what I can do," she told them, touched that in his short time as headmaster Ian had managed to garner such loyalty from his students.

"Oh, and Miss Howard?" Ryan supplicated as she dropped them off in front of the school. "You don't have to tell him that we were up there, do you? I mean, the top floor is off-limits and we weren't really supposed to be up there. I mean, we didn't do anything—"

"It's okay, Ryan," Daisy interrupted, anxious to find Ian. "I won't get you two into any trouble. If you promise to go straight to wherever it is you're supposed to be and stay there."

"Thanks," they echoed each other, relief in their voices, as they grabbed hands and ran inside. Daisy parked her car and made her way directly to Ian's private quarters.

She knocked on his door, identifying herself immediately, and was surprised at the alacrity with which the door swung open. For a minute, his face lit up at the sight of her, and then, remembering, he shuttered his feelings behind a veil of reprimand. "You shouldn't have come," he said.

Since he made no move to invite her in, she simply stepped around him and closed the door behind herself. "You were right about one thing, Ian," she said. "We don't know each other very well. Or you wouldn't have tried such an obvious ploy to get rid of me—and I would have seen through you and refused to leave!" He opened his mouth to protest, but sensing what was coming, she put up a hand to stop him. "Do me the courtesy of letting me judge what I can handle and what I can't. You may mean well by lying to me, but it only insults my intelligence. If you just want me to mind my own business, that's another story."

He gave up any pretense then and took her in his arms. "Daisy," he whispered into her hair, "this is so hard."

"I bet," she said, holding him to her, "and facing it alone doesn't make it easier. I'm not sure what I can do to help, but I've got the embassy resources behind me, and at the very least, now that I know, you can talk about it."

"Wait a minute." He suddenly realized this wasn't computing. *"How* do you know?"

"I don't exactly. I just heard from a couple of little birdies who were playing hooky on the storage floor and overheard Colette Simard and a quote unquote crazy lady say she was your wife."

"Students?" He was appalled.

"Yeah, but I promised I wouldn't rat on them. They called me because they were worried about you. I envisioned all manner of scenarios on my way over. But maybe you'd better tell me the real story. That is, if you want to. You don't have to, but I'm telling you right now that even if you don't, I'm not going to abandon you."

"I know I keep telling you this," he said, "but you are wonderful." For the first time since Sunny had walked through his door, the vise around his heart loosened just a little.

"Not so wonderful that I haven't been dumped before." She laughed. "I can understand it if I'm being replaced by a greater love. But I refuse to be skewered on the horns of a dilemma."

He tried to smile at her choice of words. He wanted nothing more than to confide in her, to forget his shame and reveal each selfish thought. Still, he felt a warning was in order. "It is true, Daisy. My wife is alive and no matter what she has become, I can never leave her."

"I know that," Daisy assured him quietly. "We weren't ready to be bride and groom yet anyway. So why don't we just see where friendship can take us?"

She made some tea for both of them, and they talked about the pressures and possibilities. He admitted that, try as he might, he could not find Sarah in the odious creature who called herself Sunny. And when he envisioned a future that forced him to be tied to her, he broke down. Daisy sat on the sofa beside him and put her arms around him, comforting him. In spite of all his protestations of duty to his wife, he could not suppress the desire he felt at her proximity. And knowing that for Ian, affection would soon be replaced by isolation, she kissed him and let him know that she would not deny his passion. They did not hear Colette enter, as she often did, with her own key. They did not see her eyes turn to hard black coals of hatred as she backed out of the room and closed the door on the embracing couple.

Colette stormed back up to the top floor, muttering under her breath. "He's like the others," she mumbled. "He can't see what I have to offer. They think a pretty package is more important than what's inside. Well, I won't believe that. I won't paint myself up and simper around. Why should I? I could be indispensable to him. I could have taken care of his undead wife for him. I could have made a life for him at St. Denis. For both of us. Instead, a lunatic and a whore take him away from me, and as usual, I get nothing. It isn't fair. I wish I could get rid of them both . . ." She stopped grumbling as she opened Sunny's door to a welcome of scatological epithets hurled in her direction. Suddenly it came to her. She could.

"Do you want to get out of here?" she asked the screaming woman when she paused for breath.

Sunny looked at her, immediately mistrustful. "What's the catch?"

"For me, none. I can just leave open the door and let you go. For you, that's another story."

"I'll take my chances. Open the door."

"Where will you go?"

"Anywhere but here."

"How will you get there? The closest town is St. Denis, which you didn't seem to like much. And even that is twenty kilometers away."

Sunny paused. The stone-faced broad had a point. "I'll hitchhike," she ventured, not quite sure of herself.

Colette shrugged. "It's late. Cars don't usually pass the school after hours. We are out of the way here."

"The hell with it. I'll walk," Sunny declared. She'd find somebody somewhere to help her out. She always did.

"There's another way," Colette suggested coyly and saw that Sunny was interested. "You need a car, you need money. I know how you could get both. There's a lady who's going to be driving out of the school tonight. You could intercept her."

"Yeah, and what? Tell her I need a loan?"

"No. Shoot her."

Sunny burst out laughing. "You're not just a prig, you're a vicious prig. Just one problem. I don't have a gun."

"I do," said Colette quietly. "I'm alone at night. I got it for protection."

Sunny looked her up and down. "I'd call that wishful thinking, honey. But anyway, I'm not the killer, Stuart is."

Colette and Ian had talked about his wife's multiple-personality problem when she had offered to help him handle the situation. She hadn't forgotten that he had mentioned one of them was a ruthless man.

"Why don't you let Stuart do it, if you can't? You could be rid of Ian, have money, a car. You'd be free."

"Yeah, sure, for how long? They put you in jail for that sort of thing," Sunny objected. But Colette could see that something was happening to her. For a second, her eyes had rolled back into her head, and she seemed to mumble to herself. She recovered quickly and acted as though nothing had happened.

"Who would tell?" Colette pressed. "Not Ian. Everyone thinks you're dead. I could convince him to let it go. He doesn't want you any more than you want him."

"You can say that again" came the response, harsh and direct. Colette did a double take, then her mouth dropped open in amazement. It was easy to believe that she was suddenly talking to a different person, wearing the same dress as moments ago but suddenly, unmistakably, a man.

"You are Stuart," she said with certainty.

"Right you are, doll. So where's this gun?"

"I will get it for you," Colette said, her excitement growing. Her plan was going to work. This one could be made to kill. And she would make certain that she or he or whatever it was would also be made to pay. With one of his women dead of a bullet wound and the other incarcerated for the crime, Ian would have nowhere to turn but to her. She headed out the door smiling. There were advantages to working with the deranged.

"And bring me a pair of pants while you're at it," shouted Stuart as she locked the door behind her.

When she returned with the gun and a pair of pants that she'd stolen out of one of the dormitory monitor's lockers, Stuart had already slicked his hair back into a ponytail and wiped the makeup off his face. He was sitting slouched on the cot with his legs apart. Once he'd put on the pants, it was easy for Colette to think of him as a man.

"When's this broad going to leave?" he asked her, checking out the gun, making sure the bullets were in place. Colette was pleased to see he seemed to know his way around a firearm.

"I don't know. But definitely tonight. Ian would never let her stay on a school night." She led Stuart to the gate and hitched it closed, explaining that Daisy would have to get out of her car to open it, and that was when he could shoot her.

"You say she's got a lot of bucks on her?"

"She is very wealthy and always carries big sums of money," Colette lied. She could see Stuart was hopping himself up. She wanted to keep him edgy, belligerent. "I have some pills," she offered. They were left over from Paul Kogan, who had taken them on occasion to keep awake for the school day after a night of carousing. Stuart grabbed them from her and studied the bottle.

"Yeah," he said, "this'll do." He popped three into his mouth and swallowed. She raised an eyebrow. He started to say something, but she shushed him. They heard voices, a car door, a motor starting, wheels moving slowly on gravel.

Ian, too, heard the car door slam and the engine start just as he noticed the small jeweler's box on his nightstand. Damn, he thought, the daisy ring. He grabbed the box and raced out the door. He'd catch her at the gate. It was a small token of his great affection, but she had more than earned it, and he wanted her to have it.

Hiding with Stuart in the bushes at the entrance to the school grounds, Colette whispered her final instructions. "She'll leave the car running. Shoot her after she opens the gate, and then you can drive right out. No one will come after you." *Not tonight, any-*

way, she added silently. There would be plenty of time for the French authorities to follow the trail. The car was almost at the gate. Colette disappeared, leaving Stuart alone, vibrating with excitement in the shadows, glad to be in control at last and taking on a task that only he could handle.

Daisy stopped the car at the gate as Colette had said she would and got out to open it. Stuart weighed the gun in his hand, getting a comfortable fit. He noticed how pretty she was, and the part of him that was a real man wondered what it would be like to make time with her. Ian would know that, he thought, and then felt a buzz in his head from the others. He snickered silently. The women were jealous. Well, as usual, he was going to help them out. She had opened the gate and was heading back to her car. He stepped out of the shadow. "Hold it right there," he said, pointing the gun at her. She gasped, and he got a little thrill, seeing her fear.

"What do you want?" her voice trembled. "My money? Take it. It's in my purse on the front seat of the car." He made no move toward the car, just shifted closer to her. "Listen, just take it . . . ," she began, and then she did a double take. Stuart shrugged. He often got that reaction from people who thought he was a man from a distance, then got confused when they saw the woman's body he was stuck with. "I know who you are," she breathed.

"Aren't you smart," he sneered. "Too bad you're also dead." He cocked the gun, and then he heard the scream and felt himself falling. For a minute, he thought he might have shot Daisy and she was screaming. He even entertained the possibility that he had screamed himself. It took him a moment to realize that Ian was on top of him, grappling with him, and that the shrieking was coming from Colette. Ian was trying to take the gun from him, but Stuart wasn't going to let that happen. He locked his grip around the gun, ignoring the voices in his head, whether from reason or the others he couldn't be sure. But he wasn't going to let anyone else command the situation. He'd been subdued too long. It was his turn to do things his way. And his way was to fight. He felt the pressure on his wrist, and only an act of supreme will kept him from giving in to the pain and letting go of the gun. Summoning everything within him, he wrenched his arm but could not free it, and in the process, lost control. The gun went off. He heard more screams, a chorus this time, and this time, his voice was among them. And then the spotlight, the beam that shone on the personality in control, was turned off, and he was gone.

"Ian?" Sarah asked, baffled, as she opened her eyes and saw that he was leaning over her. She tried to move, but he held her still, and she realized he was cradling her head and they were on the ground.

"Ssshh," he said. "Don't try to talk. Help is coming."

"Why?" she asked, then felt something sticky and warm leaking over her fingers and saw that she was bleeding. "Oh, my God." She was terrified. "What happened to me?"

"Sarah?" Ian asked, incredulous. "Is that you? Have you come back?"

"Oh, Ian, it's been awful," she moaned. "Sunny got the spotlight and started the fire. I couldn't get control for a long time. When I did, I came to find you. To tell you what happened. But I don't remember anything after I got off the plane. Did Sunny do something?"

"Yes," he answered quietly. "And Stuart."

She started to cry. "I'm sorry. I thought I was better. Whole. But they wouldn't let me stay together."

"I know, sweetheart. It's not your fault."

"Did I hurt anybody?"

"Only yourself."

"What's wrong with me?"

"You've been shot."

"By whom?"

"By me," he told her, his own eyes filling with tears. "I'm sorry, Sarah. I didn't mean to hurt you, but you, I mean, Stuart was going to kill someone. I tried to get the gun away, and it went off. Oh, God. I'm sorry."

"No," she soothed him. "Don't you cry. You did the right thing. I wouldn't have wanted to shoot anyone. It's better this way."

"An ambulance is coming. You're going to be all right," he tried to reassure her.

"Actually," she said, smiling faintly, "for someone who's bleeding as much as I am, I feel pretty good. The others have kind of faded away. Maybe you killed them. That would be wonderful."

"Yes," he echoed, "it will be wonderful. When you get better . . ."

"Even if I don't. Life was hell with them inside me. For both of us. You know that. Now they're gone, and I feel like I can finally get some peace. I'm going to close my eyes and rest now, okay?"

"Okay. You deserve it."

They heard the sirens approaching in the distance. She opened her eyes again for a minute. "Promise me you won't feel bad, Ian. You put me back together again. Made me Sarah. I love you."

"I love you, too, Sarah," he said. She smiled and closed her eyes again. By the time the ambulance arrived, she was dead.

11

In the middle of the night, the police arrived at the American School at St. Denis. Ignoring their dormitory supervisors' admonitions to stay in bed, the students had poured from the building in their pajamas, groggy with sleep but wide-eyed with wonder at the herd of emergency vehicles that snaked its way over the grounds. They were all begging to be told what had happened, and although their teachers were exhorting them to go back to bed, they, too, were curious to know what was going on. While Ian stayed with Sarah's body and the police questioned Colette, who insisted that she had broken no laws, Daisy tried a little damage control.

"There's been an accident," she announced to the group congregating on the steps, the teachers now as reluctant to go inside without an explanation as the students. "Someone Mr. Taylor knows has been hurt. That's why the ambulance and the police cars are here."

"Who is it?" one of the kids called out.

"She is not connected to the school" was as much as Daisy felt they needed to know. "I think it's safe to say that none of you were acquainted with her."

"I heard a gunshot," another child sang out and was joined by a chorus of assent.

Daisy toyed with telling them they were right but dismissed the truth as being too inflammatory in this case. "I don't know what you heard, but I can tell you there is absolutely no danger to anyone in the school. The incident is over. Now, if you'll all follow your supervisors back to your rooms, if there's any more information, you'll be told in the morning." There were a few groans and complaints, but eventually, the children were persuaded or otherwise compelled to go inside.

Breaking away from her group, Daniela came running over to Daisy. "Did this happen because we told?"

Daisy put her arm around the girl and hugged her. The air was a little cool, but Daisy knew that wasn't the cause of Daniela's trembling. "Of course not, Daniela. Don't even think that, honey. You didn't do anything wrong."

"Was it the lady in the room that got hurt?"

"Yes, but that had nothing to do with you. In fact, I'm glad you told me what you heard. Something worse might have happened if you hadn't."

"If she's dead, that means you and Mr. Taylor can—"

"Sshh, Daniela. Don't say things like that. Life doesn't work like a library book. It's not that simple."

Daniela said nothing, but Daisy could see the girl didn't entirely believe her. "You go to bed, now," she said, kissing the girl gently on the forehead. "You're still going to have school tomorrow."

"Can I just tell Ryan?" Daniela asked. "He's probably upset about it, too."

"Sure," said Daisy, knowing what it feels like to be worried about someone you love. Daniela gave her a shy hug in return and ran into the school. Daisy watched and smiled to see Ryan, peeking out from inside the door where he had been waiting, just as concerned about Daniela as she was for him. "It's not that simple," Daisy repeated to herself, but, in a way, she herself did not understand why it couldn't be.

By the time Daisy got back to Ian, the group had thinned. Although Colette maintained that Mrs. Taylor had stolen the gun from her and that she was only in the vicinity because she had been trying to prevent her from killing Miss Howard in a fit of jealousy, the police remained skeptical and took her with them for further questioning. The ambulance had taken Sarah's body to the morgue. None of them had doubted that the shooting had been accidental on Ian's part, and he had been left on his own recognizance with a request that he come in the next day to give a statement. Daisy found Ian, his bloodied arms empty, still on the ground where he had held Sarah while she died. Daisy sat down beside him and put her hand gently over his. "If you need a shoulder to cry on . . ."

"I can't cry any more," said Ian, numb.

"What will you do?" she asked, thinking it wasn't a bad idea to steer away from the emotional fallout for a moment and focus on logistics.

"I want to take her back home. She should be buried in Woodland Cliffs, not here among strangers. I've got to tell her family." He gave a sorrowful laugh. "That's going to be a hard one. Hey, Drew, I've got good news and bad news. The good news is your sister didn't really die in the fire. The bad news is I killed her."

"Don't," Daisy said. "You said yourself it wasn't really Sarah. If you hadn't been there, she would have killed me. I owe you my life."

"On the other hand," Ian said, unwilling to cut himself some slack, "if I'd kept you out of it in the first place, you would never have been in danger."

"It's over," said Daisy. "You're going to need to do your share of mourning. And then you're going to need to let it go."

"What time is it?" asked Ian. "Can I still call the States?"

"It's six hours earlier there, so you're okay. Come on, I'll go with you." She helped him get to his feet, and they trudged wearily back to his cottage.

Inside, she prepared tea, although she knew he probably wouldn't drink it, while he went to the phone. He picked up the receiver and, hesitating, put it back down in his lap, steeling himself. Then he dialed. Not intending to eavesdrop, just wanting to be sure he was bearing up, Daisy listened to Ian's part of the conversation.

"Robert, it's Ian. I need to talk to Drew," he began, forgoing any pleasantries. This wasn't the time for an exchange of small talk with the butler. For a long time, there was silence, and Daisy assumed he was waiting for his brother-in-law to come to the phone. But then she heard him gasp and begin to mutter exclamations of dismay. "Oh, my God . . . Oh, no . . . When?" She turned off the kettle and hurried into the living room, not questioning him while he was on the phone, but standing there, letting him know that if something was wrong, she was prepared to share it. "Yes, of course . . ." He was ending his conversation, "I'll take the next plane out . . . I'll let you know . . . Tell the others I'm on my way." He hung up and sat in stunned silence for a moment. She realized he hadn't even mentioned Sarah. He turned to her, and his eyes were full of tears. "It never ends, does it?" he cried.

She put her arms around him. "Yes, it does, Ian," she said with tears in her own eyes, not knowing what new tragedy had befallen him, but only that he had been hurt even more. "Yes, it does."

When he told her what had happened, that Sam and Drew had been caught in an explosion and the family was gathering to keep a vigil while rescuers searched for them in the rubble, she insisted on going with him. He protested at first, not wanting to saddle her with more of his miseries, but she gently dismissed his qualms as impractical. It would be hard enough for him to deal with the catastrophe in progress. She would handle the one that had already transpired. He could be there to support his family while they waited for the drama with Sam and Drew to unfold. She would take care of making arrangements for the casket and burial. Then, when the time was right, Ian could tell them about Sarah. Hopefully, by then, Sam and Drew would be rescued, and there would be only one reason to mourn.

It was Jack who met them at the airport. He hugged Ian before turning to Daisy. "Strange, isn't it, how fate throws people together," he remarked before embracing her as well.

"Stranger than you know," she informed him and then, at a signal from Ian, quickly told him what had happened to Sarah the night before in St. Denis.

He stood for a moment in complete and utter shock, then once again turned to his brother-in-law and folded his arms around him. "Oh, Ian. I am so, so sorry. What an awful time for you."

"I wanted you to know in case Daisy needs help. But I don't think I should say anything to anyone else," Ian offered. "Everyone's got enough to handle right now. When Sam and Drew are safe again . . ." He trailed off, knowing it was as much a prayer as a promise.

They had brought Sarah's body with them on the plane, and Daisy offered to go with the people from the funeral home that she had arranged to meet them. But Ian declined. "I'm bringing Sarah home," he said without irony. "I should look after her."

They understood and let him go alone, realizing it was something he needed to do. Jack and Daisy said little to each other as he collected the luggage and led her to his car.

"You're not upset I've come, are you?" she asked as they drove to Belvedere. With everything that had happened in the last twenty-four hours, she had completely forgotten that her relationship to Ian's family was not without its difficulties.

"Grateful," Jack assured her, setting her mind immediately at rest. "As a matter of fact, you won't be the only, shall we say, 'complication' in residence."

"What do you mean?"

"Diego Roca came with us from Washington."

She did a double take. *The* Diego Roca? Melinda's former . . . ?"

"Yeah, that one," Jack said, smiling a little. "Nico got out of the hospital the same day Sam and Drew—"

"How is he?" she interrupted, wanting to know immediately, having followed his case through Ian.

"Great. Really, really wonderful. The new kidney is functioning. There's been no rejection. He's still on some immunosuppressive drugs, so we have to watch him. But, basically, he's just like any normal two-year-old. You'll see him."

"You brought him with you?"

"That's where Roca comes in. As soon as we heard about Sam and Drew, Melinda and I wanted to come, but we couldn't bear the thought of leaving Nico. At the same time, we weren't going to bring him to the site of the explosion, and we didn't want to leave him with people he didn't know. So Diego offered to come, too, and watch Nico while the family stays with the rescue crew."

"He must have been happy to have the extra time

with his son," noted Daisy, then realizing she might sound callous added, "except for the horrible circumstances, of course."

"You're right," Jack concurred. "He is. He's going back to San Domenico when this is over, so it'll be a while before he sees Nico again. They've developed quite a bond, not to mention the fact that they now share a pair of kidneys."

"Is that hard for you?" she asked gently.

"It was at first," he admitted. "Roca's a powerful man. I don't just mean his position. He's passionate, intense. He and Melinda had a very tempestuous relationship. I was afraid, seeing me next to him, she might think she'd made a mistake."

Daisy looked at the man beside her and smiled. The window was open and his blond hair, permanently streaked by the sun, was blowing away from his chiseled face. Even tired and with a day or two of stubble, he was drop-dead handsome. And from the day they'd met as intimate strangers, she had known he was strong and honest and sensitive. She couldn't think of a more winning combination, and from what she could tell, he hadn't changed much. "You're no slouch yourself, Jack Bader. I doubt you have anything to worry about."

He laughed and said, "Sweet of you to say so. But there was the thing with Nico as well. I love that baby. I couldn't love him more if he were my own son. Hell, he *is* my son. His first word was *Dada,* and he was talking to me. But I couldn't help him. He was going to die, and there was nothing I could do. We needed Roca to save him."

"I get the picture. You can't hate a guy who saves

your son. But you can't like a guy who wants your wife."

"Insightful as usual," he joked. "But it's okay now. Life's too fragile and unpredictable for all of us. In the long run, we can't improve our fates by fighting each other. Better to just accept what comes our way."

"Words to live by," Daisy said. They had passed through the gates of Belvedere and were driving up the circular path to the front of the house. She had seen quite a bit of the world, but this was impressive by any standard. "Home sweet home," she said sardonically as they approached the mansion's colonnaded porticos. "It's hard for me to imagine Ian living here."

"I think it was hard for him, too."

"Now *she* looks right at home," said Daisy, indicating a woman, older but still elegant, who appeared to be waiting for them on the porch.

"She should," Jack explained. "That's Mathilde D'Uberville Symington. Forrest built this house for her. But I don't think she had much happiness in it. Nowadays, she seems to come back only for tragic occasions."

Jack pulled up to the front of the house and helped Daisy out of the car. He introduced her to Mathilde, and they exchanged a few words in French. Mathilde looked toward the car, and Daisy understood that she was expecting Ian to appear.

"Uh . . . Ian will be here soon. He had to stay at the airport to take care of something," she added lamely.

To her surprise, Mathilde didn't ask what it was. She didn't ask why Daisy had come. There was nothing she wanted to know until someone came to tell her that her son and his wife were alive and well. And when that happened, she would not need to ask.

"Drew? Drew? Answer me!" Sam demanded. She had woken from a thick fog of sleep, drenched in sweat, light-headed and disoriented. Becoming aware of her tomblike surroundings, it had taken her a moment to realize she was not still in some horrendous nightmare, and this was, in fact, her real life. Her husband's body, partly covering her own, seemed lifeless. She tried to move him, to shake him, but only succeeded in moving herself just enough to reverse the impact of the numbness caused by the deadweight of his body. A fury of pins and needles suffused her entire right side. For not the first time since the ordeal had began, she started to cry.

"Sshh, sshh," she heard and, filled with relief, moved her head to cover the few inches that separated them, resting her lips on his damp and salty cheek.

"Drew! Thank God. I thought you were . . ." She couldn't even say the word.

"And leave you here to enjoy this on your own? Never!"

She laughed, impressed and grateful that he still had the ability to make a joke, no matter how feeble. Hearing her laugh, his own spirits brightened. "Did you sleep?"

"I guess so. You, too?"

"Either that or I passed out."

"How are you feeling?" she asked, then started to laugh again. It was such an irrelevant question. "I mean, does your leg hurt?"

"I can't even feel it anymore. I wonder how long

we've been here." They were both wearing watches, but even with their eyes accustomed to the dark, they could not see the dials.

"It feels like days. I'm hungry."

"I'm thirsty."

"Me, too." They thought silently for a minute about what they wanted. "Drew?" Sam finally had the courage to ask. "Do you think they'll find us?"

"I think we've got a chance. We can't be all that far from the surface because we're getting a steady supply of air."

"Which means we won't die of suffocation, just starvation and dehydration."

It was a possibility, Drew knew, but it wasn't one they should dwell on. "Let's talk about the high points in our life."

"You mean give ourselves a eulogy?" Sam countered.

"No." He was determined to snap her out of it, even though being stuck in a space the size of a coffin was an understandable trigger for depression. "I mean like a top-ten hit parade of our greatest moments. I'll start. Moira's birth."

"Hmmm."

He could feel her smiling, even though he couldn't see it.

"Of course," she went on, "I was the one screaming in pain in your mother's attic, humiliated because I thought you didn't love me. So it was kind of different for me."

"Picky, picky," he teased. "But don't tell me when she came and I was finally there beside you that wasn't the greatest moment of your life."

"You're right," she agreed. "It was."

"Your turn," he said. He was exhausted with the effort of speaking. But he could tell that it was helping Sam recover her fortitude and forced himself to continue. "Greatest moment number two."

"Well, let's see," Sam mused. "I'd have to say finding you alive and well after you'd disappeared in England."

"That was good," he acknowledged. "Although, of course, you didn't have to get blown up in Harrods and taken by the IRA, as I was, to get to that particular apex."

"Point well taken," she admitted. "Although I think it's fair to say we both enjoyed being on *Donahue* afterward. What else?"

"This one is strictly mine," he said softly and a little more seriously. "Seeing you for the first time at the Millpond, looking like a water nymph . . ."

"I was wet and naked," Sam harrumphed.

"Hey," he chided, "I told you this was mine. You were the most beautiful creature I had ever laid eyes on, and I knew from that moment on that I couldn't live without you. And I still . . ." his voice faded.

"Drew?" Sam called him, alarmed. "Open your eyes. Look at me." She put her face closer to his. "Look at me," she commanded again. His eyes fluttered open. "Listen to me," she tried to sound forceful. "I don't think you should go to sleep anymore. I want you to stay awake, to talk to me."

"I can't sweetheart," he whispered. "So tired . . . Just let me . . ."

"No, Drew. I'm not going to let you slip away. You got me this far, now I'm going to get you the rest of the way. We're a team, Drew. We don't do that well on our own. And I'm not ready to give up."

"Not giving up," he said, "just resting."

"It amounts to the same thing right now, and I'm not going to let you do it." She had no idea if what she was doing was right. But she remembered reading somewhere that it was dangerous to let shock victims go to sleep because they might slip into a coma. "We'll play a game or something," said Sam growing more desperate. "What do you want to play?"

"Ssshhh," Drew said.

"No, don't shush me. I'm not—"

He put his one free hand to her lips to make her be quiet. "Listen," he whispered. She heard it then, too. A rumbling sound, then scraping, more rumbling, more scraping.

"Do you think . . . ?" she asked, not daring to believe.

"Could be," he said.

When they started to hear voices, they took turns shouting, although Sam, feeling stronger, yelled the most. It was another fifteen minutes before they got any response. But when it came, it was definite.

"We're coming to get you," someone said.

"Don't worry, we won't move," shouted Sam and thrilled as their laughter reached her. "We made it," she said to Drew, moving her head the few inches to his and kissing him fervently on his parched lips. "We're going to be all right."

It took another two hours for the rescue crew to clear a path through the rubble, removing debris like pickup sticks, piece by piece, for fear that one wrong move could bring the rest crashing down on them.

Slowly, small shafts of light filtered through their gloom, making them even more aware of how frighteningly close they had come to being annihilated. When at last the mass of concrete that had locked them into their tomb was lifted by a crane from above their heads, they had to close their eyes against the brightness of the sun and could only hear the applause and cheers that welcomed them back to the world of the living.

"Take Drew first," Sam instructed them. "He's got a broken leg and I think he might be going into shock." Weak as he was, Drew started to argue until it was pointed out that, in any event, he'd have to come out first, since he was lying on top of Sam. When she knew that her husband was all right and that they were both safe, when she had stood on wobbly legs and felt the air on her face, only then did Sam give in to the terror that she had held at bay for two days and two nights, and promptly fall into a dead faint.

When she came to, Gina was standing over her. "Welcome back," she said, smiling. "You gave us quite a scare."

"Not any more than I scared myself. Where's Drew?"

"The doctors are putting a cast on his leg. He's going to be fine."

Sam sighed with relief. She felt tired, but she didn't feel ill. She sat up and looked around. She realized she was in a hospital room. Gina noticed her alarm. "You just fainted," she told her before she asked. "You're going to be fine, too. You're both very, very lucky."

"I know it," said Sam. "We came *that* close. You were right about the Armageddon Advance, Gina."

"Yeah, Drew filled us in on what happened while you were sleeping. I'm only sorry we had to find out the way we did."

"Did anybody else get hurt in the explosion?" Sam asked, remembering the world had continued to revolve while they had been frozen in their tomb.

"There were some minor injuries. A few cuts and breaks. But because the bunker was made of thick reinforced concrete, the damage was mostly sustained in the basement where you were. The explosion did knock out all the windows and send everyone running out of the building for cover. It's probably what saved me and my pals. We used broken glass to cut ourselves loose."

"I'm sorry, Gina," Sam said, quietly remorseful.

"Are you kidding? You've got nothing to be sorry for."

"Yes, I do. I messed up. Luke saw me going off with Drew and had us followed. Someone saw us at the Millpond. I won't say what we were doing, but I can tell you it was pretty clear we weren't estranged. That's what got him suspicious and turned him on to you."

"Forget about it," Gina advised. "You got us our man. Even if he is in tiny little bits. At least he won't be preying on people who aren't as smart as you. And his arsenal is gone. Who knows what damage would have been done if he'd had a chance to use it. You did good, kid. Thanks." She started to go, then turned back, remembering something. "By the way, they're giving you a Congressional Medal of Honor."

"Are you kidding?" Sam was truly astonished. "What for?"

"I don't know. They like to do that sort of thing when someone almost kills herself while serving her country. They're funny like that. The President will be calling. Don't put him on hold." With a laugh, Gina was gone.

The news of Sam's medal was received by the rest of the family with more than the requisite pride and joy. They had gathered in the hospital waiting room, prepared to keep a vigil until both Sam and Drew were out of the woods. Their wait had been blessedly short. Honor added to relief made for a giddy brew. Hoping that the cloak of euphoria that enveloped them would protect them from the full impact of cold reality that he had to deliver, Ian told them as unsensationally as possible what had happened to Sarah.

As he had expected, it was Mathilde who took the news the hardest, but even she did not blame him for Sarah's end. "Before, she was whole only with you, *mon cher,*" she wept. "But now, she is whole for all time. Thank you for bringing her home."

"What will you do now?" Daisy asked Ian after Mathilde had been given a tranquilizer and they had brought her back to Belvedere to rest.

"I'll stay here until after the memorial service, and then I guess I'll go back to the school and salvage what's left of the term. What about you?"

"I spoke to the embassy in Paris today. They're starting to work on next year's American Film Festival in Deauville. They want me to stay in the States a while and do some screening."

"Deauville," he said wistfully.

"I know. We never made it there."

"I'd like to see it someday," he said, and she noticed he hadn't said anything about going with her. She understood. Their time had come and gone, their lives intersected but not connected. For Ian, there was still too much of the past to sort through before he could commit to a future. For Daisy, the present was too pressing to be waylaid by someone else's past.

"Go in the fall," she said, "after the summer crowds are gone. And try to go with someone you love."

It was decided that Melinda should break the news to Sam. She sat on the edge of the bed and hugged her sister for a long time. Sam could feel her shaking with relief. "Hey, come on," she cajoled. "It's always like this with the Myles militia. Every day a new adventure."

"Well, I'm about ready to get out of the business. How about you?" said Melinda, finally letting her go while she wiped away a few stray tears.

"Yeah, maybe," Sam conceded. "What about Nico?" she asked, aware that Melinda had been through a harrowing experience of her own. "Is he okay?"

"He's great," beamed Melinda. "You'll see for yourself when you come home."

"You brought him?" Sam asked, genuinely excited. The only child she loved as much as her own was her sister's.

"Yes. And Jack. And Diego."

"You're kidding! Diego?"

"Yes, and Daisy Howard is here with Ian from France."

"Jack's Daisy?" she burst out incredulously before she realized what she was saying. "I mean, his former—"

"It's quite a crowd. Of course, Mom and Dad and Mathilde."

"It's going to be quite a welcome home," said Samantha enthusiastically until she caught a look on Melinda's face. "What?" she asked. "There's something you're not telling me."

"There's another reason Jack and Daisy came." And giving her the basic facts, but sparing her the gory details, Melinda told her sister what had happened to Sarah.

Sam's eyes filled as she considered how accustomed she had become to tears. "Does Drew know?"

"Not yet. I thought maybe you would want to tell him. Ian told the rest of us after we were sure that you guys were all right. It's been an emotional roller coaster for Mathilde."

"I bet," sighed Sam, thinking that for a woman who had been raised for a life of privilege, her mother-in-law had been forced to bear a great deal of deprivation.

Alone, Sam went to Drew's room and found him sitting up in bed, his leg with the cast being propped on a pillow by a cute and more than professionally interested nurse. "I can't leave you alone for a minute," she teased gently, making the young nurse blush as she hurried out of the room. Drew grabbed her hand and pulled her down onto the bed with him. She took his face in her hands and kissed him tenderly before telling him the sad news. Then they held each other for a long time, grateful to be alive and together.

"Let's get out of here," Drew finally said, breaking their melancholy silence. "I want to go home. I want to see Moira. I want to be with my family."

"Good idea," agreed Sam. It took all of her considerable charm and powers of persuasion, but finally, with a pair of crutches for Drew and blessings for them both, they were released. Their welcome at Belvedere was heartfelt and bittersweet, and even Moira, who hadn't been told that her parents were in danger, felt how special it was to have them home. They were family, and they were together to face whatever joys and sorrows fate had in store for them.

"It isn't every day you get to see a head of state rocking a baby to sleep." The voice was throaty and voluptuous, and still pushing the stroller back and forth, Diego turned to see the tall blonde he had seen inside smiling at him. He had noticed her, not only because she was strikingly beautiful, but because she had appeared to be a little on the outside as he was, enveloped by the emotion of the family reunion, but not exactly a participant. When Nico had become fussy, he had welcomed the opportunity to take the baby out of Melinda's arms and bring him outside. He wondered if she had followed him.

"I followed you," she said, completely direct, and made him laugh out loud. "Is that funny?" she asked, curious but clearly not in the least disturbed by his amusement.

"Only because I was asking myself that very question, hoping that perhaps you had, and I find it refreshing that you would volunteer such information yourself," he explained, charmed by her candor.

"You seemed as out of place as I was."

"Again, you read my thoughts. They are generous and good people, and I share both their sorrow and their joy. But since you know who I am, you can understand why I am awkward among them. But you?" he queried.

"I'm Daisy Howard" was all she said, knowing it was all that was necessary.

"Ah," he said, understanding all. "You are the reluctant bride."

"And you," she grinned mischievously, "are the abandoned groom."

"Do you ever think about how different all our lives would be if you had not given up Jack at the altar?" he asked.

"Every day," she said.

"And do you ever regret it?"

"Not for a moment."

"Why?"

"You've seen them. Do you need to ask?"

"No, you're right. It's something to envy." There was a plaintive tone in his voice, not self-pity, but an awareness of loss.

"Or to strive for," she offered and was pleased to see his handsome, brooding features transformed with a smile.

"You make it seem possible," he said gallantly, and she took it for what it was, not just a compliment, but an invitation to try.

"Is San Domenico very beautiful?" Daisy asked, well aware of the door she was opening.

"A paradise," Diego answered. "You must see it for yourself." And without another word, they both knew that someday she would come.

"Strange, isn't it," Daisy quoted the remark she had heard earlier, "how fate throws people together?"

THE SUMMER OF L♥VE TRILOGY

by Leah Laiman

FOR RICHER, FOR POORER

FOR BETTER, FOR WORSE

TO LOVE AND TO CHERISH

Available from Pocket Books

POCKET BOOKS

982-03

ANOTHER SUMMER OF L♥VE TRILOGY

by Leah Laiman

MAID OF HONOR

THE BRIDESMAID

BRIDE AND GROOM

POCKET BOOKS

1085-02